EMBERWOOD

WITCHES OF FRIEYA: BOOK ONE

ERIN LE MARQUAND

Disclaimer: This is a work of fiction. Names, characters, business, events and incidents are the products of the author's imagination. Any resemblance to actual persons, living or dead, or actual events is purely coincidental.

Permission requests can be sent to the author:
authorerinlm@gmail.com

ISBN: 978-1-3999-3513-5 (paperback)
ASIN: B0BDNJN79F (ebook)

Editing by Brittany Corley
Chapter and scene break artwork by DesignsbyMeganTurner
Cover design by Clara Dailey

For those who have always doubted themselves.
Do the damn thing. Get shit done.
Get out of your own damn way.

"Let everything happen to you: beauty and terror.
Just keep going. No feeling is final."
- Rainer Maria Rilke

Content Warning

Emberwood is a new adult fantasy romance which may not be suitable for some readers. For a full list of content warnings, please go to the book profile on Goodreads.

Playlist

Season of the Witch – Lana Del Rey
Dance Macabre - Ghost
Darkness at the Heart of My Love - Ghost
Would? - Alice in Chains
Blessed Be – Spiritbox
Jesus Christ – Brand New
Hurt You – Spiritbox
Slither – Velvet Revolver
Still of the Night - Whitesnake
Nine Inch Nails – Closer
Highwayman – The White Buffalo
The Killing Moon – Echo and the Bunnymen
This Love – Pantera
Bird with a Worm – The Used
The Bitter End – Placebo
Fight Fire with Fire – Metallica
Funeral Derangements – Ice Nine Kills
Volbeat – Temple of Ekur
The Chain - Fleetwood Mac
Death by Water - Senses Fail
Love Bites – Def Leppard
A Little Piece of Heaven – Avenged Sevenfold
Song #3 – Stone Sour

The Realms of Frieya

Northern Realm
- Eskium
  - Duskbrook

Eastern Realm
- Arleau

Western Realm
- Zhadria

Southern Realm
- Troyla

Pronunciation guide

Frieya: Free-uh
Eskium: Ess-kee-um
Arleau: Are-low
Zhadria: Zad-ree-uh
Troyla: Troy-lah

Prologue

The woman's arms and legs were tethered to a wooden post, the soft skin of her wrists an angry pink as the rope tore into her flesh. Her gaze shot down in terror as the flames rose, licking at her calves like a hungry beast of Hell.

The whites of her eyes stood out as she shot a look from one man to another, frantically searching for someone who would douse the flames and set her free.

But she would not be saved.

An old man basked in the glow of the burning bodies, his pock-marked face illuminated by the flame. He wasn't disturbed by what he saw. No, he was amused by their suffering, gaining some sick satisfaction from their agonised cries.

His grey eyes were focused on one person – the woman with midnight black hair and eyes like ice. Her pale skin was like the moon, her snow-white flesh almost luminescent as it juxtaposed with the smoke from the pyre.

The grin on the old man's weathered face seemed to widen as the flames grew higher, charring the woman's slip, snaking up and up towards her breasts.

She screamed and begged for mercy, pleading with the man to let her go, promising she was innocent. He only laughed in response.

"Please. Please stop this," a strained voice sounded from a hunched man on the floor.

The grey-eyed man halted, looking down his nose at him. "This is better than she deserves." He grimaced as he began to walk away towards the shadows. “Get up off the floor, boy. We’re going home.”

“No! You can’t do this!” the young man yelled as he rose to his feet, shoving the old man out of the way, and dashed towards a nearby well. He frantically pulled at the rope, straining against the weight of the heavy pail, heaving it upwards as he hugged it against his chest. He sprinted towards the burning woman, throwing the water over her in one fell swoop.

The water crashed against her, dousing some of the flames.

But it was not enough.

The fire traversed her collarbone and began its assault on her raven hair, causing her to wince and crinkle her nose as the sulphurous odour intensified. She tried to look at the young man, her eyes brimming with tears as angry swirls of orange and red invaded her vision. Her wails carried on the air like the howl of a banshee echoing through the murky forest. The trees swayed and churned in the wind, creaking and croaking with every gust.

The young lad attempted to gather more water from the well but was held back by the forceful hands of the old man.

His grip was firm as he glowered at the tear-soaked face of the younger man; not an ounce of empathy in his grey eyes. “If you dare take another step, that *thing* will join her up there,” he gestured behind him, “do you understand me, boy? This is what happens when you dally with the devil.”

The fire gained strength, whipping up and over a man tied to a post beside the raven-haired woman. He writhed in agony as the hairs on his arms and legs were set alight, filling the night air with more noxious fumes as his olive skin burned.

Another woman chanted, calling upon the Great Mother to save her, willing the water from the well to heed her call, the earth underneath her to erupt.

The Great Mother didn't answer.

Instead, the flames rose higher, forcing her to release her white-knuckle grip on the obsidian pendant she was holding, dropping it to the frozen floor beneath her.

The sound of their keening voices forced bats from their roosts. The flapping wings and high-pitched screeches signalling their departure from the woods.

"Your soul is damned. I will celebrate your demise knowing I have extinguished your filth from this realm," the old man paused, staring into the eyes of the raven-haired woman. "You weren't worthy of him in life, and you will be forgotten in death." He tilted his head in the direction of the young man, who was again weeping on the ground. The old man huffed and skulked away, wiping the sweat from his brow with a handkerchief.

The young man winced as he heaved himself up from the ground and wiped the mud from his hands onto the legs of his breeches. His fingernails were filthy from where he dug into the dirt beneath him as he watched his father destroy the woman he loved.

The shadows from the flames jumped across the weather-beaten houses, casting silhouettes like couples dancing by candlelight.

But the only dance that took place that night was the dance of death.

CHAPTER ONE

Phoebe

As the only child of Rafael and Gabriella Emberwood, Lord and Lady of Eskium, I had been used to getting my own way for the majority of my twenty-five years. I wasn't a brat as such – I was grateful, humble, and conscientious, but I *was* headstrong, often refusing to take 'no' for an answer. My upbringing, combined with possessing forbidden magickal powers, meant I often wondered what my life would have looked like had I not inherited the craft from my mother or been born into nobility via my father. Whenever I pleaded with my parents to let me use my powers, they told me the same story:

Frieya was a realm of peace for many moons - the fire witches of the south, the earth witches of the east, the water witches of the west, and the air witches of the north all lived in harmony. Magick was considered a gift, handed down from mother to daughter – but not every mother and daughter. It was deemed such a blessing from the Great Mother herself that the matriarch's name was passed down through generations instead of the patriarch.

But harmony was just an illusion. The coven of air witches in the north began using their powers for evil, dancing with darkness and wreaking havoc wherever they went. As the magick splintered and evolved, it no longer resided only in women but in men too. In doing so, it fractured the elements, forging volatile and depraved power.

Chaos rained down on the Northern Realm as the darkness grew; villagers went missing, crops were spoiled, and children were torn from their homes to be forced into magick camps to be trained to fight.

After numerous failed attempts to disarm the rogue coven, Lord Quinton Whitehill sentenced all the dark witches to death, beheading countless men, women, and children with a small army. But for the coven leaders, he deemed beheading too quick an end. For them, it was to be death by fire, burning the last remnants of the coven who came to be known as The Black Cloth.

Quinton Whitehill, my grandfather, was renowned for being sullen with ice where his heart should have been. Thankfully for me, I had never met him; he had died a few years before I was born. Based on what I knew of my grandfather, I felt lucky I didn't know him.

The diabolical events incited by the rogue coven brought about the end to magick as the realm knew it. Though I carried the same fire as my mother, neither of my parents would allow me to use it for any reason – good or bad. My mother, Gabriella, ceased using her fire in her late teens after news of what happened in Eskium reached the golden sands of Troyla in the Southern Realm, where she lived. She left a year or so later and travelled to the north, satisfied that it was no longer dangerous, seeking a humbler life than the one she was destined for.

But love had its own kind of magick.

Not long after my mother arrived in the north, she met the new heir to Eskium, Rafael. My grandfather had died from a mystery illness a few months prior to her arrival, leaving the lordship of the town to his only son, my father.

Years later, despite abandoning her magick, my mother passed her tiny kernel of power to me. However, it was clear that the Great Mother had other plans – I had been blessed with fire *and* water.

Unfortunately for my parents, I planned to master both elements.

In the Northern Realm, the spring and summer seasons were brief and winter seasons long. There were months of rain, then relentless snow and ice, transforming Eskium into an icy dominion. The town was perpetually dusted in snow like powdered sugar, coating the fields surrounding Eskium Castle in a frozen blanket, shrouding the flowers in the frozen glitter of winter's sleep.

Letting out a contented sigh, I stretched and looked out of my window at the frosty hills and smiled, remembering the Yuletide ball was only a few days away.

During the Winter Solstice, it was tradition for my family to host the Yuletide masquerade ball. The castle would be adorned with holly and ivy, and burgundy ribbons, each window illuminated with a candle filling the sconces with warm, buttery golden hues, honouring the Great Mother. The scent of cinnamon and clementine would fill the corridors, coaxing me towards the kitchen to sneak a sip of Maria's homemade mulled cider. Maria Dreed, the castle's cook, often caught me mid-slurp and would chase me away from the kitchen with a tea towel, laughing maniacally as she tried and failed to whip the backs of my legs. I loved her like a grandmother – having never met my own, it was a joy to have her in the castle and I cherished her company.

I lazily walked to my bathing room and studied myself in my ornate silver mirror through eyes full of sleepy dust, noting the puffy circles underneath my eyes from a heavy night's sleep. My hair was in a loose and messy braid; most of the plaits had unfurled during the night, making my strawberry blonde hair look like a bird's nest.

After untying the remnants of my braid, I attached a lavender-filled linen bag to the taps of my copper bath and watched as the hot water soaked through the herb and filled the tub. Sprinkling a dash of vanilla oil from a tiny glass bottle, I added a generous cup of salt, creating a hypnotising swirl of white and lilac in the water. I slipped out of my silky nightgown and cautiously put one toe in to test the heat, gently easing myself into the tub – it was piping hot, just how I liked it. Reclining, I rested my head and let out a contented groan as I inhaled the relaxing floral scent – it could have been quite easy to go back to sleep.

I submerged my head, running my fingers through the knots as I soaked my long hair. After a few moments, I came back up, ready to begin my morning intentions. Clearing my mind, I focused on the way my body felt in the water, embracing the comforting warmth as it danced across my bones. I thought about lounging in the garden with Brielle and Xavien during Ostara; the morning dew on daffodils, the scent of daisies, the sway of the grass from a light breeze. Birdsong filled my ears; a charming lullaby of a blackbird or wren, and I smiled to myself as I imagined all of the negative energy leaving my body, cleansed and purified by the lavender water.

But then my eyes darted open, alarmed and alert as I launched myself up with force, sending water cascading over the edge. I had just remembered that I arranged to meet with Ezra; he would not be pleased if I was late again.

Quickly, I hauled my body out of the bath and dried myself, rummaging through my wardrobe and chest of drawers for something loose to wear, grabbing the first items I could find – woollen breeches and a cotton blouse. I swiped my heavy cloak and fur-lined boots as I made my way out of my room, before clumsily hopping into my shoes. I huffed in annoyance at having to cut my bath short – I enjoyed many pastimes, but hot ritual baths and daydreaming were two of my favourites. Today, however, my daydreaming cost me a long soak.

As I headed down the staircase, I could hear my parents talking in hushed tones at the end of the hallway. Their voices were strained, and I swore I could hear my mother sobbing. I didn't have time to investigate since Ezra would be waiting, and if I were even one minute late, I would have to run ten laps around the town square.

"I'm off to work. See you later!" I lied, calling up to my parents as I ungraciously landed on the bottom step of the stairs with a thud. When I did work, I worked in Luna's Light, the local apothecary shop. It was only for a few hours a week, far less than my parents were aware.

The heavy wooden front door groaned as I heaved it open and braced myself for the cold as a wave of chilled air hit me. I sprinted over the small moat bridge, then dashed across the lawn to the stables to retrieve my horse, Snowshoe, narrowly avoiding slipping on the ice as I ran. The mare was so white and iridescent in the sunlight that she shimmered like an opal, hues of silver, pink and turquoise glistened along her coat. Her white mane was long, and the hairs crimped as if one of the stable hands had braided it overnight and let the hairs loose in the morning.

"Good day, Snowshoe." I patted my horse gently, then smoothed her nose. Snowshoe responded with a whinny, sending puffs of hot air into the frosty breeze.

I gently eased myself atop my horse and set my course for the town square. It wouldn't be long before Ezra would be pacing impatiently, eager to dish out punishment for my poor punctuality.

The frozen air bit into my skin, and I winced as it caught my scalp, making it tingle and sting. I internally chastised myself for going out into the freezing cold with damp hair – if Maria knew, she'd be furious with me, insistent that I'd catch my death.

I signalled for Snowshoe to ride hard by prodding her sides with the heels of my boots, hoping I would reach Ezra as quickly as possible. Had I not been in such a hurry, I may have stopped to marvel at the icy fields, basking in the unusual glow as thousands of frozen droplets glittered in the midwinter sun.

As I approached the town square, the snow-covered paths became muddier, the roads covered in a beige sludge from the wheels of carts and carriages zigzagging through. I slowed Snowshoe, bringing up the reins ever so slightly. The mare's hooves clipped and clopped along the cobblestones, it was a sound I always loved.

I couldn't help but feel warm and fuzzy with contentment as I looked around the square, noting all of the festive decorations. Shops were illuminated with candles, and bushy green garlands adorned the windowsills, painting the town in festive golds, greens, and reds for the Yuletide season.

Arryn Merek, the owner of The Silver Sparrow, was supervising some of the village children as they prepared a giant wreath for the door to his tavern; a tradition of his that always warmed my heart. The children squabbled over each piece, arguing amongst themselves about who should put what and where. If I wasn't running late, I could have joined in; instead, I made a mental note to help with the castle wreaths instead.

A strained cough brought me back to the present. The source of the noise came from a slim man leaning against the wall of Arnold Leighton's leatherworking shop, his arms folded tightly against his chest, causing his muscles to flex.

Ezra Cain wore his usual garb of a sleeveless linen tunic and breeches – he never seemed to feel the cold. The winter sun gleamed off his ink-black hair, causing my eyes to trail from the top of his head to the end of his ponytail. I met him in The Silver Sparrow a few years prior. That night, my clumsiness during a drinking game caused Ezra to reveal his powers.

My mind wandered back to that evening when I had knocked over glass tankards and almost fell on top of the broken shards. Ezra stopped me from falling with just one movement of his hand, causing me to halt mid-air. Luckily for him, only my friends and I had witnessed the encounter, swearing on our lives never to tell another soul. For several weeks after, I begged Ezra to help me hone my elemental magick, promising I would never use my powers maliciously. He had been regretful for revealing his powers, but eventually gave in. He did, however, make it very clear that the training would always be on his terms, and he could and *would* end it should I give him any cause for concern.

The sound of Ezra clearing his throat – again – pulled me from my reverie. I slid from Snowshoe, grabbing her reins as I approached him.

"Good afternoon, sunshine," I smiled enthusiastically, grinning from ear to ear. I was fond of Ezra and enjoyed pushing his buttons – he was earnest and short-tempered; easy to irritate. He shifted and stood upright, the tick in his jaw signifying his typically impatient mood.

Ezra's eyes narrowed and a deep line formed between his brows. "One of these days you will be early."

"Nice to see you too, Ezra." I smirked as I mocked his glum demeanour, plaiting my damp hair into a braid.

"Less of that, Emberwood. Let's get to work," Ezra replied curtly as we walked towards our usual spot in the woods, away from the hustle and bustle of the town square.

I tied Snowshoe to a thick tree stump and retrieved an apple from my satchel, motioning for her to take it from me. The mare took next to no convincing, eagerly swiping the fruit with her mouth.

Gingerly stepping through the frozen leaves of the forest floor, my boots crunched with every step, leaving footprints in the sludgy snow. I cautiously watched my footing, not wanting to fall on my backside and make a fool of myself.

Ezra had set up several targets at the edge of the clearing. My task was to conjure flame and control its trajectory, aiming and landing only at the hay bales.

"You could at least make it a challenge, Ezra." I joked with false arrogance, scanning the four hay bales that had been dutifully positioned. I chewed the inside of my cheek - I was *actually* kind of nervous, having not made the progress I eagerly wanted.

"Don't tempt me into making this more difficult for you. Even if you manage to set all four targets aflame, I may ask you to conjure water to extinguish them," he paused, shaking his head before he continued, "I'm always saving your ass. You're still as foolish as the night I met you."

"You wouldn't have it any other way though, would you?" I replied, placing my satchel on the ground. Taking a deep breath, I readied myself. I was somewhat competent with flame but conjuring and controlling water was a different story.

Positioning my body, I distributed my weight evenly on both feet, my arms parallel to my legs.

"Remember your stance. You will not be able to control the direction of the flame if your feet do not feel as though they are rooted to the earth." Ezra paced the ground where I stood, his arms behind his back.

"They feel pretty rooted, Ezra." My voice was slightly strained as I peered over my shoulder to see where he was stalking, digging my soles even further into the icy dirt beneath me.

"Very well. Proceed."

I focused on the first bale, my gaze intense as I felt the heat rising from within, instantly thawing my chilled skin. Slowly raising my hands, I felt the flicker of heat radiating from my palms. With one swift movement, I twisted my hands in circular motions and forced a wave of flame outwards. It barely reached a few feet in front of me and fizzled out in several small patches on the ground.

"More fire, Emberwood," Ezra demanded.

"I'm trying."

The heat relented, and I threw my clenched fists down at my sides, expelling a frustrated sigh. I said aloud, "I am the daughter of the elements."

Closing my eyes, I took another deep breath and exhaled slowly, resuming my grounding stance and repositioning my hands.

The heat rose again, and I braced myself as I felt it shifting beneath every inch of my skin and bones – from my toes all the way to the top of my head. The surge of power strengthened my faith in the magick I was blessed with.

"I am the daughter of the elements," I repeated, with more conviction this time. Honing my sights on the same bale, the heat felt stronger, singeing my skin as I twisted my hands as if I were holding an invisible burning orb.

The motion that followed was violent and unforgiving. The flames escaped my palms like a projectile, a molten lance heading towards the hay. I held my stance as I guided the end of the flames outwards, sending it careening towards the target.

I let out a tense breath, smiling at my victory; I did it. The bale was ablaze, the vibrant yellow strands blackened with the intensity of my determination; it was ferocious, and the most impressive display of power yet.

“Very good,” Ezra motioned towards the second pyre, “again.”

CHAPTER TWO

Lady Gabriella

Rafael had been acting strange the last few weeks. Most nights, he had come to their bed around the witching hour, smelling of whiskey and cold air. Gabriella had tried to broach the subject with him, but he continued to distance himself from her even more.

She couldn't understand his sudden change in mood, nor could she deny the dull ache in her chest following their latest argument. The sound of Phoebe rushing down the stairs and out of the front door briefly interrupted the painful silence that followed their disagreement. Phoebe was no doubt running late for her shift at Luna's Light again.

Wiping away the tears that had escaped, Gabriella padded down the hallway, feeling the plush carpet beneath her bare feet. She swiftly descended the staircase, causing her long auburn hair to billow behind her. The smell of freshly baked bread guided the way, leading Gabriella to the kitchen to see one of her favourite people.

Maria had been the castle cook for over twenty years. She was in her sixtieth year, her short curly hair now silver and wiry, her eyes a light acorn brown. She was plump and busty; her flour-dusted aprons always looked like they were a nuisance, but they never seemed to bother her.

"Oh, good afternoon, Ella. Would you like some tea?" Maria offered with delight upon Gabriella entering the kitchen. She was the only one who called her Ella. "Dear me, what has upset you so?" Maria's eyes squinted in worry as she laid her eyes on Gabriella.

"That would be wonderful, thank you Maria," Gabriella replied, avoiding the second question as she glanced at the pies, cakes, and loaves cooling on the marble countertop.

"And some cake?" Maria smirked, knowing full well Gabriella would not be able to resist.

"Of course," Gabriella scoffed – she had never turned down a cake from Maria in over twenty years.

Maria gently transferred one of the cakes to a large plate with a floral design and placed it on the counter by Gabriella. It was a chocolate cake, with delicate ribbons of orange zest inside, one of Gabriella's favourites. Maria sliced into the cake and pulled a large slice away.

"Here you go. Cheer up, love." She looked at Gabriella with a soft smile, placing the slice onto a smaller side plate and pouring tea into a china cup.

"Thank you, Maria. What would we do without you?" Gabriella returned the smile and gently patted Maria's arm.

"You'd all be stick thin!" Maria let out a cackle and tidied away some of the crumbs from the cake.

Yes, they likely would be a little slimmer, but they'd be far less happy.

Gabriella smiled again, taking delicate bites. Maria was effortlessly maternal, much kinder than the woman that had birthed her.

"So, what's wrong then, Ella?"

"Oh, I don't want to bother you with this, Maria. You have too much on your mind already with the Yuletide ball preparations."

"You know you can tell me anything. And cooking is not a burden to me, my dear."

"I know," she replied with a half-smile.

"Is it about Rafael? He's been acting ever so strange, raiding the cellar in the early hours of the morning looking for booze like some sort of drunken teenager. But I'm not going to stick my nose in by giving advice, after all, my own marriage never lasted!" She leaned against the counter giving Gabriella her full attention.

Maria had been married to Jefferson Dreed, the town's apothecary and the owner of Luna's Light. She insisted they fell out of love many moons ago. It was hard for Gabriella to imagine anyone falling out of love with Maria; she was just so kind and considerate and funny too.

Gabriella's forehead creased, curious about her husband's antics. Rafael had never been a hard drinker. An occasional ale with his dinner or a brandy in the evening. He wasn't the kind of person to get through a bottle of whiskey every night.

"Last night I saw him staggering around, muttering something about… What was it? A black heart, I think," Maria paused, "I'm sure that's what he said. I asked him if he needed anything, but he didn't respond. So, I went back to my bed."

Maria's quarters were down the corridor from the kitchen. Her room was modest but cosy, she had been offered one of the larger rooms upstairs many moons ago, but she preferred to be close to the kitchen.

Finishing off the last morsel of her cake, Gabriella padded over to the sink to wash her plate; the contents now sitting heavy in her stomach like a stone as her mind raced, wondering what the Hell could be wrong with her husband.

"Leave that with me, Ella." Maria practically snatched the plate from Gabriella's hands.

Giving her a nod in response, Gabriella gingerly walked out of the kitchen and paused at the bottom of the stairs.

Black heart? This had to mean something. If Rafael was in trouble, she wanted to help. She didn't want him to face this battle alone – whether it was a physical or mental one. She was furious with him for shutting her out, but she was more disappointed that he didn't feel he could trust her with whatever this burden was.

As she approached the guest bedroom, Gabriella was conscious of her footsteps. Even though the hallway was carpeted, the floorboards underneath still creaked due to the age of the castle. Pressing her ear against the wood, she heard the faint sound of snoring.

She turned the handle and peered around the open door to find Rafael sprawled out across the bed, face down on the pillow. In a deep and drunken sleep, he was breathing heavily, evidence of his stupor in the form of an empty whiskey bottle beside him.

Who was this man before her? She barely recognised him; his hair was dishevelled, his beard wild and unkempt too. He was usually immaculate.

Proud. But he was now a shadow of the man he once was, for no obvious reason. *What was tormenting him?* She lightly perched on the edge of the bed and placed her hand on his forearm. Her heart ached to see him this way; she wished she knew what was wrong and what she could do to help him. *What was going through his mind?* He stirred for a few moments before settling back down again, nuzzling into the pillow. She stroked his face, her eyes trailing his masculine features. He was still so handsome, her Rafael.

"I hope you know I love you with all my heart," she said in the softest of whispers as a tear rolled down her cheek.

CHAPTER THREE

Phoebe

The night of the Yuletide masquerade ball had arrived, and the castle was buzzing with droves of townsfolk.

Every inch of the castle was adorned in festive finery, foliage, and candles; not a single surface had been left uncovered. Evergreen garlands peppered with holly and berries twined around the grand staircase, flooding the space with the refreshing scent of pine. The Yule tree stood in the hallway, over twelve feet tall, dressed in pinecones and red ribbons, amongst other things. It was my mother's pride and joy.

As Lady of the Castle, my mother was primarily responsible for arranging town events and fundraisers. She also spent many years supporting vulnerable women, mostly mothers, helping them make a better life for themselves and their children. She taught them how to read and write, as well as how to use basic arithmetic. For those interested, she also taught them how to sew, and heal minor ailments. My mother didn't believe a woman's place was rooted in domesticity. The ability to mend clothes and soothe cuts were useful skills to have with or without a husband and children, but she knew that possessing skills such as these had the power to change lives. Maria also provided cooking lessons, showing the young women how to grow the ingredients and make affordable and delicious dishes.

My mother and Maria made a great team; the Yuletide masquerade ball was the highlight of their year and not only a great example of how well they worked together but how much they enjoyed providing for others.

Maria always cooked non-stop in the days leading up to the celebrations. The kitchen was filled with various cooked portions of meats: turkey, duck, goose, and ham, as well as endless bowls of potatoes and roasted vegetables, gravies, and sauces. She had also made four types of dessert: a cream and jam sponge, a lemon cheesecake, chocolate muffins, and an apple crumble. She always cooked far too much but abhorred the idea that anyone would leave with a hungry belly. The castle usually entertained around one hundred Eskium villagers, and Maria would see everyone fed a generous portion. Second helpings were highly encouraged, much to my delight.

"Phoebe, are you nearly done? Our guests are arriving," my mother called to me through my bedroom door.

I was not a fan of dressing up; I much preferred the part of the event that involved stuffing my face and drinking so much sparkling wine that I nearly popped.

The dress that Tallulah Finnegan, the town's tailor, created this year was the most sophisticated one yet. There would be no unflattering, puffy sleeves or onerous underskirts with bows and ribbons that had been on the dresses my mother requested when I was younger. I had opted for a black velvet gown that hugged me in all the right places and pooled at my feet. It was the epitome of regality, with long sheer sleeves adorned with the finest rose gold outlines of suns and eye-watering detail along the plunged neckline.

My hair was gathered on one side in waves, with a section held in place by an ornate inky black clip decorated with the tiniest rose and clear quartz crystals.

"Yes, mother. I'm just adding the finishing touches and I will be down," I replied, placing my dark, feathered mask over my eyes and opening the door.

"What do you think?" I asked as I twirled in the hallway.

"Great Mother. *They* are going to be the talk of the town for years to come." My mother waved a finger at my neckline. "Your father will be furious."

"Then let him be furious. I'm going to go have fun with my friends." I lightly kissed my mother's cheek before I carefully descended the stairs. *It wasn't my fault I had been blessed in the bust department, so why shouldn't I show them off?*

"Oh, and Mother?" I turned and called out.

"Yes?"

"You look unbelievably beautiful."

My mother returned a smile full of warmth, smoothing down her blush pink gown.

"Phoebe, you look…Wow. I'm speechless." Tyrus greeted me at the bottom of the stairs, taking my hand in his and placing a feather-light kiss on my knuckles.

"And you look rather lovely yourself," I smiled as I surveyed him from head to toe. He was tall and lean, with sandy hair and chocolate brown eyes; laughter lines adorned his otherwise youthful face, though they were hidden beneath his silver mask. I had only seen him in formal attire a few times before, and it always made me giddy.

"You guys look amazing!" Brielle skipped around the corner with her arm looped with Xavien's. They had obviously already familiarised themselves with the bar, each with two glasses of sparkling wine in their hands.

"You are going to be very popular tonight, Bee." Xavien joked, widening his eyes and nudging Tyrus's elbow with his own. "You'll be fighting the men off when the dancing begins."

"They can certainly try," Tyrus grabbed me by the waist and pulled me closer.

"You both look ravishing," I motioned towards Xavien and Brielle as Tyrus nuzzled my neck, sending a thrill through me.

Xavien had tied his hair up into a bun and was dressed in a deep purple jacket, white shirt, and black suede breeches, and Brielle wore a silky gold halterneck gown with matching gloves which made her look nothing short of radiant. They each decided to wear a mask that matched one another's attire: Xavien wore a gold satin mask and Brielle purple velvet.

My best friend was gorgeous inside and out. Her skin was a rich brown colour, with a flawless complexion and cheekbones like petite apples beneath the surface. She usually kept her black curls short and bouncy, but for the ball, her hair was in a slick braid that encircled her head like a serpentine crown, with delicate wisps of hair circling the top of her forehead in lustrous spirals.

We had been best friends since we were young children, spending every waking moment together, playing in Eskium Castle, in the woods near the town square, or in the garden of Brielle's family home. We spent hours making daisy chains, collecting rocks and unusual stones for my altars, and weaving crowns out of lavender, buttercups, and twigs. 'Witchy stuff,' Brielle would call it. She did not possess powers like me, her mother being one of the many women untouched by magick, but she wished she did. I always reassured her that she didn't need special powers; after all, there is a witch in every woman.

I made friendship necklaces for us both, using leather cord and amethyst stones, explaining to Brielle in great detail about its power, telling her to hold onto it whenever she felt nervous or to put it under her pillow to aid sleep.

When we weren't doing *witchy stuff*, we would pick apples to snack on, climbing trees until our hands were raw from the rough bark and splinters.

One day, we had decided to build our very own tree house with bits of old wood Brielle's father had disposed of – weathered doors, worn floorboards – anything we could get our grubby hands on. The finished product was a mess, the structure wonky and unsteady, but we didn't care. Our handiwork meant we could see far across the hills of Eskium and watch the sun go to sleep, leaving behind a burst of peach and pomegranate in the sky.

Often, Xavien would join us *after we* finished all the hard work, but he would always arrive with a satchel of food, no doubt something he had taken off the windowsill of a neighbour, like a fresh pie or roast chicken legs. Xavien was the definition of mischief, and there was never a dull moment with him around.

"You're the most beautiful girl in all of Eskium," I whispered to Brielle, drifting back into the present. Brielle replied with a coy smile; she wasn't good at accepting compliments, but her body language made me think she might believe it for once.

As we entered the main hall, the smell of clementines and cinnamon filled the air, courtesy of Maria's famous mulled cider. The room was buzzing with merriment; there was plenty of raucous laughter, hugs, and clinking glasses.

I spotted Arryn Merek, the landlord of The Silver Sparrow, leaning against a wall by the bar. He stood out from the crowd thanks to his barrel-chest and arms and legs like tree trunks. He was never far from alcohol, able to drink anyone under the table with minimal effort. It was odd to see him without a tankard in one hand and a cloth in the other. He was dressed in a simple white linen shirt and dark beige leather breeches – less formal than most of the other guests, but he probably found it difficult to find a suit that fit his broad chest and shoulders.

Ivi and Olivier Blackthorn, who ran the local farm, were rarely seen in anything other than muddy boots and dirty dungarees, but they scrubbed up well. Ivi wore a plum purple gown layered with tiny black beads that dazzled in the candlelight. Her hair was braided into a low bun; it was quite the transformation from her usual messy ponytail. Olivier was dressed in a navy doublet with matching trousers, effortlessly glamorous for a farmer. They never missed the Yuletide ball, nor any opportunity to mention that they supplied many of the fresh ingredients in Maria's kitchen, taking credit for the crispiness of the potatoes, thanks to the butter made from the milk of their cows.

Glancing around the room, I noticed Ezra in a corner. He was talking to Arnold Leighton, the leatherworker, who had forgone his signature green leather jerkin and woollen breeches for a smart beige shirt and buckskin trousers.

"Go talk to Ezra," I nudged Brielle. I had been trying to get them together for a while. "Look how handsome he looks dressed head to toe in black. He's even let his hair down, *literally*."

"Don't you dare start this again tonight," Brielle elbowed back.

My smile stretched into a mischievous grin. "Come on. What's thc worst that could happen?"

"Um, I don't know? He rejects me and I'll never be able to set foot in the town square ever again?"

"I've seen the way he looks at you. Just go and speak to him."

"Phoebe, you're making it obvious." Brielle's cheeks flushed a dusty pink.

"Please, he's not even looking this way," I lied, watching as Ezra glanced at Brielle several times.

"Besides, I'm waiting to dance with Xavien." Brielle searched the room nervously, spotting him talking with a young man that worked at The Silver Sparrow. Xavien stroked his arm with familiarity, causing Brielle to frown in confusion.

Noting her puzzlement, I took Brielle by the arm and dragged her along with me to the corner where Ezra stood.

“Hi, Ezra! Hi Arnold!” The pitch of my voice was painfully high.

“I am going to kill you,” Brielle muttered under her breath through clenched teeth.

“Hi… Hi.” Ezra responded coyly, his eyes slowly drifting from me to Brielle. Arnold simply nodded, gesturing towards the bar and sauntering off. He wasn’t a man of many words, barely conversing whenever I popped into his leatherworking shop to browse his wares.

“Have you guys met, I can’t remember?” I looked at Brielle and then Ezra, knowing full well they had met several times when Brielle came by to see me when I was training with him.

“Yes. We have,” Brielle's whole body seemed to be taut with tension as she responded grudgingly.

“Yup,” Ezra answered nonchalantly.

“Well, that’s great. Oh, my parents will be here soon! I better go find them and start doing the rounds.” I quickly scarpered off, leaving my friend behind with Ezra, knowing that I would pay for that later.

My parents walked in shortly afterwards, causing an array of gasps and applause to echo around the hall. They stared at each other lovingly, their expressions full of warmth and adulation. My mother looked up at my father and cupped his cheek, gently stroking his beard with her thumb. He held her closer as he kissed her forehead, causing her to beam from ear to ear. My heart filled with joy to know my parents were still so in love after all this time; whatever I may have heard the other day was obviously inconsequential. My father had looked far more presentable than I had seen him recently, he had trimmed his beard and styled his hair, combing his wavy locks with rose oil. I still didn't understand why he suddenly looked dishevelled in recent weeks.

After my parents nodded in my direction, they moved on to chat with the townsfolk. My father loved to entertain, and he loved his people even more. Eskium adored him in return.

After he took over lordship from his father, he vowed to turn the town around and regain their trust.

My grandfather, Lord Quinton Whitehill, was known by all as an unpleasant man, 'so vile, he probably pissed acid,' many villagers supposedly said. Though he was most renowned for the witch trials, he was famous for leeching every drop of gold from his villagers, charging extortionate rent on properties and businesses, and paying his own staff way below the average coin.

During his tenure, the shops and homes around the town square were more like hovels. Buildings were run down with poor fixtures and fittings, roofs were weak, and walls crumbled. Due to the exorbitant fees he charged, many families suffered, barely able to afford food and firewood. Many harsh winters came and went, as did entire families, perishing in the bitter cold.

Once my father became Lord, he swore he would never allow another Eskium villager to suffer, taking it upon himself to assist with the rebuilding of homes, and improving insulation and sanitation. My father substantially reduced all fees; he never understood why anyone needed all that gold and abhorred the fact his own father lived a life like a king as his own people starved and froze to death.

Within months, the improvements were evident. Homes were functional and families rosy-cheeked, their gaunt faces now full of life. Businesses began to flourish, paving the way for better trade routes to Arleau, Zhadria, and Troyla. People were happy.

We made our way over to the dining hall, ready to pile up our plates with some of the delicious food Maria had so dutifully prepared. A long table stretched across the space, piled high with meats, vegetables, potatoes, pies, soups, gravies and sauces. My stomach grumbled as I spotted a huge pot of broccoli and stilton soup and the basket of freshly baked rolls beside it.

"Great Mother. I swear Maria puts dandelion dust in her food. I cannot get enough!" Xavien said with excitement, taking a big spoonful of buttery potatoes and piling them onto his plate.

"Are you accusing our cook of spiking the food, Xave?" I asked jokingly.

"Listen, I'm not saying she's a *witch* or anything," he whispered, "but I've never had potatoes like this. Ever. I wish she would give me the recipe so I can have them every day. They make me so happy."

"Even if she *did* give you the recipe, there's no way you'd make your potatoes taste *this* good," Brielle interjected as she slipped off her silky gloves and grabbed a turkey leg.

Year after year, we tried to convince Maria to join the festivities, wanting her to be spoiled with attention and praise, and to have a chance in the limelight for once. But she was insistent that she would not leave the kitchen until the ball was finished. "You never know when you might need more mashed potatoes!" She would always say. Maria had reassured us countless times that cooking for the Eskium people at

Yuletide was the highlight of her year and basking in glory was not her cup of tea.

Once our bellies were full and we had our fair share of sparkling wine, we waddled back into the main hall.

Brielle and Xavien took to the main floor first, dramatically weaving in and out of other couples in a blur of purple and gold as they danced together. You could hear their laughter above the music, which was no easy feat given the chamber orchestra providing the evening's entertainment. Xavien twirled Brielle around, dipped her, and pulled her back up towards him in an effortless move. It was impressive, considering the amount of sparkling wine and food he had already consumed.

"Why must we always eat before we dance? I have a stitch," Tyrus winced as he rubbed his side.

"Stop being such a baby." I lightly shoved him in the shoulder before placing my cheek against it and holding my body close against his.

We swayed to the music; the rhythm of the string quartet allowed for a dance that was more like an embrace. Tyrus's chin rested on the top of my head and for a few moments, I felt a sliver of that all-consuming adulation. I often wondered if I would ever feel that way about someone. Tyrus and I were close, sure, but we were very much just friends with benefits.

"May I have the next dance?" An unexpected voice sounded behind us, bringing me out of my daydream with a jolt. I turned to find a tall and broad-shouldered man offering his palm.

I was awestruck for a few moments as my eyes adjusted to the wonder in front of me. Realising my mouth was agape, I shut it with a snap, then glanced back at Tyrus, who looked perturbed and darted his eyes between the stranger and me. Then he begrudgingly gave a slow nod, and I watched as his jaw ticked, his gaze piercing through the stranger's like a hot iron before he sauntered off to Brielle and Xavien with his fists clenched.

The stranger was imposing, his muscles clearly defined beneath his black shirt. His hair was long, dark and wavy, almost curly. And his eyes – I had never seen eyes that colour before, deep blue with flecks of gold that seemed to shimmer against the candlelight in the room, made even more intense by the black leather mask that framed them. My eyes trailed down to his nose, my gaze abruptly stopping for a few seconds to admire his nose piercing, like a magpie drawn to treasure. *Gods above.*

"Y…Yes," I hesitated for a moment before taking the man's hand.

A frisson of electricity tickled my fingers and sent goosebumps up my arm as he held my palm. Glancing down, I was convinced that the sensation dancing across my skin was visible.

"I must say, you look good enough to eat," the stranger teased.

Heat filled my cheeks. His voice was unlike anything I had heard before, with just a hint of exoticism that sounded warm and inviting like the golden sands of Troyla in the south.

"You should not say such things to the Lord's daughter, especially one who is taken."

"Taken? Pity. Who is the lucky man or woman?"

I tipped my head to direct the stranger's gaze to Tyrus, who stood on the sidelines with his arms crossed, his cheeks flushed an angry red.

"You are way too good for him, you know that, right?" He spun me around before capturing me by the waist with a firm grip.

"And what makes you so sure of that?"

The heat of his body against mine was almost too much to bear, searing through the velvet of my gown.

"You have looked in a mirror before, haven't you?" His gaze casually moved from the top of my head to my mouth and then briefly to my breasts. *Subtle as a brick.*

"If you continue to flirt with me so conspicuously, then I will have no choice but to end this dance."

"Shall I flirt inconspicuously instead? I'm not sure I know how," he whispered as he placed his cheek against mine. The feel of his stubble against my skin set me aflame again, causing my pulse to thrum so violently I could feel my heartbeat in my ears.

As I went to leave, the stranger gently took me by the wrist and pulled me closer to him.

"Okay, okay. I'm sorry. I will behave."

The firmness of his chest against mine caused a flurry of butterflies to coalesce in my stomach – a riot of wings desperate to break free.

"You can barely see my face under this mask, I could be hideous." I regretted my response almost immediately.

"Even a blind man would know that you are the most enchanting woman in this room." His eyes locked with mine and my legs suddenly felt boneless.

I was clueless about the identity of this man. Eskium was a small town, and everyone knew everyone. *Who was he?*

"Quite the charmer, aren't you?" The adrenaline sent a wave of false confidence through me.

"So, I *am* charming you?" He smirked, making me fixate on his full lips.

Refusing to reply, I continued to survey the stranger, scanning his features for any sign of familiarity.

"Something tells me you're not used to being told how magnificent you are, Phoebe."

My eyes shot to his. *How did he know my name?*

"Who are you? I've never seen you before," I asked as he continued to glide me around the floor.

"So many questions." The deep timbre of his voice rumbled through him, and I felt every word against my chest, making my skin tingle beneath my gown.

I gulped as a wave of desire coursed through me. "I know this is a masquerade ball, but this *man of mystery* thing you're trying *so* hard to pull off is actually quite tiresome." I rolled my eyes and glanced away from him, soon realising that half the room was watching us. My parents looked at me curiously – I wasn't sure if they were intrigued or uncomfortable. I wanted to crawl into a hole to disappear out of sheer embarrassment.

"Are you sure about that?" he whispered into the shell of my ear, his neck so close to my face I couldn't avoid inhaling his hypnotic scent – alluringly warm with a touch of something that reminded me of spices.

I raised my chin in defiance. "Yes, I am certain."

His eyes met mine again, and it felt as though time stood still. The deep blue-veined with gold reminded me of lapis lazuli, and I peered into them quizzically, wondering if they offered the same properties as the stone: truth and knowledge.

Don't be foolish, Phoebe. This man seemed to wear deceit like a coat.

“I know you’re too good for him because any sane man would never let go of you, even for a few minutes,” he whispered again.

“Oh, so you prefer your women tethered to your side?” My tone was laced with disdain.

“Not exactly,” he paused, “I think you’re too wild to tame,” he said softly, pushing an errant curl behind my ear, “and beautiful birds don’t belong in cages.”

My heart pounded in my chest; the heat that flushed my cheeks before had turned into a wildfire.

“Think you’ve had her for long enough, don’t you?” Tyrus suddenly appeared on the dancefloor, his voice as sharp as a knife.

“Eternity would not be enough,” the stranger quipped back, holding my gaze as he released his grip and ushered me towards Tyrus. The stranger slowly walked in the opposite direction, turning back with a smirk on his face, before disappearing into a small crowd of people I did not recognise.

“Don’t let him dance with you again,” Tyrus commanded, taking me forcefully by the arm.

“Excuse me? It’s a masquerade ball, Ty. This is kind of what happens…” I peered down at the vice-like grip he had on me, irritated that he was attempting to drag me away.

“I don’t care. Stay away from him.”

“You’re being ridiculous.”

“I won’t say it again, Phoebe. Stay. Away. From. Him,” he snarled as his fingers dug into my flesh.

Yanking my arm away, I glanced down at the white impressions left on my skin from his crushing grip. I rubbed my palm over the marks, attempting to soothe the burning sensation that lingered.

"Firstly, do not ever grab me like that again. Secondly, you do not control what I do. This is a dance. The clue is in the name." My soft features became hard lines and edges.

"He's bad news, Phoebe." Tyrus's voice softened.

"Do you know him?" I asked, turning my head to see if I could locate the mystery man.

"No. But isn't it obvious? He's turned up as if from nowhere and no one knows who he is."

"Sounds familiar," I retorted.

"Please, Phoebe. Just avoid him for the rest of the night. I don't trust him."

I sighed, sauntering off to the bar to get away from him for a moment. Collecting two glasses of sparkling wine. I downed one glass and then started on the next; the bubbles burned on the way down.

"Who *was* that, Phoebe?" Brielle sidled up to me, shooting quick glances around the dancefloor.

"I have absolutely no idea." I took another long sip, then placed my glass down. I paused for a few seconds, realising I could still smell the stranger's intoxicating scent on my dress – sandalwood and spice.

"Well, seeing as you're spoken for, I'd very much like to dance with him myself." Brielle wiggled her shoulders mischievously.

"What about Ezra?" I queried, trying to spot the lithe raven-haired man.

"He is not the dancing type." Brielle let out a long sigh, then slumped her shoulders, evidently disappointed with Ezra's lack of interest in waltzing her around the dancefloor.

"Makes sense. Well then, go right ahead." I gestured in the direction of the stranger without looking at him.

Brielle's brows knitted together. "What's wrong?"

"Nothing, it's fine."

It wasn't really fine; I was all kinds of flustered. I was hot and cold at the same time, exhausted yet wide awake. *What the fuck was that about?*

"Phoebe, tell me."

"I don't know. I just feel very strange after that encounter."

"Any woman would. I mean, *look* at him." Brielle averted her gaze in an obvious movement, looking over at where the stranger stood in an alcove with several other mystery guests.

I didn't want to look at him. But curiosity got the better of me, and my eyes slowly trailed over to the corner where the stranger stood. *Where the Hell did he come from? Who were those people with him?*

Those blue and gold irises locked with mine in an instant, causing my heart to gallop in my chest in a mixture of fright and excitement. I tried my best to pull my gaze away from him, but it was like I was tethered. I was a moth, and he was one giant, gorgeous flame.

"Great Mother. I guess I'm invisible." Brielle sauntered off on slightly drunken, wobbly legs.

Reaching for the half-empty glass of sparkling wine behind me, I promised myself I would look at him only once more.

I slowly turned to face the direction of the stranger again, but he was gone.

The feeling that followed next took me by surprise. Disappointment.

CHAPTER FOUR

The stranger

I didn't understand why we needed to be here. It seemed far too risky, but *she* insisted we needed more information.

"Keep yourselves to yourselves, find out what you can, and don't cause a scene," she muttered under her breath as we skulked in a dark alcove of the castle.

That seemed easy enough.

Until I saw *her*. Phoebe Fucking Emberwood.

Gods above. She was beautiful, with hair the colour of strawberries and sunshine.

What the fuck did I just say?

She was divine, a goddess amongst mortals, with curves that could turn a clergyman away from the cloth.

I was overcome with the urge to get a closer look, to see if she was just as enchanting up close, but then *he* appeared next to her—that pathetic excuse for a man. I looked on as he held her close and led her across the floor.

"Don't you fucking dare," she snarled next to me, following my line of vision to the Emberwood woman. She gripped my arm, attempting to hold me back, but I shrugged her off.

Fuck it.

I knew I shouldn't have approached Phoebe Emberwood, but self-control wasn't my strong suit. And when better to explore my curiosities than a masquerade ball?

Striding across the room, I felt dozens of eyes trailing my every movement. Before I knew it, I was standing in front of her, asking her to dance, praying to the gods that she would oblige.

The idiot next to her stiffened. Good. He deserved to feel threatened.

She peered up at me through bottle green eyes and thick eyelashes, her face partially covered by a feather-laden mask. A gasp escaped her lips.

When she agreed with a tentative 'yes,' I took her hand in mine in a flash. A short sharp twinge shot through my fingers, along my wrist and up my arm, like a powerful shock. She seemed to feel it, too, as she glanced at where our hands met. *Odd.*

I didn't even need to look at *him* to see how much I irked him; his aura was so barbed with fury he could have sprouted quills.

Her body against mine created the most delicious friction, and my mind couldn't help but wander as the heat of my skin seeped into hers. My eyes danced over her from head to toe, lingering without subtlety on certain parts of her. I couldn't recall the last time I'd danced with a woman, but I knew then that I wouldn't forget this one in a hurry.

She was so easy to fluster. I loved that. The flush in her cheeks and underneath her collarbone was enough evidence I needed to know that I was having an effect on her. I took every chance I could to get closer, resting my face against hers, breathing in the sweet scent of her hair. Lavender and vanilla. *Delicious.*

But the bliss of her in my arms was short-lived as her insufferable bastard of a 'boyfriend' interrupted us, his deathly cold tone cutting through my stupor like a blade of ice. *Some boyfriend.*

I watched as he ushered her away, his grip on her soft flesh much too forceful. That pissed me off a lot more than it probably should have.

He muttered something to her through gritted teeth, his fingers still pinned to her arm. I should have gone over there and knocked his fucking teeth out, but I'd already drawn too much attention. I clenched my fists in protest, wishing I could steal her away from him and soothe her pinched flesh. *What the fuck was wrong with me? I didn't even know this woman.*

He stormed off, heading towards a long-haired blonde man, so I reluctantly peeled myself away from the main floor, content that the idiot had finished handling her like meat on a butcher's block.

Just as I was about to retreat entirely, I took one last look at her. I was somewhat surprised to find those green eyes locked with mine; the stubborn beauty refused to look away, luring me closer like a siren song.

Finally, she broke eye contact with me, allowing me the opportunity to sever the invisible thread and vanish further into the shadows.

CHAPTER FIVE

Lord Rafael

It was a frosty morning at Eskium Castle, and Rafael had just finished his breakfast of bacon, fried eggs, and mushrooms when one of his footmen asked to speak with him. He let out a groan as he got up from his chair, wincing as his joints cracked and popped – he was really starting to feel his age. The dull ache in his back had not ceased, a consequence of spending all night on his feet mingling with villagers during the ball. The aches and pains had been worth it – Rafael was overjoyed to have hosted such a successful event for his people, though his wife deserved all the credit.

Despite such a jubilant yuletide ball, he still thought something was wrong. He had felt it in his bones for weeks now, a sense of never-ending dread consuming him with a melancholy he had never experienced before. He did not possess powers like his wife and daughter, but he was sensitive to shifts in energy – something that began when he was a young lad that he never understood.

He knew he had to talk to Gabriella about this soon; he needed to stop shutting her out. His heart felt full recalling the way his wife looked at him the night of the ball – so many moons had passed, yet they still were infatuated with one another.

Drowning his sorrows dulled his unease temporarily, but as soon as the whiskey high wore off, it was as if someone had smothered him with a dark shroud and suffocated him.

Nighttime was the worst. When he didn't drink himself into a stupor, the castle was as quiet as a graveyard, the silence so palpable he wanted to yell until his throat was hoarse and his lungs burned.

It was foolish of him to push Gabriella away when he valued her company, and her counsel, for over two decades, but he couldn't bear the thought of burdening her with the dark thoughts that plagued his mind. He didn't know what they meant, either. *What if this was all in his mind?* He wasn't sure what scared him more.

"My Lord," the footman approached hesitantly. "Word has arrived from the town square."

Rafael's pulse thrummed violently, sending waves of panic throughout his body. He fidgeted with the hem of his shirt; he didn't understand how, but he knew it was bad news.

"One of the villagers has been found murdered."

Rafael teetered backwards, grabbing a chair to steady him. He stood frozen for a moment, trying to swallow down the knot that had formed in his throat.

"What…wh.. Who is it?" he asked, his voice suddenly raspy.

"Arnold Leighton. The leatherworker."

"Arnold? Why in the gods would anyone murder Arnold?"

"I don't know, my Lord, but whoever did it was barbaric. Jefferson says it looks like an animal savaged him."

"Are we sure it *wasn't* an animal?"

"Yes. These wounds were unnatural, my Lord. A mixture of what Jefferson called… magick and blade."

Great Mother. The last time Rafael had seen bloodshed was when the Roamers attacked the town a few moons prior.

"Find out everything you can and report to me at once." he added, "Any witnesses?"

"No, my Lord. But Arryn is the one who found the poor bastard outside The Silver Sparrow. Arnold's eyes were missing..."

An overwhelming feeling of nausea filled Rafael. *Was this what he was dreading?*

"Is the body with Jefferson?"

"Yes, my Lord."

"I will go there at once. Prepare my horse."

When Rafael arrived at Luna's Light, the apothecary shop owned by Jefferson Dreed, dozens of people had gathered outside. The sound of panicked whispers heightened the fear in his heart, making it difficult for him to concentrate. He ushered them to one side and made his way to the door. He couldn't recall which days Phoebe worked at the shop and sincerely hoped she would not be there to see Arnold's battered body.

"What is happening, m'Lord? Are we no longer safe?" a woman called out, clutching her shawl with such a fierce grip her knuckles whitened.

"We are doing what we can. There is no need for alarm." Rafael's response was firm as he rapped on the window three times. Jefferson appeared through an alcove at the back.

Rafael cautiously walked over the threshold, narrowly avoiding numerous wooden windchimes as he made his way through – a cumbersome decoration that Jefferson insisted on having to keep evil spirits away – fitting for the superstitious apothecary. Wisps of smoke funnelled from sticks of incense, flooding the small space with the strong scent of jasmine and white sage.

"He's through here," Jefferson announced.

Approaching the back room, Rafael fanned the air with his palm to free his nostrils of the overpowering smell of the incense. The room was ice cold and the sudden drop in temperature caught him by surprise, sending an unnerving chill down his spine. The room had barely been used in the time Rafael had ruled Eskium; murders simply did not take place in the town unless there was a siege, and bloodshed had undoubtedly been spilled on both sides.

A body draped in a white cloth lay atop a table against the back wall of the room; splotches of dark red blood dotted the corpse from head to toe. Rafael thanked the gods that Arnold left no wife or children behind.

Rafael warily lifted the cloth, peering slowly underneath the fabric. What he saw before him was so deeply horrific, he had to fight back the rise of bile in his throat. Arnold would have been barely recognisable were it not for his signature green leather jerkin and the tattoo on his forearm: a boar and two daggers. His skin was unnaturally grey for someone who had been dead a matter of hours as if the energy had been drained from him. Along with both of his eyes, half of his face was missing, the bone of his nose a jagged nub and a deep slash ran from his jaw to his collarbone, revealing the sinews and nerve endings of his neck.

It took Rafael several deep breaths to quell the sudden need to vomit as he scanned the rest of his body. His legs seemed the only part of his body that hadn't been maimed. "Great Mother. This is savagery, I've never seen anything like it," Rafael clasped his mouth with his palm, "patch him up as best you can so we can prepare his body for the Summerland ceremony."

Jefferson nodded, gathering vials from the shelf behind him.

"I'm going to speak with Arryn at The Silver Sparrow," Rafael announced, stomping out of Luna's Light and through the crowd of villagers who had still not dispersed.

As he hurried to the tavern, he offered only the briefest of smiles to the villagers he passed, opting to keep his head down to avoid further questions.

He spared a solitary glance at the leatherworking shop, noting the 'closed' sign and unlit candles; a solemn reminder that Arnold would never step foot in that shop again. Never make another pair of boots. Never make the saddles for Eskium's horses.

Approaching the entrance to the tavern, Rafael paused before the main door. The sight of the Yuletide wreath made his heart feel heavier than he ever thought possible. He took a deep breath and opened the door, relishing the warmth that enveloped him as he entered.

"Rafael," Arryn spoke, his voice low and sombre. "Drink?" he asked, lifting a bottle of whiskey from behind the bar, along with two short glasses.

Rafael nodded, taking a seat in one of the booths.

Arryn sat down heavily, slightly knocking the table. He placed the bottle and glasses on the table, pouring a generous measure for them both.

"Thank you." Rafael said, taking a sip, letting the strong alcohol coat his dry throat and warm his belly, "tell me what you know."

"I found 'im around six this morning when I was bringin' in the kegs. At first, I thought he was passed out drunk by the hitchin' post, but he didn't seem pissed at the ball last night, so thought it odd that 'e'd be out 'ere drunk. Then I saw the blood." Arryn's voice was shaky as he took a swig of whiskey, his face full of anguish. "So much blood, Rafael. How could I not 'ave 'eard anythin'? What if I could 'ave helped him?" He scraped his fingers through his shaggy grey hair, then hung his head dejectedly.

"I don't think anyone could have helped him, Arryn. We don't know where and when he was killed. But we do know that the wounds were borne of magick."

"The wounds… they were… brutal, Rafael. Who… or what could do somethin' like this? How could it be magick?" Arryn got up from the booth and plodded over to the bar, depositing his empty glass on the side.

Rafael's leg bounced beneath the table. "I don't know. Jefferson is going to inspect his injuries further and report his findings to me."

Arryn folded his arms across his broad chest. "The villagers are starting to panic. Some 'ave already fled to Arleau and Zhadria. Murders don't happen 'ere, Rafael. We need to find who did this, and quickly."

"I know. Please, be on your guard and let me know if you see or hear anything odd in the tavern. I mean it. Any folk you've not seen before, or anyone acting strange, tell me immediately." Rafael rose from his seat, his gaze fixed on Arryn.

Arryn gave a nod and shook his hand.

As Rafael rode back to the castle, thoughts of Arnold's battered body flashed in his mind, filling him with that sickening sensation all over again. His mind drifted to his family, then terror hit him like a brick in the face. *Whoever did this to Arnold could come after Gabriella or Phoebe.*

He nudged the horse with the heel of his boot more forcefully than he usually would, but he needed to get home. The wind whipped at his face as he picked up speed; plumes of dust kicked out underneath the horses' hooves, leaving a cloud in its wake.

Outside the castle stood a postmaster, shifting from foot to foot as if he stepped on hot coals.

Rafael's heart rate thundered again. *There's something wrong. I can feel it.*

He jumped down from his horse and rushed over to the man.

"A parcel for you… m'Lord," the postmaster hesitantly passed Rafael a wooden box.

"What in the gods is wrong with you, lad? Pass it here!" Rafael scowled at him and snatched the box.

"N…nothing, m'Lord. Good day to you." He scurried away, half sprinting down the hill.

Rafael shook his head. He was about to open the box where he stood, but he glanced around the grounds at the castle staff going about their duties and decided it would be better to inspect it privately.

He ventured to his study instead. Taking a seat in the leather chair behind his desk, he opened the box. The lid slowly opened with a metallic creak.

Two eyeballs. And a blood-soaked note.

Eyes for you to see.

He peered back at the glassy, bloodshot globes staring at him, the brown of the irises dull and devoid of any previous human ownership.

Arnold's eyes.

His hands shook violently as he read the note again.

Gabriella strolled in as he went to wipe his mouth with a handkerchief. She was seemingly unaware of any disturbance from Rafael. Shoving the box to one side, he hoped to attempt at covering it up under a stack of papers.

"You look like you've just seen a ghost, Rafael." Gabriella reached for him, but he flinched.

"It's…it's nothing. I just need to lie down," his voice was hoarse as he fought against the rising bile in his throat.

"Rafael, please," she pleaded with him, grabbing hold of his arm. "Tell me what is going on! I've had enough of your misdirection. I am your wife. You can tell me anything. Please. Tell me."

Rafael considered guiding her out of the door and locking himself inside, but he was tired. Tired of feeling whatever *this* was. Tired of shouldering the burden alone. "A villager… has been murdered," he announced reluctantly, averting his eyes from his wife, not wanting to see any alarm on her face.

"What?! Who?" Gabriella's eyes were wide in shock.

"Arnold Leighton."

Gabriella gasped, covering her mouth with her hand.

"But that's not all," he added, hesitantly passing the wooden box to his wife. "This just arrived. Be warned, Gab, it is gruesome."

She tentatively opened the lid and nearly dropped the box onto the floor.

"What in the gods?!" she screeched.

"They belong, *belonged*, to Arnold."

Gabriella held her palm across her mouth in shock. "Why would anyone want to kill Arnold? Desecrate his body this way?"

"I don't know. But the feeling of cold lead in my stomach makes me think that he won't be the last."

CHAPTER SIX

Phoebe

"Hold on – did you say eyeballs?" Xavien covered his mouth as he dry heaved.

"Yep," I replied, chewing my lip as I tried to distract myself from the gruesome images plaguing my thoughts.

"Bloody Hell. What is going on? Poor Arnold." Brielle got up from the armchair she was sitting in and sat next to me. She rubbed my arm reassuringly. "Are you okay?"

"Mmhm. I'm just… In shock. And a bit scared, to be honest."

"It's okay, Phoebe. It's probably just a one-off and someone has played a sick joke," Tyrus sat on the other side of me, enveloping me with his arm.

I glared at him, wondering how he could refer to mutilation and murder as a "sick joke."

"I feel frightened for my parents. What if something happens to them?" My voice was barely audible.

"Don't think like that. It will be fine. Whoever this evil fucker is will get caught soon," Xavien's smile was pensive as he handed me a cup of mead, motioning for me to take a sip.

"Hey, I know what we should do," Xavien announced, rubbing his hands together, "I've just acquired some exquisite silverleaf." He waved a hessian pouch at us, his face the picture of mischief.

"Fuck it, why not? I think we could all use the distraction." Tyrus added, glancing in my direction like he was checking for my approval.

"Sure," I replied unenthusiastically, glancing down at my hands in my lap. Smoking silverleaf was not the wisest choice but I needed to do *something* to take my mind off what happened.

"Xavien, not all traumatic events need to be treated with dodgy substances." Brielle's leg bounced nervously.

"Oh, come on! We used to smoke this all the time when we were teenagers," he protested.

"We're not teenagers anymore," Brielle huffed.

"Brielle, relax. You don't have to join in if you don't want to. But it could really take the edge off." Tyrus started to help Xavien grind the silverleaf into finer flakes, ready for the sycamore pipe.

"Why the Hell would anyone murder Arnold?" Brielle pondered, fetching a plate of grapes, cheese, and bread from the kitchen.

"I don't know, but maybe we should talk about something else? We're supposed to be having fun and distracting ourselves from the bloodthirsty murderer." Xavien shook his head in annoyance.

"Very well, pass it to me then." I extended my palm towards Xavien, taking the pipe and resting the funnel between my lips. I took one long intake of breath, held it for a few seconds, then exhaled slowly, causing small puffs of smoke to escape my nose.

"Oh, that is gooood," I giggled, handing the pipe back to Xavien.

"Please tell me that hasn't hit you already?" Xavien chuckled, looking between his friends.

"Hey! It's been a while since I smoked this." I said with a grin, making myself comfortable on the sofa.

"Do you remember when Tyrus ended up in Olivier and Ivi Blackthorn's farm the last time we smoked this?" Xavien slapped his thigh as he let out a dirty and contagious cackle, which set the whole group off laughing.

"Not just the farm. The godsdamn pigsty!" Brielle motioned me to hand her the pipe – she was never one to be left out of anything.

Tyrus threw his arms up in the air. "Okay, okay. I'm not the only one who has done something stupid on the leaf."

"Olivier found you cuddling the pigs, Ty."

"Pretty sure it was a goat, actually," he corrected.

Xavien snorted loudly, barely able to catch his breath from laughing so hard.

"And what about you, Bee?" Brielle nudged me.

"What about me?" I raised my eyebrows as I flicked my braid over my shoulder.

"Lemon cakes and... what was it? Custard tarts?" Tyrus enquired with mock obliviousness.

"Oh my gods, I forgot about this!" Brielle shrieked, excitedly clapping her hands together. "You broke into Moira's shop and stole her entire stock of lemon cakes and custard tarts!"

"And Moira caught you red-handed," Xavien added.

"I was hungry!" I whacked Xavien with one of the cushions, sending his long blonde hair flying in all directions.

"You argued… that you didn't know what she was talking about whilst your mouth… was covered in custard and powdered sugar!" Brielle could barely finish the sentence, pausing every few seconds to stifle her giggles.

"Oh, but they were SO tasty."

"You got us banned from there for months!" Xavien yelled, prodding me playfully.

"And what about little Miss Innocent over here?" I tilted my head towards Brielle.

"I am the most well behaved one out of this group." She raised her chin in defiance, taking a short puff from the pipe.

"Lochlan Kier?" I added, falling back against the cushions and throwing my head back in laughter.

"Oh, yes! La la Lochlan," Tyrus teased, clasping his hands together like a lovestruck damsel.

Brielle was unamused by the taunting, ignoring Tyrus's impression of her.

"In her defence, he had been writing her love letters for years," Xavien put his arm around Brielle reassuringly.

"That may be so, but I'm not sure he appreciated the midnight serenade."

Brielle tried to keep a straight face as Phoebe continued with the story. "You sounded like a dying animal!"

"Fine, fine. Your turn, Xavien Thorne. Let's talk about *your* embarrassing story," Brielle quipped back.

"Me?" Xavien feigned ignorance, clutching his chest in mock surprise.

"Oh yes, perhaps the best one of all," I said with a smirk, sipping from a glass of water, "*you* rode your horse *naked* through the town square."

We all burst into hysterical laughter as we recalled the chaos that followed Xavien's nude adventure. Remembering the gasps from some of the older villagers and the eyes of the younger women and men loitering in the square – their gazes lingered for longer than what was appropriate.

Xavien *was* gorgeous, with hazel eyes and the fullest lips I had ever seen. But I certainly never saw him that way; he was like the brother I never had—a mischievous, troublemaking shithead, but like a brother, nonetheless.

Friends since we were both knee-high to a grasshopper, Xavien was a frequent visitor to the castle when he was a young child, accompanying his mother, who had started working as one of the gardeners.

We would often play hide and seek, and Xavien would always cheat, hiding somewhere outside even though that was against the rules. I always found him within minutes, his strikingly blonde locks giving him away.

Eventually, I invited Xavien whenever I went to see Brielle. He loved causing mischief, playing pranks on villagers, and pinching treats. Some days it would annoy me, but never Brielle; she became fond of Xavien in more ways than one. To this day, Brielle fell fast, and she fell hard.

"We have gained quite the reputation in Eskium," Brielle sighed, wiping away a tear.

I smiled as I looked at my friends, so content in their company, despite the anxiety and dread of recent events that still lingered when the room fell silent for a few moments.

Brielle and Xavien simultaneously yawned and glanced at one another; they were so in sync at times it was bizarre. I often caught Brielle staring at him with eyes brimming with adoration and longing and wondered when Brielle would realise that she and Xavien would never be a *thing*, knowing that he was not interested in women, no matter how beautiful or charming they were.

"Bedtime, I think." Brielle yawned again and stretched her arms.

"Same, my bed is calling, and I can't risk another naked horse ride," Xavien joked.

"Goodnight, guys." Tyrus and I replied in unison.

The silence that followed their departure upstairs was stifling. Tyrus and I had not spent time alone in a while; he had gone to visit family back in Arleau for some time.

He scooted closer to me on the sofa, putting one arm behind my head as he stroked my forearm with his free hand. The look in his eyes conveyed a hunger I had almost forgotten.

"Ty… We probably shouldn't, we're both high as Hell, and you know what happened last time."

The last time we had been intimate after the leaf, I snuck Tyrus into my room at Eskium Castle. After a few minutes of groping and kissing, we both fell off the bed, landing on the wooden floor in a clamorous heap. My mother came hurtling in and discovered Tyrus on top of me, and I was naked from the waist up. Thank the gods it was my mother and not my father, as Tyrus would have been castrated on the spot.

"I only want to kiss you," Tyrus murmured, stroking my hair.

"Oh."

Tyrus moved closer and placed a tender peck on my lips. He retreated, leaning back, but I grabbed him by the collar of his shirt and pulled him towards me. His grip on the back of my head became firmer as my tongue met his, tasting the remnants of silverleaf, a heady mixture of herbs and citrus, as it danced along my tongue.

Within seconds, we were undressing one another, sleepily slipping off each other's shirts and resuming the kiss, our hands on the sides of the other's face.

I reclined back into the cushions of the sofa, bringing Tyrus with me, wrapping my legs around his waist and linking my arms around his neck. Heat pooled low in my belly, and I sought friction, bucking my hips to grind against him.

Although I was enjoying it, my mind was distracted, worried that Xavien or Brielle would walk in on us. We probably wouldn't notice their arrival because we were high as kites until it was too late.

Tyrus interrupted my train of thought by planting kisses down my neck and then over the flesh of my breast that was fighting to escape my bralette.

"Tyrus. We shouldn't." I gripped the side of his face to force his gaze to meet mine.

"I know. I'm just reacquainting myself," his voice was muffled as he continued to traverse my breasts with his mouth. "You will be the death of me," he whispered, peering up at me for a moment before resuming his torturous exploration.

CHAPTER SEVEN

Phoebe

"I need cheese scones. And I need them now." I groaned as we dawdled along the cobble path of the town square, clutching my grumbling belly. Silverleaf always made me ravenous the following day.

It was early in the morning, just after eight, and the streets were quiet. Most of the villagers were gathered at the fruit and vegetable market around the corner, which meant there wasn't a queue outside Moira's.

"Oh my gods, I hope she has those waffles!" Brielle jumped up in excitement, clapping her hands together like an elated child.

We approached the bakery, and I went to push the door but was met with resistance. It was still locked. *Strange.* The bakery should have already been open for business.

Cupping my hands on either side of my face, I pressed against the glass and peered through the window, puzzled by the silence of the shop.

Then, I noticed something on the ground, behind the main counter – an arm flailed out as if the person had fallen, the wrist adorned with several colourful bangles.

Moira.

"Look! That's Moira!" I yelled and grabbed Tyrus by the arm, tugging him towards the window to inspect for himself.

"Fuck, what should we do?"

"Let's try forcing it open," Xavien suggested, pushing the sleeves of his green woollen cardigan upwards; he readied his arms.

Xavien shoved his right side against the wooden door, along with Brielle. Several heaves later, there was still no sign of the door giving way. It was no use; the door wouldn't budge.

"I can try to melt the lock?" My voice was a low whisper. I knew I shouldn't use my powers outside of the training grounds, but this was an emergency, and it would take too long to request help from elsewhere.

My friends nodded in unison.

"Okay, crowd around me."

Taking a deep breath, I steadied my feet as I swivelled my right hand and coiled my fingers. Tiny ringlets of fire emerged from my fingertips, and I focused the flame into a minuscule jet of power. The heat licked at the lock, melting the gold into thick, metallic globules. A few more seconds of intense heat disintegrated the inner mechanism.

"Good job, Bee." Xavien lightly patted me on the back.

I eased the door open and rushed inside, Tyrus, Xavien, and Brielle were closely behind.

"Moira? Are you okay, Moira?" I tentatively called out as I peered behind the counter. The stench of copper burned my nostrils.

"Oh my gods!" I shrieked, letting out a gasp as I stumbled backwards and knocked into Tyrus.

Brielle clutched at her pendant, sending panicked glances to the rest of our group.

"What… What the Hell happened?" Xavien asked as he peeked over the counter before covering his mouth.

There was blood everywhere. Something truly horrific had happened to Moira, leaving her with the most gruesome injury I had ever seen – a gaping hole in her chest and splintered ribs, as if her heart had been ripped out of her chest cavity.

"We need to hurry and get back to the castle to inform my father." I looped my arm through Tyrus's and motioned for my friends to follow.

I burst through the main door of the castle, panting from the exertion of running most of the way home.

"Father! Father!" I shouted, trying to catch my breath as I rushed into the kitchen, then to the dining hall trying to find him.

Sending a panicked glance towards my friends, who were close on my heels, a deep crease lined my forehead at the eerie silence of the castle. Just as I went to rush up the stairs to look for him in his room, my father's voice sounded from behind his office door. I sighed, relaxing a fraction. In my fretful state, I hadn't thought to look in the most obvious place.

"In here, Phoebe." His voice sounded strained.

I headed towards the office. "Father, it's Moi–" I stopped mid-sentence as I passed through the doorway. Freezing in place, I was taken aback by my father's sloped shoulders and bloodshot eyes; my mother stood beside him with a worried look etched on her face.

He stood there, pale and tense, as he unfurled a piece of paper and presented it to me, his eyes drawing my attention to the bloodied box on his desk.

A red heart to replace the black one in your chest.

Another note. Another body part.

This time a heart.

"Father, I know who this belongs to," I said shakily, breaking the silence as Xavien, Brielle, and Tyrus charged into the room; they were short of breath from trying to keep up with me.

"What in the gods do you mean?" My father looked at me incredulously, concern etched his features when he met my eyes and saw the pale look of my friends.

"We went to go and get some snacks from Moira's bakery and…" my voice trailed off as nausea began to build in my throat.

"And?" My mother urgently queried, standing beside my father, gripping his arm.

"Moira's dead. We found her behind the counter of the bakery with a massive hole in her chest," Tyrus interjected.

Brielle clutched Xavien's arm, tucking into him as if huddling for warmth. Tyrus reached out for my hand, but the touch I returned was limp.

"What in the gods is happening?" My father snarled, crumpling the note in his fist. "I need answers and I need them now!" He thumped the desk, causing a handful of items to rattle and topple over.

“Fetch Jefferson, and hurry,” my mother said, commanding the footmen in the hallway to bring the apothecary to Eskium Castle.

“What is this person trying to do to me? What have I done that is so awful they would purposely send me severed body parts?” My father poured whiskey into a glass and threw the liquid back.

Xavien tilted his head, eyeing Brielle and Tyrus, signalling for them to leave the room to give us some privacy.

“I do not know, my love. But we will find out.” My mother stroked his arm, trying to provide a slither of comfort.

“In all my years as Lord of Eskium, I have never experienced anything like this. I am good to our people, Gabriella. Better than the other Lords and Ladies of Arleau, Zhadria, and Troyla.”

The look on my father’s face filled me with sadness.

“Could it be a competitor? Someone who wants to be Lord and is trying to scare you into stepping down?” My mother asked.

“But who, Gabriella? Who is interested? We had an election not so long ago and no one else came forward. None of the villagers appealed against the continuation of my lordship.”

My mother paused, biting her lower lip apprehensively as my father thundered up and down the floor.

“Father, wearing the rugs down will not help. We must formulate a plan!” I attempted to step in his way to halt his pacing.

“A plan, Phoebe? A plan? What do you suggest? We have absolutely no leads. No evidence. Just two dead villagers!”

"Some tea and biscuits," Maria announced as she shuffled into the room and hesitantly placed a tray on the table. My father glared at her as if she had brought him another sundered body part.

"If the wind changes whilst you continue looking like that, you'll forever have a face like a slapped arse," she huffed and shook her head, then waddled out into the hallway.

I took three cookies and slumped down into an armchair. My mother looked at me like I was mad, her eyes asking, *"How could you eat at a time like this?"* I shrugged in response, chewing enthusiastically.

The sound of the front door creaking open startled everyone, causing many of us to jump up from our seats.

"Jefferson, through here," my father called out.

I watched through the doorway as Jefferson awkwardly greeted Maria. He looked as though he was going to hug her, but gently patted her arm instead. I wondered whether it was difficult for them to see one another, even though they separated some time ago.

The apothecary entered the room, dressed in vibrant colours, his hair characteristically wild.

My father motioned towards the bloodied box on the table as the quirky apothecary walked across the room.

"I don't understand… None of this makes sense." Jefferson paused as he lifted the wooden box and squinted his eyes, taking a closer look. "Each body part has had different methods of removal. It doesn't seem as though the mutilation has been carried out by blade alone." Jefferson frowned as he combed his fingers through his long white beard.

"What does that mean?" I asked.

"I believe this is dark magick... I haven't seen this since..." Jefferson trailed off, walking over to his bag of supplies and rummaging through the various bottles.

"Since when, Jefferson?" My mother asked nervously.

"I need to retrieve Moira's body and inspect it further." He hurried out of the room and disappeared out the front door, leaving us with more questions than answers.

CHAPTER EIGHT

Lord Rafael

Rafael and Gabriella barely slept, each one tossing and turning throughout the night. He had rejoined his wife in their bedroom; she was frightened, and he could not leave her to fret alone. Phoebe did not seem as bothered; her snores travelled loudly from down the hall.

"What are we going to do?" Gabriella looked up at Rafael, her hand resting against the rise and fall of his chest. He glanced at his wife, feeling pained by her distraught expression.

"For the first time in forever, I do not know." Rafael pulled Gabriella closer to his chest as his mind raced. *What if they come for us next? What if they hurt Gabriella? Phoebe?* Visions of their bloody bodies filled his mind. He scrunched his eyes to will the images away.

"I think we have no choice but to begin questioning the villagers," Gabriella added.

"You cannot be serious? I will lose any loyalty that still lingers after this if I treat everyone as if they were guilty."

"How will we ever find out if we don't start asking questions?" Gabriella sat up, and continued, "We should at least question those who spoke to Arnold at the ball. Find out if anyone saw him leave."

"This is not the way we do things, Gab. This cannot be at the hands of one of our own, it must be an outsider."

There is no way it is one of the villagers – Eskium is a peaceful town; its people are good. What about that chap who danced with Phoebe, and the people he was with? Who were they?

"You have no proof to the contrary," Gabriella replied, a hint of frustration in her countenance.

"Then I will find it."

The following morning, the Emberwood family sat at the dining table in silence. Rafael and Gabriella pushed the food around their plates with disinterest. On the other hand, Phoebe slurped down her porridge and started on a small bowl of fruit, interrupting the quiet.

"Gods, girl. I envy your iron stomach," Gabriella said with a smirk.

"Food is comforting to me," Phoebe replied, shoving another grape into her mouth.

A knock sounded at the dining room door.

"Come in," Rafael beckoned, sipping from his cup of tea.

A postmaster stood awkwardly in the doorway.

"What is it?!" Gabriella barked, irritation from her lack of sleep evident in her tone.

The postmaster shakily handed an envelope to Rafael. He took two quick steps backwards and rushed out of the door.

Rafael looked down at the parchment, eyeing it carefully.

It was sealed by a black sigil—an eye inside a four-pointed star.

Gods, no.

He glanced at his wife and his daughter, hoping to hide the panic on his face, and shoved the paper into his coat pocket, then stood up to leave.

"Where are you going? What is that?" Gabriella shrieked after him.

"Leave me be, Gabriella!" he snapped back at her.

He stormed into his office and slammed the door, retrieving a letter opener from the top drawer of his desk. It was a golden-bladed article with four small rubies: a gift Gabriella had given him on his fortieth birthday. His chest ached to recall that day and the smile that adorned his beautiful wife's face.

Rafael took a deep breath and exhaled slowly. He gently slid the blade beneath the seal and opened the letter; the wax cracked and gave way.

Greetings, Lord Rafael.

Have you enjoyed my gifts? I certainly enjoyed retrieving them for you.

If you want the butchering to stop, you will pay me fifty thousand gold coins. Meet me at The Silver Sparrow one week from now. Alone.

If you do not deliver the payment, I will continue slaughtering your villagers, then I'll come for your precious Phoebe and that whore you call a wife as well. Your castle will be nothing but ash and ruin if you do not comply.

You have been warned.

Rafael staggered backwards. The Black Cloth was back. And they were after him.

He paced the floor, scraping his fingers through his hair.

Striding over to his desk, he grabbed the decanter and poured whiskey into a glass, his hand so unsteady he nearly dropped it. He threw back the deep amber liquid, then poured another. It burned on the way down, providing a temporary reprieve.

What was he going to do? He couldn't tell Gabriella. Besides, he didn't have fifty thousand gold coins. The Yuletide ball was not the most economical of affairs, plus the lands were nowhere near as fruitful in the winter season. Years ago, he reduced the taxes to help families make it through the harsh frostbitten months with enough food in their bellies and logs for their fires. He would have nowhere near that amount until Beltane, at least.

His heart pounded so viciously Rafael felt light-headed. His palms were clammy, and moisture had not returned to his mouth despite the two glasses of whiskey. Rafael didn't think he had more than ten thousand gold coins on hand. He scrambled through the desk drawer in search of the key to his chest, pushing papers and trinkets aside with no regard. A metallic clunk sounded, and he clumsily snatched up the key from the floor.

"Fucking Hell!" he yelled, falling to his knees to reach the key under his desk. He darted across the room and frantically clawed at the chest, missing the lock two or three times thanks to his shaking hands.

On the fourth try, he was successful; inside, as expected, lay a mound of gold coins, and in one corner there was a small collection of glistening crystals. Perhaps he could soften the blow by giving this person some of the family jewels. There were a few small rubies and sapphires – they had to be better than nothing. He gathered the jewels and placed them in his pocket, fetching a large burlap sack from the coat hook on the back of the door to scoop the coins.

CHAPTER NINE

The stranger

Things were getting out of hand.

It was never supposed to be this way. Now the blood of two innocents had been spilled, their bodies mutilated for her entertainment.

It was only supposed to be *him.*

That's what she told us.

I wish I had never agreed to this.

I needed to try and get her to stop. She'd gone too far.

CHAPTER TEN

Lord Rafael

Rafael awoke just before dawn covered in sweat. His pillowcase was drenched, along with the bedsheet. But he was more disturbed by what jolted him awake: a dream. No, a nightmare.

An old man had appeared before him, covered in a dark shawl. The knuckles on his fingers were gnarled like a withered and ancient tree; each one adorned with gold and platinum rings. Rafael's rings. The old man laughed and bellowed, repeating the words "ash and ruin" over and over again when a young woman walked out of the shadows behind him. She looked just like.... Her hair was midnight black, her eyes an unusually pale blue. As Rafael went to ask the old man a question, a grey-haired woman wearing a black veil walked up to him, poking and prodding him as if she were inspecting a piece of fruit for rot.

"The apple doesn't fall far from the tree," she sneered, floating over to the old man and the young woman. He swore he knew all three of them but couldn't place it; their faces were all partially hidden.

A sickening feeling swelled within him, tying his stomach in knots. Dread always seemed to find him, even in his sleep. It continued to gnaw at the frayed ends of his sanity.

Suddenly, the realisation hit him. The old man was someone he knew well. It was Jefferson Dreed.

He shot up out of bed and clambered to his dresser, yanking out breeches and a shirt. He hopped into his boots and threw a heavy cloak over him and made his way downstairs and out of the castle.

Rafael arrived outside Luna's Light just as the sun rose, coating the town square in a buttery glow. It was deathly quiet, many of the villagers were all still likely fast asleep, but he had to wake Jefferson up. He slammed his fists into the glass door of the apothecary shop, causing the bell to shake on the other side.

"Jefferson! Get up! I need to speak with you. Urgently!" he shouted, looking up at the small window above the shop where Jefferson lived. He pounded his fists again. The edge of his palm stung from the coldness of the glass.

Jefferson appeared in the doorway at the back of the bazaar, a silhouette that would not have been easy to identify if it weren't for the wild hair he was renowned for.

Shuffling towards the entrance, he tied his robe. "What in the gods are you doing, Rafael?" he asked through strained eyes, opening the door to him.

"You were in my dream. My… my nightmare," Rafael stammered his reply through laboured breaths.

“You came here at this hour to tell me that? Have you lost your mind?!” Jefferson’s face was thunderous.

“No. No. Something bad is coming. And you have something to do with it.” Rafael stumbled through the doorway, pushing his way past Jefferson.

“I have no gods damn idea what you’re talking about and think you need to go home and sleep off your whiskey,” Jefferson replied, trying to usher Rafael out of the shop.

“You are connected to all of this, because of...” He stared at Jefferson, his eyes lingering on his features.

“You’re talking nonsense Rafael. I should give you some cloveroot to clear your booze-addled brain.” Jefferson began to retreat to the back of the shop.

“You are harbouring a dark secret, Jefferson. And soon we will all find out what it is.”

“Dark secret? You had a nightmare, it doesn’t make what you saw real. Not that I even know what you’re talking about! How dare you wake me at this hour and accuse me of such things! I’ve known you since you were a young lad!” Jefferson walked back towards Rafael, shaking his finger at him as if he were scolding a child.

“But I apparently don’t know you at all.”

CHAPTER ELEVEN

Phoebe

"What's wrong? Your power seems… off lately." Ezra queried with hesitance, looking at my hands. I glanced down at my palms, frowning as I turned them over. "I don't know. I'm just worried, I guess, and it's making my magick… different."

During the last few training sessions, I noticed that my fire magick had become unpredictable. Sometimes it would appear as gentle licks of flame on each fingertip; other times, it would rush out of me so fast it knocked me backwards. But that wasn't the only odd thing. My water magick had started to emerge more often – only minuscule misty spheres like tiny glass baubles – but it was more than I had been able to conjure before. Before the murders started happening.

"Let's try your water again," Ezra suggested, adding more logs to a pile for me to practice.

"Set this aflame, then douse it with your water." He pointed towards the target and then took a step back.

My magick had been present for as long as I could remember, brewing beneath my skin like simmering water in a pot. When I was a child, I would often light the candles in my bedroom to test the magick, flooding the space with beautiful golden light. I did it several times, darting from one candle to another, blowing them out, and then setting them alight again.

Some evenings I would make a game of it, twirling my hands in the air as if I were a conductor and the flames were notes of music. Over and over again, I would shoot the flames out of my fingertips, creating my own smouldering symphony. I never dared to try anything more out of fear of getting into trouble – it wasn't until my early twenties that I decided to push those boundaries further, knowing I no longer answered to my parents.

I knew I was blessed with fire *and* water magick because when I was about ten years old, I had put out the flames that skirted along a tea towel that Maria had left by the hearth in the kitchen. The cloud of mist was nothing compared to my fire, but it was strong enough to suffocate the flames and stop them from spreading. I was tempted to push my power further, but Maria abruptly entered the kitchen, flailing her arms at the sight and smell of smoke. My heartbeat galloped in my chest, thundering against the cage of my ribs. But Maria didn't suspect anything; despite me standing there clutching a half-burned, half-soaked tea towel to my chest.

"Phoebe?" Ezra's deep voice broke the silence.

"Sorry. I was just thinking," I fiddled with my amethyst pendant, rolling it between my fingers.

"Shall we stop training today? You seem too distracted." Ezra folded his bare arms with zero indication he was even slightly cold.

"No. No. It's fine. Let's continue." I readied my stance, pushing the soles of my boots into the snow-laden earth to anchor myself. Taking a deep breath, I motioned my hands forward and sent a wave of fire towards the log pile, setting it aflame in one fell swoop.

Ezra paced alongside me, watching intently. "Now your water."

I hovered my hands outwards, watching in awe as tiny droplets of moisture appeared at my fingertips, like morning dew on spring daffodils.

"More," Ezra ordered, his tone firm.

My fingers wiggled, and mist appeared in front of my palms; a silvery cloud floated mid-air. I swept my hands from side to side, willing the element to set its course for the fire. It would never be enough to douse the flames. Determined to succeed, I had to try harder.

Taking another fortifying breath, I relaxed my shoulders and focused on the fire. But instead of a rush of water, I felt a staggering sensation of dread, causing a chill to creep down my spine. My mind flooded with images of blood and gore; a hollowed-out chest, devoid of a heart. The stench of copper invaded my nostrils. A sharp, metallic tang hit the back of my throat.

Before I knew it, I had summoned an enormous ring of water, twice my height. It churned in a spiral above my head, violent yet controlled. I gawked at my creation as my face dampened from the spray.

"Phoebe! Stop this. Now!" Ezra grabbed me by the arm as he shouted at me.

"I don't know how!" I screamed in response, my eyes darting between Ezra and the water.

"What were you thinking of when this appeared?" His grip moved to my shoulders, and his dark brown eyes seared into mine as the water pulsed above us.

"Umm," I hesitated, panicking as I tried to recall what had been going through my mind. "Moira! What happened to Moira. All the blood. The smell of it. Everything."

I peered up at the ring of water again, aghast at my own power. Ezra released his grip on me and took a step back, his mouth agape. I couldn't tell if he was terrified or awestruck – perhaps he was both.

Closing my eyes, I raised my arms above my head and willed the water to obey. The spiral began to hiss and spit as its structure weakened, fighting against me.

Ezra lightly patted my back and whispered, "You can control this. I know you can." He took a step back as I expelled a painful cry, using every ounce of my strength to move it, twisting my fingers as it began to funnel downwards. The water started to fall to the ground in thick sheets of liquid, splashing as it hit the icy floor.

My legs began to tremble, and I slid back, my feet struggling to grip the icy sludge beneath me. In one forceful motion, I pushed the diminished ring of water into the fire, soaking the pile in a single wave.

"Why don't you stay at ours tonight? It's late and you shouldn't walk home alone, not with everything that's going on," Tyrus asked as he linked his arm with mine. I nodded, my mind still wandering as I recounted the water I summoned earlier that day.

We strolled down the cobbled path of the town square and down a narrow side road which led to Xavien and Tyrus's house. The outside was plain with simple beige mortar and windows framed with dark wood. Nestled next to the little tailoring shop owned by Tallulah Finnegan, the mustard yellow awnings and flower boxes filled with pink and white daisies of her home created a shocking contrast.

"The spare room is in a much better state than when you last came over. We even have *curtains* now, thanks to this generous fella," Xavien said, slurring with a hiccup. He swayed as he tried to elbow Tyrus shortly before failing to open the door with his key.

"Out of the way, pisshead. Let me do it." Tyrus gently nudged Xavien and unlocked the door with his own key. Brielle steadied Xavien, gently holding his elbows with her palms.

The heat swept over me as I walked into their main room. The warm air was like an embrace, soothing my ice-stung skin and seeping into my chilled bones.

"Wow, you guys really have put some effort into this place." My eyes darted around the room, taking in the new patterned rug, the plush burgundy cushions and the paintings on the wall. *How the Hell could they afford all this?* Tyrus's eyes widened, looking surprisingly concerned at my prolonged observation.

"More drinks, yeah?" Xavien staggered; removing his long navy wool coat seemed to require great effort.

"Just one, then I should head off to bed. I am exhausted." I peeled off my boots and wiggled my toes as they started to regain feeling after the brisk walk from The Silver Sparrow.

Xavien poured brandy into four goblets, barely spilling a drop, much to my surprise.

The dark honey-coloured liquid had quite the kick, warming up my stomach instantly.

"So, are we going to talk about the blood-soaked, mutilated elephant in the room?" Xavien asked, hiccupping again. Brielle elbowed him, signalling her annoyance.

"Drop it, Xave. It's not the time," Tyrus glanced at me warily.

"There's a murderer on the loose, targeting innocent villagers and sending their body parts to my family home. Where would you like to start?" My tone was cold, making Xavien shift in his seat.

"I was only messing around." Xavien shot a nervous look towards Brielle, seeking reassurance. He was probably surprised by my curt response. He knew it wasn't like me to be so blunt.

I contemplated telling him that he didn't always need to fill the silence with jokes, but I knew it would only wound him.

"That's it for me tonight, thank you anyway," I said instead, setting the goblet down on the low table, no longer in the mood to be in anyone's company.

"Ty?" Xavien said pleadingly.

"Nah, I should really get some rest too. I've got to run some errands early tomorrow."

"Guess it's just me and you then again, Brielle," Xavien said as he poured another drink into their goblets.

Brielle chuckled as she grabbed a cushion and hugged it against her chest. "Go on, but only one or two more."

"Night." Tyrus added, following closely behind me. Xavien and Brielle nodded, exchanging sheepish grins as our footsteps headed up the creaky wooden stairs.

I paused outside the spare room door, hesitant to go inside.

"Goodnight, Phoebe." Tyrus's voice was hushed, causing me to jump.

"Oh, uh… yes, goodnight, Ty," I said as he looked at me in bemusement, turning the handle of his door and walking inside. A gentle click confirmed that there would be no invitation to enter, and he wasn't interested in anything other than sleep. Sighing deeply, I tried to dampen my disappointment and made my way into the spare room.

It was far more welcoming than the last time I slept over. There were two single beds, with aquamarine and grey quilts and soft, white pillows. Indeed, they had put up curtains; they were thick and oat-coloured, which took the chill off the windows. I was impressed.

As I began to undress, I realised I had no nightwear. My blouse would suffice, if necessary, but the room was chilly, and I needed more layers. I rummaged through the ivory dresser, which sat between the two beds in the hope of finding *something* that I could wear to sleep. Opening the top drawer, I was delighted to find a selection of casual shirts, some chunky knitwear, and some more blankets. I smiled to myself – Xavien loved woollen jumpers and cardigans, so it was no surprise to find a pile of them neatly folded. I lifted out the first one on the pile and pressed it against my body, seeing how long it would be – it was large enough that it would fall just past the tops of my thighs and cover my modesty from Brielle, who I expected would share the room with me later.

Settling into the bed nearest the window, I was surprised to find that the sheets were crisp and smelled like citrus. *How in the gods did these two get so domesticated?* I pulled the quilt up to my nose and turned over onto my side, facing away from the door.

Thoughts of Tyrus drifted into my mind again. Yes, I wanted to be alone, but I also needed to feel safe. I wondered if being wrapped in the warmth of his arms would soothe the panic that had started to creep in. It had been a while since we last lay with one another; the only intimacy we had shared recently was the silverleaf-induced make-out session on the sofa a few weeks prior.

I smiled as I sat up, knowing my curiosity had always gotten me into trouble. I shifted out of bed, tiptoeing across the floorboards. Gingerly opening the door of the spare room, I slipped out into the dark corridor, nearly screaming as I collided with a dark figure in front of me. Tyrus.

"What the fuck are you doing? I nearly died on the spot," I hissed through a whisper that should have been a shout.

"I could ask you the same thing, Phoebe." He placed his hands on the wall on either side of me.

"I wanted to see you." I replied, trailing a finger down his stomach.

"I didn't really think it appropriate to make a move on you with everything that's going on. And you seemed off earlier, so…" Tyrus replied, taking my hand and slowly kissed each finger.

So, he had been thinking about it too.

"Surely that's up to me to decide." I looked up at him through my thick eyelashes. "Not even a kiss?"

He moved closer, his breath passing my cheek and moving to my neck, planting gentle kisses along the way that made me tremble. I put my fingers through his hair, gripping him as he kissed my collarbone.

"You're expecting a kiss? Where?" Tyrus teased as he spoke against my skin. Taking hold of his face, I pulled him into a kiss, causing a low rumble to sound in his throat. He pushed me against the wall, then drove his hips into mine.

We moved together, clumsily shuffling across the hallway in the darkness.

Tyrus fumbled for the door handle to his room as his lips stayed locked on mine, hurriedly pushing me through the open door and closing it behind him, not once letting go of my mouth or body. I shoved him up against the door this time; my palms pressed firmly against his broad chest. I reached down towards the top of his breeches and attempted to untie them.

"Stop, Phoebe." Tyrus placed a firm hand over mine, a steely expression consuming his features.

"...What?!" I couldn't contain the surprise in my voice or face.

"Are you sure you want to do this?" he asked, still holding my hands.

"Are you kidding?" I took a step back, dumbfounded by his abrupt change in mood.

"I don't want to take advantage of you," Tyrus said in response, brushing my hair off my shoulder.

"You're not taking advantage of me. I want this. I need this," I said, taking a fistful of his shirt in my hand.

"You're not thinking clearly. You're only doing this because you want a distraction."

"And *so* what if I am? It's my choice how I go about *distracting* myself, Tyrus." I took another step back, eyeing the evidence beneath his breeches. "I can tell you want this."

"Oh, for the love of the gods. I'm trying to be a gentleman here!" He threw his hands up in frustration, causing me to flinch.

"I don't want you to be a gentleman, Tyrus. If you don't want to fuck me, then I'll find someone who does." I turned to leave, reaching for the door to make a dramatic exit. Tyrus's large hand pushed against it, shutting it with a heavy clunk. He pulled me back towards him, grabbed my face with both hands and kissed me like he meant it.

"You tell me if you want to stop at any point." Tyrus spoke as he kissed, his lips already slightly swollen from the bruising clash of our mouths.

"That's not going to happen. But thank you for your chivalry," I replied, pushing him towards the bed.

Tyrus sat upright with his back flush against the headboard; eyes fixed on me as I straddled his thighs, hitching the shirt above my waist. He grabbed the soft flesh of my hips, pulling me closer.

As I began to unbutton my shirt, Tyrus froze. His eyes glazed over.

"Ty? What's wrong?" I nudged his shoulder. He said nothing in response.

"Hello? Are you okay?" I nudged him harder, grabbing him by the shoulders and lightly shaking him. He murmured something under his breath, but his voice was too hushed to hear the words clearly.

"Tyrus, speak up. I can't hear you." I grabbed his face in my hands and forced him to look at me.

Finally, his eyes met mine, and he opened his mouth to speak, and whispered, "Get out of my head."

CHAPTER TWELVE

Lord Rafael

One week had passed since Rafael received the anonymous letter. His time was up. He felt physically sick, unable to eat his usual cooked breakfast that Maria had prepared. Wiping away a bead of sweat from his brow, he did one last check of his inventory.

The sack struggled with the weight of the coins. Maybe it would have been easier if he just took the chest, but that would have made it more evident something was amiss.

There was a knock at the door of his study. Rafael darted a panicked glance as the doorknob turned, the sound of a metallic whine making his skin crawl.

"Your carriage is outside m'Lord." A footman peered around the door.

"I'll be right out." Rafael patted the pockets of his jacket, feeling for the rubies and sapphires. He scooped them out and dropped them atop the pile of gold coins. Making his way out the door, he struggled to support the weight of the sack on his right shoulder.

“I’ll take that for you m’Lord”. The same footman tried to relieve him of the heavy bag, but Rafael abruptly stepped backwards for fear he would see the contents.

“I’m fine, thank you.” Rafael responded bluntly, trying to maintain composure.

“If you insist, m’Lord. Where are we going today?”

“Town square. The Silver Sparrow. I have a business meeting with local merchants,” he lied.

“Very well, m’Lord.”

Rafael stepped into the carriage, hurling the heavy sack onto the plush leather seats. He sat down with such a heavy slump that it startled the horses. Soon the sound of gravel under hooves filled the silence, and Rafael gripped the bag next to him.

The journey was roughly ten minutes by carriage, but it felt like Rafael had been travelling for hours. The snow-capped hills did nothing to soothe his soul as his mind flitted from one intrusive thought to the next – images of his family crying in distress, or their lifeless bodies.

The carriage turned into a windy narrow path leading to the town square’s outer quarter. Overhanging branches thick with snow pelted against the windows, causing Rafael to jump in fright. His nerves were shot after a week of unrelenting dread.

Suddenly there was a loud thud, followed by shrieking and whistling. The sounds of branches breaking echoed through the woodland. Rafael peered outside each of the windows, thinking the carriage had hit thicker branches. But when the carriage lurched forward, he had an awful feeling the footman was no longer seated.

“Aghhh, please! Don’t hurt me! Nooo!” There was a guttural sound, then a wail. Rafael reached for the dagger that was sheathed against his calf inside his boot; it wouldn’t do much against bandits, but it was all he had.

Leaning over to the window on the other side of the carriage, he went to turn the handle as a large red palm slammed against the glass—a blood-covered palm. His eyes widened in shock and he clambered backwards. Rafael didn’t have a chance to think about his next steps, the door was ripped open with force, tipping the carriage to one side. Two figures in thick black hoods stood before him. He did not know whether they were men, women or beasts, but at that moment, he knew that it was not the work of bandits. He glanced at the emblem on their clothing, a symbol embroidered into the lining of the cloak: an eye inside a four-pointed star.

The Black Cloth.

In a matter of seconds, Rafael was hauled out of the carriage by the lapels of his jacket.

“I love family reunions!” said one of the figures with a devilish grin.

Family reunions? What in the gods did that mean?

The first two figures dragged him along by his arms; his legs left a trail in the mud behind him as he kicked out furiously. The third person retrieved his sack from the back of the carriage and followed behind. They stopped once they reached a nearby cave. Rafael tried to wriggle free and snarled, “Don’t you know who I am?!”

Their laughs were maniacal as they hurled him to the ground, making him land awkwardly on his elbows.

A feminine cackle echoed in the cave.

A young woman stalked out of the shadows looking like death incarnate. She was raven-haired, which shimmered with blue and green hues like a magpie's feather; her eyes… icy blue. She was dressed head-to-toe in black, a wraith in female form.

"Long time no see, huh father?" Her expression was malevolent as she kicked his leg with the pointed tip of her high-heeled boot.

He stared at her with such incertitude she threw him to the back of the cave in a swirl of violent wind with one effortless glance. Rafael winced at the pain in his back. *Oh, gods. It can't be her, can it?*

"Don't you recognise your own daughter?" she sneered and strode towards him. He frowned at her, his eyes darting from her hair to her eyes to her alabaster skin.

She released her invisible hold of him, and he fell to the floor. Crouching down beside him, she waved a lit torch by his face, surveying the details of his features as if trying to will memories of him to appear in her mind. The heat from the flame licked at his cheeks.

"You're not… Surely, you aren't…" he whimpered, his voice breaking.

"Do you see me now, father?" she slinked around him like a cat.

Great Mother. It was his first child. His secret *child.*

"Ina… What? How?" He gulped, trying to clear the knot in his throat. "Why…Why are you doing this?" He grimaced through gritted teeth as he tried to regain some balance, seeking purchase on the mossy wall behind him.

"Why? Because you let my mother burn and did NOTHING! Because you couldn't stand up to your pig of a father. Didn't take long for you to forget about us though, did it? Living a wonderful regal life with that sap Gabriella and your pathetic excuse for a *second born* daughter *Phoeeebee,*" she said her name mockingly in a child-like voice. "Luxury and peace all these years, whilst I had to grow up alone and fight tooth and nail to survive, competing with rats for food."

"I never wanted that to happen to you or your mother... I… I loved you. My father said he would kill you if I didn't let him...take your mother's life. I… was promised you would be cared for. I paid the matron at the orphanage a substantial sum…" Rafael's head hung dejectedly, his eyes lined with silver as tears began to escape.

She huffed. "Oh, a *substantial fee*. That makes it okay then."

"Please. You must believe me."

"I hear her screams in the back of mind every day and night. Screams that you could have stopped. But you did nothing."

Rafael stared at his estranged daughter, trying to recall how she looked when she was a child, when she wasn't *this*.

"I tried to stop it!" his voice boomed, causing her to bristle.

"You weren't *man* enough to protect us, then you palmed me off to a total stranger," she paused, "not good enough, *father*." She spat the last word at the ground as if it were poison on her tongue.

"I'm… I'm sorry. I'm so sorry." Rafael pulled his knees to his chest.

"Why didn't you try to find me?" she asked as she turned her back on him, a hint of sadness laced her words.

“I did. I promise I searched for you. I went back to the orphanage, but it wasn’t… there. It was destroyed, as if a storm had passed through.”

She whipped her head back in the direction of her father, causing her pitch-black hair to swish over her shoulder. Her rouge-lined mouth twisted into a wolfish grin. “Oh yes. That was quite a *storm*.”

“There’s no way there’s fifty thousand gold coins in here, Briar,” one of her henchmen yelled, interrupting her locked gaze with her father.

“Briar? Why are they calling you Briar?”

She ignored him.

“This is all the gold I have. Please, take the rubies and sapphires too,” Rafael's voice croaked as he peered over at the sack, watching the group of men and women rifling through it.

“Add salt to my wounds,” she sneered through gritted teeth. “But the gold was just a ploy to get you here.”

“What more do you want from me?”

“Oh,” she paused, lips curling upwards into a lupine grin, “I want you to suffer."

CHAPTER THIRTEEN

Phoebe

I returned from training with Ezra just before dusk, treading crunchy grey snow through the front door.

To no surprise, dinner was ready for me as I plodded to the dining room. After another gruelling day honing my magick, I was exhausted, covered in soot and ash. I knew Maria would be unimpressed by my appearance, but I was too hungry to bathe first.

"Good evening, my dear," Maria cupped my cheek with a smile, "Gods, you look frightful. What have you been up to?"

"Oh, thanks. Um, I was experimenting with some potions at work," I lied.

Maria nodded. "Is that so?" she asked, a hint of scepticism in her tone.

Maria didn't suspect anything, did she?

"Tonight is beef wellington, roast potatoes, and green beans. One of your favourites." She placed the warm plate of food in front of me.

"You are the best, Maria." I grinned at her as I inhaled the rich smell of the roasted meat. Picking up a gravy boat, I dutifully poured generous layers of the golden-brown sauce over every piece.

"Do you want food with your gravy, Phoebe?" Maria scoffed sarcastically, one hand on her hip.

"I can't help it if your gravy is just as tasty as your food, Maria."

"Okay, fine. I'll let you off."

"Where are my parents?" I looked up, wiping crumbs away from my mouth.

"Your mother is upstairs working on that patchwork quilt of hers. I've not seen your father since this morning. He was in a funny mood again and didn't finish his breakfast."

I nodded as I chewed, groaning blissfully at the perfectly cooked meat. I assumed my father's business meetings had overrun, or he decided to grab dinner elsewhere.

"Right, I'm going to rest for an hour. Let me know if you need anything." Maria trotted towards her room, humming quietly.

As Maria closed the door behind her, I smiled. Everyone always felt a little lighter after a meal from Maria; I was sure she was sent by the gods themselves.

Hours melted away.

I had fallen asleep in the bath. Again. *I had to stop doing that.*

It must have been late as the candles in my bathing room had reduced to waxy puddles, and my skin was pebbled with goosebumps from the chill of being in the now lukewarm water. I shivered as I towelled the ends of my hair and pulled out a fresh nightgown from the dresser. The silky fabric felt soft against my tired muscles after a long day in my practice gear.

My bed could not be more inviting. My goose feather pillows were like fluffy clouds beneath my head, my thick quilt so warm it felt as though another person were with me. I was so exhausted from a gruelling day at the training grounds, my arms and legs heavy from the strain, that within minutes, I drifted off into the most peaceful of slumbers.

I awoke to the sound of horns. And shouting. *What was going on? What time was it?* I rushed towards my window and yanked the curtain back.

Was this a nightmare? I couldn't believe what I saw. Pinching my palms to the point of pain, I willed myself to snap out of the dreadful dream.

I rubbed my eyes so hard they burned, pulling a few eyelashes by accident, making me wince. It wasn't a dream. No. It was my father, and he was slumped against the low wall of the small bridge that covered the moat, broken, bloodied, and screaming in agony.

I ran out of my room and almost collided with my mother.

"Phoebe! Stay in your room. It's not safe," my mother yelled, grabbing my hands.

"It's father! He's outside. Something terrible has happened to him." I gripped my mother's forearms and tried to push her away so I could free myself from her hold.

She relented, and we ran down the stairs together, reaching the front door of the castle, hurling it open.

“It's our Lord. He is gravely wounded. Fetch a healer!” a footman shouted amidst the chaos.

“Father!”

"Rafael!"

We sprinted over and knelt on either side of him, crashing to the frozen ground. I felt my face drain of blood as I surveyed his injuries.

“Who did this to you?” I yelled as I tried to force down the nauseous feeling creeping up my stomach and throat. My heart raced violently, fighting against the cage of my ribs.

My father’s cries were blood-curdling as he writhed on the floor in agony. His arms and legs were broken, his face was bloody and blotchy, and his eyes were wild with terror. I tried to hold his hand, but his movements were too erratic. Instead, I smoothed the sweat-soaked hair away from his forehead and told him that everything would be okay.

“Where are the gods damned healers?” I roared, head snapping from one footman to the next.

My father managed to mutter a response to us, looking to his left, to me. His eyes were wet with tears, and his voice ragged. “It’s too late for the healers. Phoebe… You need to speak to Jefferson… But promise me you will flee this place with your mother soon afterwards. Please. I love you, my sweet girl.”

“I love you, father… What do you mean? What does Jefferson have to do with this? Flee? I… I promise.” I spoke through the tears, the words barely comprehensible as I tried to understand what he was saying.

He slowly looked to his right. “My dearest Gabriella, my love until the end of time.”

My mother gripped him, trembling with despair as he recoiled in pain. Our eyes averted downwards, noticing a mark had been scorched onto his forearm. An eye inside a four-pointed star. "This can't be what I think it is?" Gabriella asked through ragged breaths. "The sigil of The Black Cloth."

Tears fell down my father's cheeks, soaking through the dirt and blood that had dried. His skin was like water-starved earth, faint cracks forking down each side of his face.

It was only a matter of minutes later that he drew one sharp breath and turned his face up to the sky. We focused our attention on his face and then his chest, frantically observing his breathing.

His chest no longer rose and fell.

He was gone.

My mother's agonised cries pierced through the stillness of the night, causing echoes to reverberate off the stone walls of the castle.

The numbness that followed enveloped me in darkness, suffocating, silencing, and blinding me all at once. Robbed of my senses yet my limbs felt heavy as if my clothes were waterlogged and weighing me down.

I stared at my father, unable to comprehend what I was seeing. Unable to fathom that it was real. *He was just here. He was talking. Breathing. This isn't happening. This cannot be happening.*

His eyes still peered up towards the sky, his lips curved as if he'd had the courage to leave the realm with a slight smile on his face.

He can't be gone.

Barely able to catch my breath through the tears, I inhaled air in painful gulps. I gently closed his eyes with my fingertips and glanced down towards the left breast of his jacket, where a folded wadge of paper protruded from the pocket. Moving my gaze to my shell-shocked mother, I read out the message on the blood-soaked parchment.

Gabriella, Phoebe,

I have let you down. I have hidden the truth from you.

I am writing this to you as I prepare to meet with someone dangerous.

I received a letter a week ago from the supposed murderer, demanding payment of fifty thousand gold coins or they would storm the castle and kill us all. I have no choice but to meet with them in the hope we could end this mess.

I have a bad feeling about this. If I do not return to you, I hope you will at least see this note and know I will be eternally sorry. Please stay safe.

I love you both more than there are stars in the sky.

Rafael

The paper crinkled in my shaking hands.

An overpowering feeling of dread mixed with anger began to build, filling me with an agonising urge to set the letter on fire.

I stared at my father once more, surveying him from head to toe. Only then did I notice something glinting on the ground beside him. A blood-red coloured orb the size of a small gemstone pulsed with light and hummed with a disturbingly low sound. I rolled the orb between my thumb and finger, my eyes entranced by the movement and noise.

"Phoebe, put that down!" my mother yelled, launching herself towards me, swatting it out of my hand. The orb flew out of my grip, but it hovered mid-air instead of falling to the ground.

We both crouched and covered our faces with our forearms as the orb pulsated violently.

A feminine voice filled the air, ethereal and unnerving. It echoed around us like a siren's lament.

"Ahhh, you have discovered my Nuntius Crystal."

The voice was sultry with a venomous edge.

"Clever little contraption, don't you think? Allow me to introduce myself. I'm Briar. Rafael's firstborn child. Surprise!

Rafael was a coward. Weak. Pathetic. Yet he had the audacity to bed Zayla, Leader of The Black Cloth. My mother. I have collected his blood debt. But I am not satisfied. Nowhere near satisfied. I will be coming for you both. You can try to run, but there is nowhere in this realm where you can escape me."

Within seconds, the crystal exploded, sending thousands of tiny crimson shards flying outwards straight into our path. We ducked and dropped to the floor, narrowly avoiding being hit by the fragments. I peered through my hands, attempting to see if it was safe for us to stand. The shards remained on the ground, their original bright ruby colour now a diluted red.

My chest heaved as I checked my mother for injuries. She was okay, but an odd sensation clawed at my skin, stinging me like sunburn.

It was my fire. And it wanted to play.

CHAPTER FOURTEEN

Lady Gabriella

Gabriella had not slept more than an hour or so a night since her husband's death and the subsequent attempt on her life and that of her daughter. If fear did not prevent her from resting, the sounds of Rafael's agony kept her awake.

The days that followed were a blur. Visitors came and went. Letters and flowers arrived at the castle. Endless flowers – so many that the scent of them became nauseating. Gabriella appreciated the thoughtful gestures, but all they did was remind her of the void left behind. Rafael was gone, brutally murdered, by the hand of a young woman she knew nothing about, from a love affair he had kept secret for over twenty years. A love affair with the leader of The Black Cloth of all things.

Gabriella felt guilty for feeling angry with him; the pairing happened before they met, it was not like he had been unfaithful. *But he lay with a member of The Black Cloth and hid the fact he had another child.* She felt a tinge of jealousy and disgust; she was heartbroken that Phoebe was not his firstborn, this creature named Briar was.

In between ripples of grief came waves of anger – anger so violent it took all of Gabriella's strength to keep her powers at bay. She hadn't called upon her magick since the days before she met Rafael, but she could set the entire castle aflame with the despair she felt about losing him.

She imagined hunting Briar down and burning her from the inside out until her eyeballs bubbled in her skull. *Why take his life? Why now?* She had so many questions her head throbbed.

Maria tried to help her through the grief with endless pots of tea and bowls of food, insisting on her special blend of herbs to ease the tension in her temples and jaw. But Gabriella would often take a few sips, and nausea would overpower her, forcing her to push the cup aside and leave the tea to go cold.

Gabriella sloped to the guest bedroom, where Rafael had intermittently slept. On the bed lay his dressing gown, made of thick navy wool with the faintest silver thread, and a book, its leatherbound edges worn from years of use. She glanced to the bedside table, where a near-empty bottle of whiskey sat. Her heart sank at the sight of it, a harsh reminder of her husband's final weeks leading to this. *What must have been going through his mind?* An overwhelming feeling of guilt consumed her. *If he had told her about this, maybe she could have helped.*

She traced her hands over the soft dressing gown, then lifted it to her chest, hugging it tightly as she sobbed into the fabric. It still smelled of him – his eucalyptus and cedarwood scent clung to the fabric. She inhaled deeply, closing her eyes, imagining he was in the room with her. Lifting the covers of the bed, Gabriella slid in between them, her arms still tightly wrapped around the dressing gown. Her hand hovered over one of the pillows. A few days ago, his head had been resting there. Now he was gone. Forever.

That moment, the reality of his permanent absence came crashing down upon her. She felt her heart break. Every essence of what she had known for over twenty years was gone in a flash—ripped from her. Her world turned upside down and destroyed.

CHAPTER FIFTEEN

Phoebe

Between sleepless nights spent comforting my broken mother and avoiding my friends, I found solace in my training with Ezra. I felt confident that my mother was safe, with additional wards placed around the castle and increasing the number of footmen and guards.

I needed to do something to quell the rage that had started to consume me. The hatred and anger was so intense it turned poisonous. It was leeching, burning, and taking every drop of joy that remained.

The only thing I had left was my power. But it had changed, evolving into something more violent and unpredictable.

Before my father's death, my power simmered beneath my skin. It was there, gently ticking away, but now it was searing, biting at me as if it had fangs. Each twinge of pain pushed me closer to the edge.

I wiped the sweat from my forehead, still panting from the exertion of setting all the pyres aflame at once – something I had never done before.

Ezra was unhappy with me after I continuously ignored his requests to stop, forcing him to pin me to a tree with a swift burst of air. When he agreed to help me, Ezra was insistent he would halt training should I give him cause for alarm. My current episode, combined with the time I summoned a gigantic ring of water – power that had barely materialised before – made Ezra nervous. My emotional turmoil causing my power to flare had done just that; causing him such alarm that I had forced him to use his powers against me.

"Ezra, let me go. I promise that I won't do that again," I pleaded with him, trying to wriggle free from the hold his power had on me.

"You cannot be trusted, Phoebe. I know that your heart is broken and you're trying to mend it but abusing your magick will not change what happened," Ezra paused, releasing his invisible hold of me, "doing this will not bring him back, Phoebe."

He was usually a man of few words; what he said stung. I knew I couldn't bring my father back, but I could avenge him. And I would do it with or without Ezra's training. Spending hours every day trying to perfect my craft was not just so I could release some of my rage; I was doing so to prepare for retribution.

I had already started to meet with villagers in the town square, calling men and women to arms to avenge the death of their lord. Dozens upon dozens gladly pledged their allegiance, recalling the many years of generosity and kindness my father bestowed upon them. But many were still hesitant. The Black Cloth wreaked havoc and took lives many moons ago; there was no telling what this new generation of dark witches would do.

But I was unfazed by what I knew of their ilk. The stories my parents told me were like fairytales compared to the horror of my father's passing.

An hour or so later, Tyrus, Xavien and Brielle arrived at the clearing where I had been training, their expressions were solemn when I finally stopped to look at them. I couldn't recall the last time I saw them – a week ago, maybe two. I had avoided their visits to the castle and their invites to the pub; I hadn't felt the need to go out when there was so much to be done, nor did I want to exchange our usual pleasantries as if everything was fine. It should not have come as a surprise to them that I didn't wish to sit around getting high on silverleaf when the *thing* that murdered my father had not yet answered for her savagery.

I didn't want to see them; I couldn't face it. Being in their company meant I had to put on a brave face, make idle conversation. Seeing them would be a devastating reminder that my father was still alive the last time we were together. I turned away, rolling my eyes in annoyance.

"I am so, so sorry." Brielle was in tears as she pulled me into a tight embrace. Tyrus and Xavien followed shortly after, Tyrus lingering longer than the others. I fought against the urge to push them away, suddenly feeling overwhelmed.

"Is there anything we can do?" Tyrus asked, gently stroking my arm; but I flinched from his touch. He continued, "You never let us come to the castle to see you." I looked at him quizzically, recalling his bizarre behaviour when I saw him last and the unsettling words he muttered. *Who was he talking to when he said, 'Get out of my head?'*

"You can help me get revenge." I said with as much conviction I could muster.

Xavien let out a timorous laugh. “You can’t be serious?”

“I’m deadly serious.” I replied through gritted teeth, adjusting the sleeves of my blouse, rolling them to rest at my elbow.

“What are you planning to do?” Brielle sent an anxious glance towards Xavien, then fiddled with the amethyst pendant at her neck.

Waving a quick goodbye to Ezra who was breaking down the pyres he built, chucking the charred pieces of wood into bushes, I headed out of the grounds. “I’m going to kill Briar. And all of her vile followers.”

“What the fuck, Phoebe?” Brielle exclaimed, rushing after me. She halted, then waved coyly at Ezra before returning to my side.

“Phoebe, you’re not a murderer.” Tyrus pulled me back by my elbow. “You’re going to get yourself killed.”

“Perhaps. But I’ll go down swinging. Hopefully with Briar’s severed head in my hands.”

There was a stunned silence.

“Well on that positively delightful note, shall we head to The Silver Sparrow? I think we could all use a drink,” Xavien said, interrupting the painfully long silence with his characteristic wit.

The Silver Sparrow was busy as usual, with patrons at every table, and people standing shoulder to shoulder at the bar. The warmth and hum of the place were stifling at first, but we managed to find a table at the back in a cosy alcove away from the buzz of the main floor. Xavien made his way through the crowd to the bar, squeezing between two portly men who were busy discussing their recent success at the auction house around the corner.

I didn't say anything; I was too distracted with visions of Briar's demise, imagining the pain I wanted to inflict upon her. Brielle and Tyrus exchanged a concerned look, studying the expression on my face. I hadn't realised they had been trying to talk to me.

"It's okay, Phoebe," Brielle said reassuringly, "take your time."

Nodding at her with a half-smile, I scanned the tavern, and searched for my blonde-haired friend. Xavien had been gone a while. My leg bounced as I grew more impatient – I had not signed up for sober silence.

"So, how are things with Ezra?" Tyrus's voice pierced through the silence at the table, taking me out of my murderous daydream with a question I had been meaning to ask for a while. He placed his hand on my thigh, instantly providing me with a comforting warmth that slowed the frantic bobbing of my leg.

Brielle's face lit up at the mention of Ezra's name. "How did you know?"

The ice that had formed around my heart thawed ever so slightly. I was happy my friend had finally found someone.

"That good, huh? I'm pleased for you. I really am." I reached over to Brielle and squeezed her hand attempting to show her that I meant it.

"Maybe we can arrange a double date?" Brielle clapped her hands together excitedly, a hopeful look on her face.

"I can't imagine Ezra enjoying that," I replied, arching a brow. We knew how much he liked to keep to himself. He had been a solitary creature for as long as I'd known him, drifting through life like a stray cat.

"He has started to get used to my sunny disposition," she said, beaming from ear to ear.

"Don't all rush at once," Xavien shouted at us sarcastically with a grin on his face; he struggled to carry four large tankards of beer, two in each hand. He set them down on the table with a glassy thud, pockets of foam and dribbles of liquid escaped and pooled on the wooden table. "Fuck, it's busy in here today."

He scooted across the bench and sat in the empty space next to Brielle.

"A toast," Brielle announced, raising her tankard and looking at me. "A toast to Lord Rafael. One of the greatest men I had the fortune of knowing. He had a heart of gold, and the purest of souls. This town has lost a true gentleman." She blew out a long breath, pushing down her own wave of emotions, before she continued, "He will be Eskium's hero until the end of time, never forgotten, and eternally missed."

I swallowed down the lump in my throat as my eyes began to burn, tears creeping up to the surface. Turning to Tyrus next to me, then glancing at Xavien across the table, I saw the tears welling in their eyes too. It was enough to break down the barrier I had built, causing floods of tears to escape.

"May Summerland welcome him and may we be graced by his spirit again," Tyrus added, wiping an errant tear from the corner of his eye

We clinked our tankards together, a pensive smile on each of our faces, with eyes red from the tears we all had shed.

Being consumed by my grief and rage made me feel more connected to my father in some way as if the suffering validated my loss. I felt guilty for feeling any flicker of enjoyment that relishing any slither of happiness would be betraying him; maybe if I maintained a sombre demeanour, my father would feel just how much I missed him. Maybe he'd understand that my life would never be the same without him and that losing him had forever changed who I was. *How long will I mourn him*? I suppose I will mourn him forever. Some days it may feel like being buried alive, fighting as more and more layers of dirt and earth weigh me down, and all I see is darkness. Other days it may feel like taking a deep cleansing breath on the first day of autumn, inhaling the fresh air as the wind picks up the burnt orange and gold leaves, reminding me of the beauty of Mabon. The Wheel keeps turning whether I'm drowning in despair or blissfully content.

"Thank you. I'm sorry… about how I've been behaving," I spoke with my voice low and unsteady, glancing morosely at each of my friends.

"You have nothing to apologise for," Tyrus replied, gently nudging my elbow with his. "You don't have to punish yourself for wanting to have fun, or to feel happy."

I couldn't find the words to respond, so I shrugged with a half-smile and a slight nod.

"Let's drink until we can't feel our faces anymore," Xavien raised his tankard high in the air with an enthusiastic grin on his face. The alcohol sploshed in the tankard, narrowly missing Brielle's face.

"Not this again. Watch those bloody tankards!" Brielle pulled Xavien back down into his chair.

The four of us laughed, knocking back the pale amber liquid, and giggling as our empty tankards collided when we placed them back on the table.

Tyrus jumped up with a sense of purpose, hands on his hips. “My round.”

My eyes followed him as he walked away. So much had happened in the two years I’d known him. He had turned up out of the blue, a wanderer from Arleau in the east – a shameless flirt, attempting to woo me every time we bumped into one another in The Silver Sparrow. It didn’t take long for me to finally agree to courtship; he was so persuasive he could sell water to a fish. He soon became an integral part of our group, which was no easy feat given the strong bond between Brielle, Xavien and me.

“So… Are you and Tyrus still…?” Brielle grinned with a slight mischievous look in her eyes, and I realised I was smiling.

“Don’t even go there, Brielle Tierson,” I snapped back half-jokingly.

“You could do with the distraction, Phoebe.” Xavien winked, glancing at Brielle from the corner of his eye.

I glowered at him. “I am going to hurt you.”

“It’s been a while. I’m sure he’d drop his breeches for you in seconds.” A maniacal laugh escaped Xavien’s mouth, and Brielle hushed him with the palm of her hand.

“Shut the fuck up!” I whispered, kicking him under the table.

“Ouch!” Xavien dramatically rubbed his leg. “I think it’s broken.”

“Stop dicking around. Do not bring this up again once he’s back.” I pointed a finger at him with mirthful eyes.

“Don’t bring *what* up again when *who* is back?”

Tyrus suddenly appeared at our table, a large tray of drinks in hand.

My cheeks warmed with embarrassment. He scanned our faces with a puzzled expression, hopefully unsure of what we had been discussing before he returned with a tray of drinks.

"Bloody Hell, that was quick." Xavien raised his eyebrows; his eyes widened in awe – it had taken him twice the time to be served.

"I think the barmaid likes me." Tyrus smirked, eyeing me as if trying to gauge my reaction.

"You know there's only four of us, right?" Brielle gestured towards the variety of drinks. "How did you afford all this?! Wine, whiskey, *moonberry shots*. Ugh, gross." She shuddered. "Gods, we're going to be hungover tomorrow."

"Well, seeing as Phoebe is signing our lives away with the war on The Black Cloth, we might as well have at least one more great night to remember before we end up feeding the worms in the Eskium earth." Tyrus joked, placing a shot in front of each of us, his eyes drawn to mine.

We each raised a glass and clinked them together, shouting, "For Eskium! For Frieya!"

Tyrus's eyes flickered towards me, "For Lord Rafael. For Phoebe."

Several hours had passed, and it was now closing time at The Silver Sparrow. There were a handful of other patrons left, some slumped against the warm stone walls, others snoring in front of the roaring fireplace. We begrudgingly gathered our things and made our way to the exit. Xavien stumbled every few yards, knocking into wooden chairs.

I felt lighter after some much-needed time with my friends; the alcohol certainly helped take the edge off my sorrow and seething rage.

As soon as we ventured outside, the brisk air hit me like a frosty slap across the face. The temperature was much colder than when we first arrived, the wind so icy it stung my nose, lips and cheeks, no doubt painting my face in a pink tinge. It sobered me up almost immediately.

"You coming back to ours?" Tyrus glanced down expectantly at me, my arms now wrapped around his waist.

"Do you want me to?" I replied coyly.

"What do you think?" Tyrus smirked before placing a soft kiss on my lips.

CHAPTER SIXTEEN

Tyrus

What a night. Tyrus moved his arm over to the left side of the bed, hoping to find her still laying there. Instead, the bed was empty. Cold. He scanned the room, wondering where she was… Perhaps she'd gone to the bathing room to freshen up. Either way, he was happy that they had not been interrupted again; the odd voice that invaded his mind before had remained dormant. *What the fuck was that, anyway?*

He hadn't the slightest clue what it could have been, but it felt all too real, as if someone had burrowed into his mind and made themselves at home. Pushing those thoughts away, Tyrus focused on finding Phoebe. He gently eased his legs out of bed and picked up the discarded clothing from last night, a reminder of their lustful encounter. He adjusted himself before he left his room, the evidence of his wandering thoughts apparent underneath his breeches.

Padding across the creaky wooden floorboards of the hallway, he ventured to the bathing room. There was no noise; perhaps she'd fallen asleep in the tub –

she was always doing that. He chuckled to himself at the thought, lightly knocking at the door, but when no reply was given, he slowly turned the handle, preparing himself for what lay beyond.

But she wasn't there.

Feeling a mixture of disappointment and frustration, he huffed and made his way downstairs. *Why did she get up without saying anything?*

Xavien and Brielle were still fast asleep and sprawled across the sofa. Xavien's wild blonde hair covered half his face; an arm slumped over Brielle, whose head was nestled on his lap. Brielle bolted upright, grabbing a blanket to cover her legs; she had only been wearing a vest and undergarments.

"What the fuck are you doing lurking around, Tyrus?!" Brielle barked, startling Xavien awake. They hurled themselves away in opposite directions, embarrassed by their half-dressed proximity to one another.

"Have you seen Phoebe?" Tyrus asked, itching the back of his head.

"Nope. We've been asleep. Didn't hear anything." Xavien replied awkwardly.

For fuck's sake. She left without saying goodbye.

"Did you two, uh, have some fun last night?" Brielle said with a wink, combing through her tight brown curls with her fingers.

"Time for breakfast." Xavien peeked outside the window, seeing the sun high up in the sky. "Or lunch, I think," he added, interrupting the awkward silence, jumping up from the sofa and slipping past Tyrus on the way to the kitchen. Tyrus followed.

"Why does Phoebe always do this?" Tyrus asked with frustration etched in his tone; he fetched eggs from the countertop to start preparing breakfast.

“Why are you fretting so much? You know she's going through a lot, Tyrus.” Xavien replied, chopping some mushrooms alongside him. “Maybe she just needs some time to herself,” Xavien added reassuringly, throwing the sliced mushrooms into a hot pan with butter in the hearth.

Tyrus chewed on his bottom lip, unable to shake thoughts of doubt from his mind.

CHAPTER SEVENTEEN

Phoebe

The next morning, I left Tyrus and Xavien's house in a hurry, not wanting to linger too long. No one was awake yet, so I had to sneak quietly out the door; Xavien and Brielle were cosy and dishevelled on the couch. Who knew the antics they had gotten up to last night; I had been too preoccupied with Tyrus.

Instead of returning home, I went to Luna's Light seeking a potent elixir. I visited Jefferson Dreed a few days after my father's passing, demanding answers. After all, my father told me in his last few moments to speak to him. I had absolutely no idea why but I was determined to find out.

Why would Jefferson know anything?

And he didn't.

He very much insisted that he didn't know why my father made such a plea. But I felt ill at ease – something was amiss.

In the meantime, I was on the hunt for something to weaken Briar's powers, to render her defenceless.

I had overheard a conversation in The Silver Sparrow about an elixir that was around at the time of the witch trials. Supposedly, it could melt the flesh off a dark witch, eye-watering yellow in colour with a stench like burnt hair and vomit. I wasn't sure if what I overheard about the elixir was true, nor was there any guarantee that Jefferson would possess something so powerful. I scanned the wooden shelves for it, my fingers dancing over glass vials of all shapes and sizes.

"Phoebe… It's a surprise to see you. You know you don't need to do any of your shifts, please only come back if and when you're ready." Jefferson studied me warily, ceasing to stack items onto shelves.

I nodded toward Jefferson but didn't respond, continuing to peruse the various bottles.

"Are you looking for something in particular?" He smoothed his wild grey beard nervously, pensively walking around the wooden counter to stand closer to me. "Perhaps some twilight powder to help you and your mother sleep?"

Jefferson had owned the shop since my father was a young lad; my father always spoke fondly of the apothecary. It was hard not to like Jefferson. He was a vibrant, whimsical, eccentric character known for his colourful wardrobe, often wearing a green velvet waistcoat and pale blue shirt. His trousers were always slightly creased and just a tad too long, and the bottoms always pooled over his chunky brown boots.

"I'm looking for something that melts the flesh off a dark witch." I said so casually I didn't recognise my voice.

Jefferson's jaw dropped. "D-d-d-on't be ludicrous!" he stammered. "Why in the name of all the gods would you need something like that?"

"You know that The Black Cloth are back and they killed my father. I must do something about it."

"Phoebe, I can't let you do this, this is dangerous business. There is no coming back from this… You don't know what you're getting yourself into."

"I know exactly what I'm getting myself into, Jefferson. And I will do whatever it takes to avenge my father." I lifted my chin with a motion that made me feel taller and braver.

"Now fetch me the elixir I'm talking about, or I will start breaking every vial in this place."

Jefferson was crestfallen, staggering backwards and bumping into the counter.

For a moment, I felt guilty for being so harsh, but a soft heart and weak conscience would get me nowhere.

He paused. "Very well."

Jefferson headed towards a room at the back of the shop, shaking his head. I could hear the clinking of glasses and the shuffling of boxes. He walked back out with one palm-sized receptacle of bright yellow liquid.

"How much?" I asked confidently.

"Two thousand gold coins." Jefferson winced, seemingly preparing for a disgruntled response.

"Interesting. I know for a fact that nothing in here costs that."

"Then perhaps you should acquire it elsewhere or put an end to this tomfoolery!" Jefferson's eyes did not move from mine as he firmly placed each hand on the counter.

"Fine. I trust these are equivalent to two thousand gold coins. Probably even more." I slid a blade across the wooden countertop: my father's letter opener—solid gold, with rubies adorning the hilt. Jefferson's eyes widened in surprise as I delved into my satchel and gently placed a handful of gold and platinum rings on the counter, each with a different stone or crystal.

Jefferson's eyes darted between me and the rings, and he stifled a cough, as if his throat was too tight when he spoke, "Did these belong to your father?" He pushed the items towards me as he shook his head back and forth sombrely. "I will not accept them."

"You will. And you will not speak a word of this to my mother." I gingerly nudged the items back towards him with my right hand.

"You are putting me in a very difficult and dangerous position, Phoebe."

"Don't you want them to pay for what they did? Put a stop to these remorseless lunatics? Do you think the bloodshed ends with my father? Mark my words, The Black Cloth will not stop and they will be back. And when they return, they will come for all of us."

He gulped; his eyes wide in shock at my outburst.

"Well, what's it going to be?" I asked, adjusting the satchel on my shoulder.

Jefferson gently slid the blade off the counter and scooped up the rings, depositing them in a drawer beneath the counter, then locking it.

"I will never speak of this to anyone. And you will not tell anyone that you acquired that elixir here."

"Deal." I turned on my heel to leave, looking back over my shoulder as I spoke, "Jefferson?"

He paused and sighed, clearly exasperated. "Yes?"

"What is this elixir called anyway?"

"Widow's Kiss."

Looking down at the bright yellow liquid, I thought of my bereft mother. "Widow's Kiss, indeed," I whispered, exiting the shop.

I would not be able to keep the promise I made to my father – the promise to flee. No, I would stay and fight.

CHAPTER EIGHTEEN

Lady Gabriella

Phoebe was spending more and more time away from Eskium Castle, leaving Gabriella to sit alone with her thoughts all too often. It was after six in the evening, and she had not yet returned for dinner.

She rarely missed dinner unless she was out with her friends and lost track of time.

But I asked her to be home before sundown or to send a messenger if she would stay out for the night. Fear suddenly invaded every rational thought in Gabriella's head.

When Phoebe was still not home at six-thirty, Gabriella sent one of the footmen into the square to look for her, terrified that Briar may have already struck. If she was safe, she could only be at a few places: Luna's Light, The Silver Sparrow or Tyrus and Xavien's house. If she was not safe, well, Gabriella didn't want to think about that; Phoebe could be anywhere. She started to pace the floors, chewing her nails, willing the heat in her palms to settle – a sensation she hadn't felt in many moons.

When the footman returned a short while later to let her know Phoebe was drinking in the tavern with her friends, Gabriella felt so overcome with relief she could cry, the heat in her hands instantly relenting.

After checking that enough guards were posted around the castle for the third time, she decided to retire upstairs, the anxiety had overwhelmed her to the point of exhaustion but not enough for her to switch off and fall asleep.

Her patchwork quilt was a form of therapy for her. She tended to it time and time again during sorrowful moments; besides, it wasn't going to make itself, and she had spent a full year on it already.

She gathered up her materials and set herself comfortably in the velvety marine-blue armchair of her craft room. This room was one of the few places she found solace; the other was at the kitchen countertop with Maria, eating one of her homemade cakes. The thought of Maria's cakes had her wondering if there were any in the kitchen that she could grab before she attempted to sleep; her food somehow always soothed the soul.

Gabriella was working on adding floral details to a yellow patch of fabric when a ferocious gust of wind burst through the door. She threw her arms over her face to shield her eyes from the blast, dropping the needle and thread into her lap; she didn't know what in the name of the gods was happening. It wasn't stormy outside; the window wasn't even open. Apprehensively, Gabriella moved her arms away from her face and adjusted her eyes to the twisting black winds around her and looked up. A feminine form, cocooned in a swirl of silver grey that seemed to shimmer like shards of broken quartz.

Great Mother. *What was this creature?*

"Oh sweet, sweet, Gabriella. So pleased to meet your acquaintance," the young woman said through a saccharine smile, bowing and extending a hand to shake hers as the winds died down. "I'm Briar."

Gabriella's jaw dropped; she couldn't believe her eyes. She often thought about what she would do when she finally met the woman who killed her husband, but as Gabriella looked at the woman in front of her, all her vengeful thoughts vanished, and she was frozen in fear.

"Get away from me, monster." Gabriella recoiled, pushing herself off the armchair and backing up until she felt the bookshelf behind her, digging into her back. "How did you get in here?"

"Sshh shhh. You're wailing just like your dozy guards," Briar whispered, slinking across the floor like a cat. "And as for your wards? Pfft. Pathetic."

Wards? We didn't have any wards.

"Get out of here before I end you," Gabriella threatened, sounding more confident than she was. She discreetly fetched a crochet hook from the woven basket behind her.

"Ooh, I do like a bit of *fire* in a woman. Maybe dear old papa and I weren't so different after all?" Briar shifted slowly towards her, lifting her chin with a crimson-taloned finger.

"Don't touch me with your wretched hands." Gabriella pulled her head away from Briar's touch, moving herself along the bookshelf behind her, using her hands as the only guide.

"But my hands are *so* good at what they do." Briar raised an eyebrow mockingly. "I'm taking you far away from here."

"Like Hell you are," Gabriella screeched, shoving a pile of heavy bound books in Briar's direction.

"A game of kiss chase? I love it."

Gabriella's expression was as cold as steel, her eyes searing through Briar like hot iron. She kept her fists clenched at her sides, knowing that if she released her fire, she might never be able to control it.

Briar was like a predator teasing its prey, pacing in front of her, peering out into the hallway. "Where is that *darling* daughter of yours?"

"You leave her out of this, you bitch." Gabriella grew furious at the mention of her daughter, and launched herself at Briar, her hands clamping around her throat.

"Gods, you do know what I like, don't you? Harder, please." She shoved Gabriella against the wall with minimal effort.

"Oh, the things I'd like to do to you. I don't normally fuck older women, but I can make an exception." Briar slid her fingers down Gabriella's midriff, stopping just above her belly button. "I must say, Daddy dearest had impeccable taste."

Gabriella's face contorted with disgust.

"Shall I inflict pain or pleasure? Maybe I'll give you both." Briar laughed wickedly, throwing her head back.

"You will burn, just like your mother," Gabriella roared, her hands rising above her head, drawing upon the fire from the candlesticks around her. She gathered every flicker of flame and sent a molten wave towards Briar.

Briar dodged to the side, narrowly avoiding the hit as it crashed into a bookcase, sending burning papers flying in all directions.

"Gods, you are a gorgeous family, aren't you? You don't have a younger brother, do you?" Briar taunted.

Gabriella sent another fiery ball of energy towards her, this time hitting Briar right in the chest. The flames singed her black silk blouse, leaving a burn in the fabric.

"That was one of my favourite blouses, you silly old bat." Briar brushed herself down, not noticing the second wave heading towards her. She fell backwards at the sheer force of its power, knocking into the picture frames on the wall. She landed with a thud, surrounded by pieces of broken wood and glass.

"Vile cretin," Gabriella sneered as her eyes scanned Briar's limp body. As she reached down towards Briar's head with a blazing palm, her feet were knocked out from beneath her by a heeled boot. Briar was on top of her in seconds, pinning her wrists to the ground.

"That tickled." Briar planted a long lick along the side of Gabriella's face, scraping her tongue from her jaw to her cheekbone.

"Get the Hell off me, you cursed bitch, before I burn those dead eyes from your skull." Gabriella headbutted her, leaving her with a bloody nose. Briar wiped the scarlet bead away; her eyes fixed on Gabriella's.

"How very dramatic. It's going to take a lot more than this to hurt me, but I do love seeing some zest in you, *Ella.*"

Gabriella froze.

"Your little kitchen *friend* didn't appreciate my visit." Briar beamed at the pained expression on Gabriella's face.

Playing with the air she conjured in her palm, Briar edged closer to Gabriella. "We'll see how she fares at Duskbrook Manor."

"You better not hurt her, I swear to the gods."

"The gods won't help you." Briar turned on her heel, swaying her hips as she skulked across the floor. "She's safe. For now. Until I decide what I'm going to do with her. You could of course accept your fate as my prisoner in exchange for her safety."

"I will never be your prisoner."

"Then I guess Maria is going to become very familiar with my hungry rats." Briar made a biting sound, then expelled a devious laugh.

Gabriella rose, her body encased in orange, red and white hues. She was pure fire—pure rage. She screamed so loud the windows of the craft room shattered, sending shards flying. The wave that followed was unrelenting, burning through everything it met in its path.

Everything but Briar; she was surrounded by a silvery grey barrier, protecting her from the flames.

"Your castle *will* be nothing but ash and ruin. And it will be at your hand," Briar snarled.

Gabriella stared at her in horror as the fire whipped around them, snapping at their heels and seeping into the hallway.

"Oh, you didn't know? Fire cannot kill me," Briar sneered as she dragged Gabriella into a foggy vortex, trapping her within.

Gabriella clawed at the gauzy mist, gasping for oxygen as her vision began to blur, clouding her eyes. She was like a helpless fly, caught in the web of a black widow spider.

"Shall we go on a little adventure?" Briar jeered, snickering as she swept them both out of the castle and into darkness.

CHAPTER NINETEEN

Phoebe

I decided a slow walk home would be a good idea, even though the tips of my fingers burned from the cold. Fifteen minutes into the journey, I started to regret my choice; my body ached from lack of sleep. Another fifteen minutes or so I would be home where I could soak in the bath, with piping hot, lavender-infused water.

The smell of smoke filled my lungs as I approached the foot of the hill leading to the castle. I wrinkled my nose, scanning the rolling fields and small patches of woodland for signs of a fire, yet nothing seemed amiss.

It wasn't until I reached the peak of the hill that I discovered the source of the burning smell: Eskium Castle.

Running as fast as I could, my limbs strained with the slight incline of the hill. My heartbeat thundered in my chest, adding to the nauseating feeling of panic that worsened with every laboured step.

"Mother! Maria!" I screamed out, desperate for someone to answer, as I lowered my satchel to the floor. I couldn't see any of the castle staff either. *Gods, had everyone perished?*

"Mother, where are you?!" I attempted to approach the entrance to the castle, but the heat from the open front door was overwhelming. Smoke billowed out, angry black and grey swirls suffocating the stone walls.

Tears filled my eyes as panic overwhelmed me, and I continued to scream, aghast at the wreckage that was my family home. I looked down at my open palms, furious that I had not yet mastered water.

I peered upwards to the top of the castle, the smoke burning my eyes as I tried to look for any sign of their escape. Twisting my fingers, I prayed to the gods to help me douse the flames, but only small spheres of mist appeared at my fingertips. Throwing my arms down at my sides, I let out a pained sound as the reality of what was in front of me came crashing down. *Why can't I summon water as I did before?*

Feelings of regret began to seep in, crawling over my skin like spiders – I should have stayed home. It was foolish to assume my wards and extra guards would have been enough to stop an attack.

As I went to take a step backwards, I tripped, barking out a curse as I stumbled, sending me crashing to the frosty ground in a clamorous heap.

The fall knocked the wind from me, forcing me to lay still for a few seconds to quell the nausea that had begun to build. Heaving myself up, I took a greedy gulp of the frigid Eskium air. I scrabbled along the floor and began to shovel snow with my bare hands, desperate to find out what had caused me to trip. My hands burned from the chill, sending stabbing pains through my fingers. One last dig through the snow revealed a body – one of the guards. His skin was mottled, pink and blue from winter's kiss of death, his beard and eyebrows thick with ice.

Crawling on my hands and knees, I found another snow-covered mound. My heart pounded violently in my chest as I raked my fingers through the icy blanket, wincing as it stung my flesh. Using my forearms instead, I pushed snowfall aside, revealing another guard. A puddle of crimson pooled underneath his body, staining the frozen floor like red wine on a white shirt.

The sound of crunchy footsteps and the humming of voices creeped up the hill, forcing me to move my chilled bones.

Villagers had come to see where the smoke was coming from.

"Go and fetch all the pails of water you can carry! Quickly!" ordered one of them, herding the handful of men and women towards the castle's well.

"It's no use – it's gone," my voice cracked as I held in a sob. "I think my mother is still inside." I crumpled and fell to my knees. Warm tears streamed down my cheeks, thawing my gelid skin.

"Miss Phoebe, we will do what we can. Your mother may not be d –" the villager looked panicked as they took a breath, and continued, "Perhaps she has found a place to hide, or she escaped."

I sincerely hoped that my mother did manage to escape, and Maria too. *But why wouldn't she be here now, outside, calling for help?*

Looking around me, I was numb with the shock from what was unfolding before my eyes. The burning castle, the panicked villagers throwing pails of water at the savage flames, the stables—Snowshoe! I forced myself to get off the frigid ground and sprinted towards my horse, who was frantically bucking against the gates.

"Snowshoe, I'm so sorry," I whispered through heavy sobs as I untied her from the pen and walked her out towards the path. "Please help me untie the other horses," I asked a young man standing nearby.

It wasn't until Snowshoe was standing in the light of day that I noticed something – a bloody handprint marred the right side of her otherwise pristine white coat. A chill crept over me. I cautiously placed my palms over the horse, scanning her body for any injuries or other ominous symbols, then led Snowshoe round by her reins so I could look at her left side.

"Oh dear gods," I mumbled to myself.

A symbol. In blood.

The Black Cloth sigil.

A paralysing current of dread ran through me, wrapping me in a clammy and cold sweat.

"Miss Phoebe – your horse! What the…?" yelled a villager, smoothing Snowshoe's nose to soothe her.

Eskium Castle, now fully aflame, began to crumble. Only a charred skeleton remained. Over twenty years' worth of memories were up in smoke.

I didn't know what I was going to do next. The only thing I knew was that Briar would pay for this. And soon.

"I need your help." I demanded breathlessly as I barged through the door to Luna's Light.

Jefferson spun round from one of his shelves, his eyes wide with confusion.

"Gods, what now?" he responded with a bluntness in his tone that made me grit my teeth.

"My mother is gone," my voice broke; I couldn't believe the words that left my lips.

"Phoebe, what do you mean? What has happened?"

"The Black Cloth… They attacked the castle. My mother is gone. So is Maria," I slid to the floor, my legs too weak to keep me standing.

"Gods, no. No, no, no." Jefferson shook his head in denial; he started to pace and pinched the bridge of his nose.

"Jefferson. Tell me everything you know. You were around at the time of the dark witch trials in Duskbrook, yes?"

"Why are you asking such a question?" he replied, bumping into the shelf behind him as he retreated further.

"I need to know where to find them. The Black Cloth." I stared at him, desperation clouding my features.

"It was nearly thirty years ago, Phoebe. Who's to say this new group resides there?" He wouldn't look at me, nervously fiddling with the buttons on his shirt cuffs.

"Tell me what you know. Now." I pulled myself up, keeping my eyes locked on him. Taking a step toward him, I pulled a dagger from my pocket and pointed it at him. A pang of shame hit me as I saw the fear in Jefferson's eyes.

"Really, Phoebe? You would maim me for this information? Your father would be so disappointed."

"How dare you speak of my father!" I roared, taking a step closer. "I suggest you think very carefully about what you say next."

Jefferson paused as indecision flashed over his face. "Okay. Okay. Fine! I'll tell you what I know."

Relaxing my arm, I held the dagger in a loose grip at my side.

"There was a place, in the town of Duskbrook. Uh…Duskbrook Manor. That's where the leader of The Black Cloth… Zayla, used to convene with her brothers and sisters of the craft." He paused for a few seconds as if he was carefully considering what he was going to say next. "She wasn't always a bad woman… She should not have died as she did..." Jefferson trailed off.

I couldn't help but notice the way his face changed; the mention of Zayla's name seemed to cause him a great deal of pain.

"Well, Briar Ravenquill, is now leading this new coven. She claims to be the daughter of my father and Zayla. She is the one who murdered him," I interjected.

The blood had drained from Jefferson's face, making him look sickly. He fumbled for a stool and perched on it. "No… No, that's not possible. That's… That's not her name. That *wasn't* her name. And she died a few years after her mother."

"Are you okay?" I asked, noting how he hunched on the stool and stared off into the distance.

His bushy white eyebrows were drawn together, and he twirled his beard, gazing into nothingness as he sat there deep in thought.

"Jefferson?" I asked again, placing my palm on his hand. "What is it?"

"I… I can't… I don't know…" he mumbled.

"Did you know Zayla?"

His pale blue eyes shot up to meet mine. I had never noticed their unusually pale colour before.

As I went to speak again, Jefferson placed a palm on my hand. "You cannot do this alone, Phoebe."

"I will not be alone. I will travel with Tyrus, Xavien and Brielle at first light, along with any able-bodied man or woman who wishes to join us."

A sigh escaped Jefferson as he pulled several vials from beneath the main counter.

"Then I am coming with you."

I no longer had a home. My father was dead. My mother and Maria were missing.

Tyrus, Xavien and Brielle were all I had left, though I was grateful I had anyone, especially friends I considered family.

Tyrus and Xavien had suggested I move in with them, telling me the guest room was mine. I was immensely grateful for the gesture; without it, I'd be sleeping in the stables of Eskium Castle.

"If this is a one-way trip, then I get to open my most expensive bottle of wine, right?" Xavien casually declared, pouring red wine into glasses for everyone after I had just laid out my plans to sack Duskbrook.

"I guess so," Tyrus replied, taking a sip.

"Listen. We may not have magical powers, but we know how to fight, how to use weapons," Brielle added; she was nowhere near as confident about this as she tried to make us believe. She gripped her amethyst pendant tightly, betraying her true emotions.

"I know what I am asking of you all. So if you decide you cannot join me in this, I will understand." I glanced at each of them for a few seconds, praying to the gods they would fight with me.

Xavien's usual youthful face looked tired. "And hate us forever? You'll come after us and set our arses on fire!"

I chewed the inside of my cheek as my mind raced, suddenly feeling fretful about how I had dragged my friends into danger.

"We're not letting you do this without us." Tyrus leaned over to me, placing his hand on my forearm. Noting the warmth of his long and calloused fingers, my mouth quirked up into a smile.

"We leave at first light."

We arrived at the town square just after sunrise, there were dozens and dozens of armed men and women, some with ornate daggers, gargantuan axes, and menacing polearms, others with simple farming tools like forks and spades. My heart swelled with pride at the loyalty and bravery of my father's people.

I stood atop the ledge of a water fountain, trying to gain some height so I could address the crowd.

My heart raced so fast I could hear my heartbeat in my ears.

"I cannot thank you all enough for joining me in this fight. I do not know what horrors await us. I must warn you, this will be treacherous."

The crowd remained eerily quiet, causing me to fidget nervously.

I inhaled deeply and counted, fiddling with my amethyst pendant.

Inhale.

One.

Two.

Three.

Four.

Five.

Exhale.

"We all know that The Black Cloth has returned. They killed my father and I have every reason to believe they have my mother. And Maria."

The crowd gasped. Panicked eyes shot from one person to the next.

"I will find a way to bring them to their knees, to break them. I will end them all if it is the very last thing I do." I paused, scouring the crowd for signs of doubt.

"Do you know what they did to this town?! They're evil. We'll never survive!" a villager yelled.

"And what about their magick? We can't fight against magick!" another person called out, causing a weave of nods in accordance.

"We can," I said with conviction.

"How can you be so sure?" a young lad walked forwards, squeezing between a few people standing near the front.

"Because the Great Mother blessed me with fire."

Flames appeared one by one at each of my fingertips.

"Gods save us!" a woman screamed, grabbing hold of the man next to her.

"Do not be afraid. I am not like them. I will use my power to save us, to save Eskium."

"How can we trust you?!"

"Because she is now the heir to Eskium," Brielle announced. "She is good like her father. Humble like her mother. And strong in her own right. She is kind, a wonderful friend, and a great neighbour. And she loves this town."

Tears filled my eyes. I didn't feel deserving of such kind words, nor had I considered that I would take my father's mantle.

I continued. "I am not like The Black Cloth. I am not my grandfather. Only the guilty will pay for their crimes. Eskium will not suffer any more bloodshed at the hands of this scourge."

The crowd murmured, shuffling as they considered my words.

"What say you?!"

The crowd erupted with roars. "For Lord Rafael! For Phoebe! For ESKIUM!"

CHAPTER TWENTY

Lady Gabriella

When Gabriella awoke, she had no idea where she was, and her hands were shackled. She surveyed her arms and legs, surprised that her injuries were minimal, only scrapes and bruises caused by the skirmish at the castle.

She expected Briar to have maimed her further while she was unconscious. Actually, she didn't think she would ever be aware of consciousness again. She thought she would be in Summerland, preparing to reincarnate and hopefully rejoin her beloved Rafael in whichever form the gods deemed worthy.

The stone walls dripped with moisture, green from algae and mould layering the surface. The wooden beams above were weathered and riddled with holes from woodworm and covered in cobwebs. Dozens of tiny black spiders skittered in and out of the gaps. *Where was she? A dungeon? A basement?*

Gabriella laid atop a heap of blankets, one small comfort in this damp room. A single candle on a brass-coloured dish cast a golden light, warming the otherwise bleak space; she was grateful for any small amount of light and minuscule hum of heat. She tried using her powers, but only minute puffs of smoke escaped her palms. She didn't know what these shackles were made of, but they nullified her fire. They were a dark metallic colour, and felt rough against her skin.

"Comfy in there, Ella?" A familiar voice jeered through the metal window hatch of the door.

"What do you plan to do with me?" Gabriella snapped back.

"I haven't decided yet. I like seeing you bound though. It's giving me *all* sorts of ideas." Briar raised her eyebrow suggestively as she pressed her face against the hatch.

"Do you not grow tired of your empty threats? It's becoming quite dull. I might die from boredom instead." Gabriella knew she should stop mocking her, but she made it far too difficult to stop.

"Oh, sweet Gabriella. They're not threats. If you ask nicely, I'll make them promises instead."

Gabriella rolled her eyes; she was running out of energy to respond to Briar's attempts to intimidate her.

"What, no retort? Aw," she whined, "No fun."

Gabriella continued to ignore her.

"Very well. Rest your pretty little head. Tomorrow, I have need of you."

Gabriella sat up to enquire what she meant, but Briar slammed the window hatch shut.

Have need of me? Gabriella had come to realise that with Briar, that could mean any number of things. She shifted back down into the threadbare blankets. It wasn't pleasant by any stretch, but she was thankful she was able to lay on something.

Her mind drifted to Phoebe. To Maria. *Where were they? Were they dead? What of Eskium Castle?* When Briar swept them both up in a whirl of shimmering grey smoke, Gabriella had only caught a glimpse of the destruction – destruction she caused because she lost control. She felt great shame at her weakness, their family home crumbled to ash and it was her fault.

Gabriella slept fitfully, nightmare after nightmare tormenting her with images of Briar and the fires burning at Eskium Castle. The very real possibility that her daughter was dead, as well as Maria. She tossed and turned, thrashing amongst the blankets. She thought the nightmares that followed her husband's murder were sickening, but these were something else. Sharp claws tore at her flesh. Beaks as black at midnight pecked at her eyes. Ravens. Flying at her face in a fit of black feathers, claiming her sight. The sound of Briar's maniacal laughter echoed in the distance. Phoebe's face reeled in agony. Her body pinned to a table as she was poked and prodded. A tall man dressed in black stood in the corner of the room, eyes shimmering like sunlight on the ocean.

Gabriella was startled awake by the sound of the door unlocking.

She could not tell if it was daylight; there were no windows in her cell. She pulled the blankets up towards the bottom of her chin as if it would protect her somehow.

It was only one of Briar's guards.

"What do you want?" Gabriella sniped.

“Charming,” a skinny, bald man replied, taking cautious steps towards her with a bowl of something.

“Eat this,” he said, pushing the bowl into her hands.

“I will do no such thing.” Gabriella knocked it away, sending it flying across the room. The bowl smashed as it hit the wall, causing thick and creamy globules to drip downwards and pool onto the cold ground.

“Guess you’ll starve then.”

The smell was familiar. Comforting. The scent of oats mixed with honey, blueberries and almonds. Maria made porridge like this at Eskium Castle.

“Who made this?” Gabriella bellowed.

“I believe you’re familiar with her. Mary, is it?

“Do you mean Maria?

“Ah, yes. Maria.”

Gabriella was a mixture of horrified and relieved. Maria was alive.

“Don’t look so terrified. We have need of her services if we’re to take Frieya.”

Gabriella’s throat bobbed.

“What do you mean ‘take Frieya’? And what could you possibly need Maria for? Are you and your rabble of lunatics not able to cook your own food?”

“Briar plans to take Eskium imminently, and once that frozen shithole is hers, she’ll move south to claim the rest of Frieya.”

Gabriella felt physically sick. She thought everything that had happened so far was about Rafael not protecting them. No. Briar had much grander plans: domination.

“And as for your cook, Maria. Well, I think we all know that she’s not *just* a cook is she, Gabriella?”

She stared at him as if he were speaking a different language. The guard laughed so hard she thought he would fall over.

"You mean to tell me you don't know?" he replied with a smug grin.

"What the Hell are you talking about?"

"Maria is no ordinary woman. She's a *Kitchen Witch.*"

She took a long time to reply, mulling over the words in her head.

"That's impossible…" her voice was barely audible. *Great Mother. Had she been using magick in her food all this time? Was she a spy?*

"I suggest you don't swat away the next bowl I bring you." The guard sauntered off, chortling as he strode through the heavy door.

Magick had rarely been seen or heard of since the witch trials, but there were rumours that some continued to use their powers. *But why did Maria hide her magick from her? Did she have something to do with Briar finding Rafael? His murder?*

She shook her head aggressively. No matter what magick Maria used, Gabriella refused to believe she played any part in her husband's death.

Maria was like a mother to her: loving and devoted. Gabriella thought back on the last two decades with Maria as not only her cook but her confidante. The closest thing she had to a mother after leaving her own behind in Troyla. Maria had been there at Phoebe's birth, had wiped the sweat from her brow, held her hand, eased the pain…

Gabriella rubbed her temples as a headache began to creep in. Her mind drifted immediately to what normally helped—Maria's tea. *Dear gods.* It was a concoction of a vast variety of herbs, spices and fauna.

Exactly the kind of thing a Kitchen Witch would make.

But Maria was trying to help her… Her headaches did ease when she didn't push the tea away. Nothing made sense anymore. Gabriella pulled her knees to her chest and sobbed. She longed for Rafael. For Phoebe. For all she knew, she was now alone in this wretched world, a pawn for her husband's bastard daughter.

For the first time in many moons, Gabriella felt truly hopeless.

CHAPTER TWENTY-ONE

Phoebe

I led a group of around fifty strong through The Mossfall Thicket, a bleak and misty wood that cleaved through the lush and fertile lands of Eskium like a festering wound. Swaths of ghostly black trees and rancid swamps encompassed the main path through.

The journey would be half a day's trek on foot if we continued without stopping.

"Fuck, it stinks." Xavien heaved, covering his mouth and nose with his cloak.

"Almost as bad as you," Brielle teased; she could never resist the urge to make fun of him.

"How much further, Phoebe?" Xavien asked, glancing at me as he tried to hide the worry on his face.

"An hour or so, perhaps." I looked beyond with a forlorn expression, scanning the path ahead.

I was astonished by the number of men and women who pledged their allegiance to my father, to me. Behind me followed villagers, mercenaries and noblemen and women of all ages, from sixteen to sixty, some skilled with swords and daggers, but many were just humble labourers who spent their days on the farmlands or selling goods at the market. They were skilled in many ways but unlikely to have seen bloodshed, let alone be the cause of it.

My eyes lingered on my friends; my heart ached with pride. None of them had magick in their veins, but they joined me on this cursed crusade without hesitation.

Xavien, who was skilled with axes, had fought in a few skirmishes but nothing on this scale. He had learned to use weapons after sneaking into many of the guard's training sessions at the castle. He always worked so well with Brielle; they were symbiotic in more ways than one, fluid in their movements and sure in their steps.

Brielle, who favoured dual daggers, was as quick as a cat. Her parents had trained her when she was a teenager, wanting to ensure she would always be able to defend herself should she need to. Her cunning proved useful against the bandits they encountered last year. The bandits had casually entered The Silver Sparrow, masquerading as harmless Eskium townsfolk; their motives were driven by greed – to raid the coffers of the tavern and pillage any other items worth stealing. Brielle had noted their suspicious behaviour within an instant, spotting one of them talking to Arryn whilst another scooped gold coins off the counter. She crept up behind one of them, her daggers at the throat of the lead brute. She had pushed her blades into either side of his throat hard enough that he knew she wasn't fucking around. The trickle of piss that escaped his breeches was evidence enough.

Then my eyes landed on Tyrus, a talented bowman who had been instrumental in felling the Roamers who had infiltrated Eskium from the west two years prior. The Roamers were a band of nomadic barbarians with a thirst for blood and hunger for riches. Tyrus stood alongside my father and his men when the savages stormed the various villages, their blood ignited by the thought of killing and pillaging innocents. But the people of Eskium escaped with minor injuries that day, and with no casualties. The Roamers, on the other hand, were cut down, annihilated, extinguished from the realm. Their primitive weapons were no match for soldiers of Eskium; their corpses littered the fields in their dozens, morbid evidence of their failure.

Tyrus was held in high esteem from that day onwards. He was borderline legendary, stories of his almost majestic skill told to children before bedtime. That battle was two years ago, but he had barely touched his bow since.

My legs grew weary, having walked for hours and hours.

The clearing where we would do some last minute preparations was up ahead; the deathly black branches of the trees retreated, revealing a blush pink sky, rosy like sun-kissed cheeks. Although it could only have been early afternoon, Duskbrook seemed like the kind of place that only saw daylight for a fleeting moment.

I could tell we were close. The hairs on my arms rose, the feeling of eyes all over my body felt like hundreds of ants crawling across my skin. I swore I saw glinting yellow flickers in the brush on either side of me but attempted to shake it off. I internally reassured myself for being so foolish when I realised they were eyes—feral eyes.

Just as I had convinced myself to calm down, a blood-curdling shriek sounded from the back of the group.

"Great Mother," I murmured, petrified of what would happen next.

A hulking abomination loomed over several villagers, gore dripping from jagged teeth, with pus-filled pustules all over its body. Before anyone had a chance to react, the creature lunged for one of the men, teeth gnashing at his neck. Blood sprayed in all directions, a horrific scarlet shower covered those that stood nearby.

Then chaos erupted – people started screaming, and everyone began to run, trying to escape the wretched beast.

People were knocked over, trampled on and thrown out of the way as the monster approached, blood soaking its unsightly mouth. It swiped with gnarled talons, black nails scraping against the back of another villager. Their wail was horrifying as the monster continued to shred them, ribbons of flesh falling away from their back like torn silk.

"We've got to get out of here!" Brielle yelled as she readied her daggers, one in each hand.

"No shit!" Xavien retorted as he tightly gripped the handle of his axe.

Tyrus nocked an arrow and released one after the other, rapidly and with precision. Each one found its target, hitting the beast in the neck, chest and stomach.

The pain-filled snarl that followed pierced the air as the beast swayed and pulled at the arrowheads lodged in its flesh, swiping at men and women who stood nearby.

It teetered on the spot as it broke off each arrow, leaving the sharp tips buried in its rotting skin. It let out another pained howl, causing the birds in the trees to disperse into the sky in a flurry of dark feathers.

As the beast began to falter, a figure appeared on its haunches, swiftly moving from its calves to its back.

Brielle.

She plunged two daggers into either side of its neck, sending spurts of blood into the fetid air. She twisted each blade, lodging them deeper. The beast attempted to grab her to send her flying, but Xavien skidded across the forest floor and swiped each leg with his axe. There was a sickening crack as its ankles splintered and its body gave way, falling to the ground in a booming thud.

But as it fell, it caught Xavien in its grip, squeezing his body in the palm of its giant hand, causing Xavien to howl in agony. Brielle stabbed at it, jabbing its flesh over and over again.

"Let go of him!" she shrieked, carving through its rotting skin with both daggers. I joined the fray not caring what revealing my magick would do; I sent a fireball into the creature's head, encasing it in flames. One villager ran at the sight of my flames. "Witch! She's going to burn us all!" he yelled, barrelling into others as they fled in the opposite direction.

The beast finally dropped Xavien but swiped him as he fell, causing him to land with a painfully heavy thud. He cried out in pain, gripping his left arm – blood poured from three deep slashes. His arm was a gnarled mess, revealing torn muscle and tissue.

"Xave, Xave! Talk to me." Brielle grabbed him by the shoulders and tried to pull him closer.

The abomination flailed and shrieked, batting at its head to snuff the flames. Its skin sizzled and popped as the fire continued its scorching journey over its bloodied body. The beast tried one last time to strike at us, but it was no use. The wounds inflicted were too much, and it let out a disturbing groan as it took its final breath and crashed to the muddy ground.

What the fuck was that thing?

Tyrus and I rushed to Xavien and Brielle's side.

"Xavien – show us," I commanded, trying to keep my voice steady despite knowing that the wound would be gruesome.

He reluctantly let go of his arm, hissing and wincing.

"It fucking destroyed my arm," he muttered dejectedly as tears fell down his face.

"It's okay, it can be fixed. It's fine, Xave. You're fine." Brielle tried to reassure him.

"It's not fucking fine! I can't feel it. Gods, I can't feel my arm," the fear in his voice caused my own heartbeat to hammer in my chest, turning my blood cold. I looked around frantically for Jefferson, lost in the chaos.

"Xave, take this between your teeth," Tyrus handed him a piece of wood, "I'm going to lift you up and take you to a healer."

"No. No. No. No." Xavien attempted to shake his head, as the blood seemed to drain from his face, making his complexion look sallow.

"Xavien, we have to move." Brielle stroked his hair.

He stared at her as he placed the wood between his teeth, biting down hard as Tyrus scooped him up into his arms.

He bit down harder on the piece of wood as it muffled his cries; his eyes wide in agony. Tremors wracked his body before he went limp, and he passed out.

We quickly approached the exit of The Mossfall Thicket, sprinting for the remainder of the journey, terrified that more menacing creatures would appear. As we stepped over the threshold between the forest and the ghostly village, the outlines of dwellings became clearer, revealing weather-beaten wooden houses lining the path into Duskbrook. Their ghostly silhouettes overpowered the small square, framing the grounds in macabre shapes.

It seemed impossible that anyone had ever lived there, but if I had learned anything recently, it was 'impossible' was just a word.

We passed under an arch formed from thick branches of two trees: one on either side of the road ahead, the gnarled branches framing the next stretch of path. I looked up. Skeletons hung from the ancient tree, warnings pinned to their off-white bones with rusted nails: *The Black Cloth sees all.* Ice filled my veins as I considered how they met their demise.

Did Zayla hang these people? Or had they already been killed and this was a warning? What if this was Briar's doing? My eyes roamed the two figures, noting how the ivy leaves twined through the rib cages, snaking through old bones and tattered remnants of clothing. No – it couldn't have been Briar; it seemed unlikely that this barbaric act had been carried out recently. The fact that warnings had been pinned to the bodies made me believe they had been killed before, then put on display to terrify anyone who wandered into Duskbrook.

"Love what they've done with the place." Brielle replied sarcastically as her eyes hovered over the hanging remains of some poor soul, holding onto Xavien's hand as he was transported via cart. Luckily Jefferson had joined the group and had come equipped with an array of healing tonics and supplies and treated the wound as we travelled.

Xavien slipped in and out of consciousness as the pain overwhelmed him. His arm was in a bad way, but if the tonic Jefferson gave him worked, combined with the salve smeared onto his skin, it was possible it could be healed.

The morale of the villagers accompanying me was audibly weakening, the rotten monster that had claimed the lives of half a dozen of the group worsening their fears. I was furious I could not keep them safe.

"Is it too late to turn back?" one villager said to another, their whispers much louder than they must have realised.

"I think we've made a terrible mistake," another added.

I halted, turned towards the men and women of Eskium and took a deep breath.

"I know you are scared. I know this place is the embodiment of evil. But think of your lord, as he lay dying. He fought for you. He would still fight for you now."

A hum of murmurs rippled across the crowd.

"To be scared is to be human, it does not make you weak. Wield your fear like a blade."

I observed Tyrus; his expression was tense, his body language skittish. He remained silent. *Was he frightened?*

Brielle added, "We are of Eskium blood, and we will not falter!"

"And if it goes really tits up, you could just run," Xavien muttered, regaining consciousness at an opportune moment.

The crowd rallied, raising an array of weapons above their heads, symbolising their accordance.

Rarely did Xavien's sense of humour ever prove useful, but at this moment, it thawed the ruinous reality of tackling death head-on, laughing in its face.

I decided to let the group rest for a short while before we continued. We were about a short distance away from the manor, and darkness had fallen upon Duskbrook. The sky was an inky indigo colour; stars dotted the dark sky like flecks of yellow-white paint.

Tyrus suggested scouting ahead to gather more intel, and I agreed.

Hesitantly, we made our way towards the gates of the manor, Tyrus kept his hand lightly placed on my lower back as we walked, providing a comforting warmth against my chilled skin.

"Look. Up ahead," I motioned, crouching behind a bush and pulling Tyrus with me. Swaths and swaths of dark cloaked figures huddled in groups outside.

"Fuck, how many is that?" I whispered as I tried to peer over the bush.

"Must be about twenty or so." Tyrus replied, his eyes squinting. "Briar is obviously the most powerful one, but if we take out the others first, we might be able to gain an advantage."

"How do you know?"

He didn't answer as he continued to look at the figures.

"I'll create a diversion, draw some of them in the opposite direction." He began to shuffle forward.

"Tyrus, wai –" Before I had an opportunity to grab him, he was gone, slinking through the shadows like a fox after a hare.

I caught one last glimpse of him before he slipped through the open gate into the darkness ahead.

Tyrus had been gone an excruciatingly long time. My back ached from being crouched for so long, and my fingers were numb from the cold; I cupped my hands and blew hot air into them, hoping to combat the lack of feeling.

I didn't know whether to go after him or run back to the group and storm the manor. I glanced between the gates and the narrow path to my right and back again.

"Fuck," I whispered to myself, deciding to gather up the group and press ahead. Maybe Tyrus had not yet returned because he just needed to lay low for a bit, or maybe he'd had to rethink his strategy once he was closer.

I turned to make my way back to the group, but I couldn't move, as if my feet were glued to the earth. Then suddenly, I was thrown up into the air by a brutal force, making my stomach flip. Shrieking in terror, my ears rang like a bell as my head spun. I came flying back down, hitting the half-frozen mud underneath with a violent thud. Clutching my ribs, I roiled from the stabbing pain beneath my breast. Gods, my ribs felt like they were on fire.

I rolled over onto my back and looked down, clutching my left side. Seconds later, my world went dark.

CHAPTER TWENTY-TWO

Phoebe

"Wakey, wakey." A saccharine voice echoed in the distance, a feminine but insincere lilt in the tone. I could barely reply, let alone move my body. I frowned as my eyes tried to adjust to the odd sepia light in the room. The last thing I remembered was Tyrus slipping through the gates.

"Who are you? What the fuck are you doing?" I battled to haul myself up, wondering why it was so difficult. I soon realised that I had been restrained; my wrists and ankles had been tied to a table.

"Surprise, little sister! Well… Half-sister, if we're going to be precise." A pale face appeared above mine, so close our noses almost touched. The woman's irises were such a pale blue they were almost silver, like icicles.

"Did you have a little tumble?" she asked mockingly.

Gods no. That voice. Briar.

How? What? Where was Tyrus?

Peering through gritty eyes, I took in the details of the room. The light was low but warm, shrouding the space in a brownish-grey colour. Tall, antique candlestick holders adorned every surface, the brassy tones muted by the dribbles of wax that had dried to them. The walls were lined with deep burgundy textured wallpaper and dark wooden panels, making the space seem smaller than it probably was.

"We should really let one of the healers look at her injuries." A familiar voice sounded.

"What the fu - ? Tyrus? Is that you? What's going on?" I asked, but he turned away from me so I could no longer see his face. *What the bloody Hell was happening?*

"Oh, naïve little Phoebe. Tyrus has been *sooo* helpful," Briar sneered, slinking over to him, putting her fingers through his hair. He barely flinched at her touch.

"Ty, what is she talking about?" I darted another look his way, staring angrily at the back of his head.

He ignored me again.

"Tyrus, fucking answer me!" I bellowed as the fire beneath my skin began to simmer.

"Phoebe, lovely Tyrus here is one of my trusted advisors." The arrogance dripped off Briar like oil.

No. It couldn't be possible. No way could this be possible. This was a nightmare. It had to be.

I continued to stare into the back of Tyrus's head, scowling at him in a mixture of confusion and anger. The seething torment in my eyes could have burned a hole through his skull.

Why wouldn't he look at me?

"What a foolish girl you are. How do you think all this was possible? Tyrus has been invaluable, haven't you, Tyrus?" She stroked his hair with such familiarity it made my stomach lurch.

I tried to hold back the tears as my voice broke. "This isn't real. This can't be real."

"I can see Tyrus feels horrid for betraying you. I know you've been friends a while." *Friends? We're more than friends.*

A door creaked open, and another person entered the room. A tall, olive-skinned man with dark brown, wavy hair tied up in a messy bun; he had deep blue eyes and a trim beard. If I wasn't in the middle of trying not to throw up, gouge my eyes out, and crawl into a hole to die, I might have been able to appreciate just how attractive he was. *Wait a minute. Do I know that face?*

"Is someone going to tend to her wounds? She's been here hours," the stranger asked. If I didn't know any better, he almost seemed concerned. His voice was outlandish, with an inflection that was unlike the Eskium accent. "In my own time, yes. I enjoy watching her writhe around. These Emberwood women really do make me tingle." Briar glanced over at Tyrus, whose back was still turned away. "Why does it bother you so much, Asher?"

"It doesn't. But she may die before you get what you need. You've no idea of the internal damage your recklessness caused. It'd be a great waste," he replied, rolling up the sleeves of his black shirt, revealing thick forearms covered in tattoos I couldn't properly see in the candlelight.

Briar scowled at him; the look she gave him was murderous. "Recklessness, Ash? Watch your tongue."

"Tyrus, tell me what the fuck is going on. Now." I pulled against my restraints, beads of sweat dripping down my face as I fought against the pain, trying to grip onto lucidity. "Why aren't you saying anything, what is wrong with you?"

Briar stroked Tyrus's arm, taunting me with the gesture. "He doesn't want to talk to you."

"I'm not talking to you, bitch," I hissed through gritted teeth.

"He no longer has need of you, now that you're here."

"Liar! I know Tyrus. He would never do something like this. You must have put a spell on him."

Briar threw her head back and howled with laughter for an uncomfortably long time. "You've read too many folktales, girl. I don't dabble in amateur spells. I deal with *real* magick."

"Release me and we'll see how *real* your magick is." I was desperate to get out of these restraints.

"You are feisty, like your mother. I liked her company too, until I got bored of her," she said as she laughed again.

I stiffened. My mother. *Was she here?*

"Where is she?!" I roared, my heart racing with concern for my poor mother, wondering if she was hurt.

"Oh, you know I can't tell you that. Besides, she will never *see* you again, pretty little bird," Briar jeered. "She is pretty, isn't she, Asher?" She gestured towards me.

He didn't respond, standing there with folded arms and a steely expression.

"Tyrus, you spineless fucking shit. TELL ME WHAT IS HAPPENING," I yelled as I felt the heat bubble at my core, like boiling water on the verge of overflowing.

"Your powers won't work here, save your energy," Asher spoke softly, walking over to me and lightly pressing my shoulders down onto the table. His eyes lingered over my body longer than what would be considered polite. Or appropriate. A galvanising scent of sandalwood and spice overwhelmed me.

I frowned at him, brows pinched together in puzzlement, homing in on his vibrant blue and gold eyes.

"What do you bastards want from me? You won't let me fight, you've restrained me, you have taken my mother… Just get on with it and fucking kill me already, you cowards."

"I'm not letting you go to waste. I'm going to take your powers. *Then,* I will kill you."

She was beautiful for a vile bitch. Skin like porcelain, with icy eyes lined with kohl and full ruby lips. Her hair was the blackest of blacks, shiny like the surface of a mirror. How she could have even been a half-sibling was a mystery, her cold yet alluring features the opposite of my rather warm and plump ones.

"You told me you would spare her life. We had an agreement," Tyrus bellowed, speaking for the first time.

"Down, dog." Briar turned her eyes towards him, and with a languid glance, she brought him down and pinned him to the floor via his knees. "You betrayed your best friend. Your *lover.* All for the promise of your sister's revival. You signed the Emberwood girl's life away the moment you made that deal with me, boy."

"You said you just wanted her powers – you didn't say you were going to kill her!" Tyrus screeched as he crawled to Briar's feet and tried to reach for her.

“Silence!” Briar barked in response, shoving Tyrus off her ankle.

He clawed at his throat as the air was ripped from his lungs.

She continued, not bothered by him, “One more word from you and next time I will not let go.”

Looking away, she released her hold of him. Tyrus clambered on the ground, gasping for breath.

“You did all of this for… for WHAT?” I yelled in disbelief. “How could you do this to me?” My voice was not my own, full of pain and loathing. My heart began to crack, splintering into jagged fragments. If this was betrayal, it felt like dying.

Briar approached my side, twirling her fingers as air and smoke whipped around her fist. I looked up at her in sheer terror as I felt an intense burning sensation radiating from my chest, stinging between my breasts. Flickers of flame danced in the air, corkscrewing until they reached Briar’s knuckles, seeping into her skin. She breathed deeply and grinned, euphoric in the knowledge that her plan was working.

The room began to spin. I wanted to vomit from the pain, the dizziness.

She was absorbing my fire.

I don’t know how much time had passed since I arrived, but I struggled to remain conscious. Briar had tried and failed to take more of my power as I fought against her, using every ounce of my strength to hold her back. I had never encountered such power; despite everything, I would not give up that easily.

"That's enough for today." Asher put a firm hand over Briar's, breaking the siphon.

Her face contorted with incredulity. She turned toward him, her tone oozing with malice as she said, "Do not ever interrupt me again, Asher. Need I remind you that *you* serve me, not the other way around."

An uncomfortably long silence followed as they stared at one another, each one too defiant to stand down.

Briar hissed through clenched teeth, expelling a frustrated growl. "Fine! Put her in her cell." She rushed out of the room, her long black hair billowing behind her.

I sighed in relief, but I wasn't naïve enough to think that my suffering was over. I closed my eyes for a moment, but warm hands startled me, making me jolt upwards as much as the restraints would allow.

"Woah, now. Easy… Easy." It was Asher; he was gently untying the buckles at my wrists and ankles, cautious of the sore flesh there. He winced, as if he shared my discomfort.

"I'm not a fucking horse," I sneered at him and his patronising tone as I tried and failed to haul myself up. My forearms shook with the strain; my upper body strength had become non-existent.

He smiled softly, then scooped me up into his arms. I let out a yelp as my feet left the ground.

"What the Hell do you think you're doing?" I asked demandingly, thumping his chest weakly with my fist.

"I'm attempting to carry you to your cell."

"Put me down, I can walk."

"You're not a horse and I'm not a punching bag. Stop it, or next time I'll throw you over my shoulder," he said, mouth set in a firm line. I would have liked to see him try and manhandle me; the arrogant bastard didn't know what he was getting himself into.

Asher carried me down a short corridor before stopping outside a heavy wooden door with a hatch for a window. He nudged it with his hip, causing it to fling open and whack the wall. The clunky sound of his boots on the stone floor echoed as we entered, emphasising the emptiness of the space.

The room was dark, with only a simple bed with a small table to the left of it, and a chamber pot in the corner opposite of the bed. A tiny white candle sat in a brass dish on the table, the orange light flickering gently as he set me on my feet.

"Cosy," I mumbled sarcastically as I walked over to the bed, immediately missing my plush quilt and fluffy pillows from home. *Home.* A deep ache settled in my chest at the thought, and I scrunched my eyes to stop tears from escaping. *Would I ever make it out of this?*

"Listen, princess, you're lucky you even have a bed." Asher's voice cut through my daze, drawing my attention back to his unearthly presence.

"Lucky? You call this," I gestured around me, "lucky?"

"If you behave, I'll bring you some more blankets. Deal?" he said, readjusting his shirt which had ridden up slightly, revealing just a whisper of olive skin.

"Fuck off, you insufferable prick." I glowered at him, wishing I could smack the stupid smile off his face.

"Good night to you too. Sleep well, princess." He gave me one last sickening grin and left, closing the door behind him with a loud clunk.

I shuffled over to the door and tried the handle, letting out a frustrated groan when it wouldn't budge –

of course, it was locked, but I felt obligated to check. I made my way back over to the bed, my legs dragging from the exertion of the day as if they were waterlogged. Perching on the end of the bed, I hissed, wincing as the hard frame dug into the backs of my legs.

Studying my palms, I grimaced at the dried dirt and blood from the battle with the monster – and the lack of power. I tried to summon my fire, but it did not appear. It only sizzled beneath the surface, as if it was pressing up against an invisible wall.

Scanning all four corners of the room, I wondered if any wards had been planted or if they had used a different form of spellwork. I wanted to check every inch of the room for signs of weakness, for gaps in any magick, but my body and mind were exhausted. I vowed to rest for a few hours, then I'd investigate further.

Laying back on the bed, I pulled the thin blanket over me and allowed the darkness to swallow me, making me drift off into a fevered sleep.

A gentle tap on my back roused me.

"Sit up. Drink." The voice was unusual and velvety like melted chocolate.

I turned around, then gripped the cup with two shaking hands, my fingers overlapping the stranger's. For a moment, I could have sworn I felt a pulse of electricity jump from their skin to mine.

"What in the gods is this?" I asked, wincing at the bitter concoction, which tasted like a mixture of grass and strong alcohol.

"To help ease the pain," said the deep voice again.

It took me a few moments for my vision to adjust fully in the darkness and realise who the owner of the voice was. *Asher.* I pushed myself backwards on the bed, my back flush against the wall, letting out a strained groan as a stabbing pain across my ribs overpowered me.

"Are you here to poison me?" I asked, spitting onto the floor and wiping my mouth with the back of my hand, hoping to discard any remnant of the drink he gave me.

"Why would I bother poisoning you? You're knocking on death's door already," he replied, lips curved into a grin.

"Then why are you trying to help me?" I glanced between him and the cup in his hand.

"I'm trying to ensure you stay alive so Briar can finish what is necessary."

He motioned for me to take another sip, but I refused to move.

"*Then* you will kill me. How noble."

"I won't be the one to kill you." Asher glared at me, his face stern. "Now let me see your side."

"Piss off," I said, folding my arms across my chest. The motion sent a sharp pain to my ribs. I tried to hide the wince that attempted to creep on my face.

"Phoebe. Do as I say."

It felt strange to hear him say my name; the command in his tone made me want to comply.

What was wrong with me?

I flinched as I pulled up my mud-stained blouse, doing my best to avoid touching the angry swell of flesh just below my left breast.

"The quicker you heal and regain your strength, the sooner this will be over," Asher spoke softly as his eyes roamed the subtle freckles that peppered the porcelain skin, starting beneath my breast and all the way down to the soft creases at my hip. He cleared his throat with a short and sharp cough, then lightly trailed his right palm over me, barely making contact. His throat bobbed as a strange expression of concern and intrigue consumed his face.

"I thought you were supposed to be helping, not ogling me." I scowled at him, disgusted by his obvious leering.

His eyes widened in surprise as if he didn't realise that he was paying far too much attention to my body.

"Your ribs are broken. I'll fetch one of the healers," Asher announced, getting up from where he was crouched beside the bed. Gods, he was tall.

"No, thank you. I think I'd rather die here. I'm not giving any of you dickheads what you want." I attempted to shift down the bed, but the flare of pain overwhelmed me with nausea, stopping me in my tracks.

"Language, lady."

I shot a murderous look his way. "I'm no lady." Gods, how I wished I could wipe that stupid grin off his face, but then his gaze seared into mine, and it was like time stood still—those eyes. Deep blue and gold, like sunlight on a stream.

"If you don't let someone tend to you, you are going to die in agony," Asher replied, folding his arms in protest.

"I'm dead anyway. What difference does it make?"

"Lover boy may be able to convince her to spare you. But you need to be a damn sight healthier than you are now if you are to survive the siphoning."

"He is not my *lover boy*. Not anymore. I don't know who *that man* is." My stomach dropped as I thought of Tyrus and his betrayal. *Did I even know him at all?*

"Maybe not. I *do* find it interesting that a lover would do what he's done to you. But he took his sweet time betraying you, maybe he did *actually* fall for you." He let out a low, breathy laugh; the sound sent a shiver down my spine.

"I'm so glad this is amusing for you. Just leave," I said with a sigh as I tried to get comfortable on the small and scratchy cot.

"If you won't allow one of my healers to tend to you, then I'll have to do it myself."

If Asher wasn't one of my captors, I might have allowed myself to blush at the devilish look he gave me.

"I will not let you touch me."

"I wouldn't be so sure," he raised an eyebrow. "Stop being stubborn and let me try to help you."

"The only way you could help me is if you and your band of thugs dropped dead right now."

Asher paused as I considered my options. The pain was excruciating, and I had no idea how long the siphoning would take. How long it would be until I was killed off like my father.

"Fine… But get on with it," I said, scooching to the edge of the bed, wincing as the movement jolted my ribs.

"Impeccable manners, Miss Emberwood."

I rolled my eyes at him. *How is it possible for someone to be* this *much of a pain in the arse?*

"I'll be right back," he announced, leaving the room.

His sudden absence made me feel peculiar, leaving me with a sensation akin to an itch I couldn't scratch.

Asher returned about fifteen minutes later, his arms filled with various vials and ointments, some cloth, and a pestle and mortar.

"Have my people been captured too?" My voice was shaky, and quiet; I was terrified of the answer. *What would happen to them now that I am gone?*

"The way through has been blocked by The Black Cloth. They cannot pass," he replied, walking over to a side table.

"No one was injured?" I asked, sounding hopeful for the information he would give me.

"Not that I know of."

At least they had not been hurt trying to save me.

I watched him as he sorted through the vials – a variety of small glass bottles filled with a mixture of substances I couldn't identify.

"Why do you even work for Briar anyway? You obviously have a tiny speck of humanity in that black heart of yours."

"Black heart? How macabre," he said with a smirk as he uncorked a small glass vial, emptying seaweed green powder and what I thought was salt into the mortar, along with something that looked like olive oil. He started to grind the ingredients into a paste; his jaw flexed each time he twisted the pestle.

"My parents were killed in the witch trials, along with Briar's mother. They were all murdered at the command of your grandfather." He looked into my eyes intensely, and I sent a panicked look his way, concerned about the substance he was about to put on me, along with a pang of guilt at his reference to my grandfather. *How did he feel knowing who I was related to?*

I had no love for my grandfather; had I known him, I'm sure I would have hated him too. I shouldn't suffer persecution because of his wrongdoings.

"This should help with the swelling," he halted, gesturing towards the paste he had just made. I reluctantly gave a nod to continue.

Asher dabbed the mixture lightly along my ribs, his hands surprisingly gentle, making it impossible not to notice how warm he was, almost unbearably so. The heat from his fingertips provided a comfort I didn't know I needed, relaxing my body and distracting me so much I hadn't realised he had continued his story.

"I grew up with Briar in an orphanage; we became more like siblings. But the pain she suffered at losing her mother the way she did and being abandoned by her father, *your* father, festered into something much more than just feeling unwanted. Unloved."

"You think her killing my father was justified because she felt unloved? She tortured him. Mutilated his body." I was stupefied by what he had suggested. *Oh, you grew up without a father? Guess that makes it okay to cut people up and murder them!*

"I didn't say it was justified. I'm trying to help you see how she has become the way she is." Asher seemed slightly frustrated with me, letting out an exasperated sigh.

"How can you live with yourself knowing what she does to people? Knowing that you're playing a part in all of it?"

"I had, *have*, no one else, nowhere to go. When I was a kid, I discovered I had powers like my parents. But I couldn't control them. She helped me."

"Being alone is better than being a monster."

"You've been privileged enough to have never needed to choose between the two." he said, holding my gaze with an intensity that made me squirm. His words cut through me like a hot knife through butter – he was right. I had never known what it was like to struggle, to have felt unloved or unwanted.

I shifted on the bed, curious about the exotic man in front of me. Like a brother to Briar, and complicit in all her wrongdoings, but beneath all the complexities, there was something about him. Something very vulnerable. Relatable.

"So, what power do you possess?" I queried, attempting to change the subject.

"It's derived from air magick. *Shadows, specifically.*"

I shivered. "Oh, brilliant."

Asher laughed. "What?" he asked, his lips curving upwards.

"Shadows? What the Hell can you do with shadows?"

"Would you prefer it if I could summon unicorns and gooseberries?"

Raising my brows at him, I scoffed. "Well, obviously."

"Shadow magick is not *all* ghouls and frights. I manipulate the darkness, commune with the dead, help lost spirits travel across the nether realm to Summerland. Those that cannot or will not transition, well, I summon them for… darker delights."

"What in the gods…" My eyes widened in surprise. I had heard about the kinds of horrors the air coven inflicted on the north from my mother and father, but I had no idea they were capable of magick *that* dark.

My mind drifted to my father, I had no idea if he was at peace or not.

“Could you speak to my fa-?”

“Don’t ask me that,” he interrupted.

“Why?”

“I do not talk to anyone about their dead relatives’ movements beyond the veil, regardless of how pretty the requester is.”

Heat flushed my cheeks. *He thinks I’m pretty.*

“Are you really flirting with me even though I’m wounded, mourning my murdered father whilst being held captive by my evil half-sister?”

“Why? Is it working?” he smirked at me–that wicked grin, so sinister yet seductive at the same time.

“It’s weird. And you’re disgusting.” I averted my gaze, dismissing his flirtations. Deep down I knew I could not deny that he was an incredibly handsome man.

“That’s not a no.”

I took a deep breath, pushing down the wave of anger and frustration that threatened to spill over.

“I know you from somewhere,” I announced abruptly, focusing on each part of his face. From those enchanting eyes to the nose piercing, down to the dark and wiry hairs of his beard that framed a strong and masculine jaw. *That nose ring…*

“What makes you think that?” His mouth curved into that disarming smile again.

“Don’t play games with me, arsehole.”

“That foul mouth. Hard to believe you’ve been living like a princess in a castle.”

“I’m not a princess! And you know nothing about me.” His assumption of my character was starting to piss me off.

“Hold still whilst I wrap your ribs.”

I looked down at where he had reached out. His skin was a dark tan colour and prominent veins threaded from his hands and up his forearms, which were covered in swirls of ink. Peering up at him, I said with as much conviction as I could muster, "You've touched me enough today, thank you."

His eyes trailed my body from head to toe, burning an invisible path on my skin.

He tipped my chin with the most delicate touch of his forefinger, angling my face making it near impossible to look away. "Trust me, if you ever truly let me touch you, you will beg me to never stop."

My jaw dropped in shock at the audacity of his words. *Did he* want *to touch me? Hell, did I want* him *to? Snap out of it, weirdo.*

"So, on the topic of touching. How is the traitor in the bedroom?"

The personal question startled me, rattling my nerves like metal on metal.

"I refuse to answer that. Especially when *you're* hiding something." *Earlier when I told him I knew him from somewhere, he did not confirm or deny it.*

"That says it all. He doesn't look like he knows his way around a broom closet, let alone a woman." He huffed a breathy laugh.

"Do you usually pester your prisoners like this?"

"No. But none of our prisoners have ever been as enchanting as you."

My stomach tingled with butterflies. *Gods above, this fucking guy.*

"Right, enough flirting with me. Your ribs need to be wrapped and you're going to let me do it."

"Ugh!" I groaned, overcome with annoyance. I *was the one flirting?*

He tilted his head expectantly. “Miss Emberwood.”

“Gods, you’re insufferable. Fine.” I lifted my arms, pulling my blouse upwards ever so slightly. I stifled a gasp as his head hovered close to mine, winding the bandage around my ribcage several times. Each wrap of the cloth caused his hair to sway. *Hell, he smelled good—warm, masculine.*

“I suggest you try to get some sleep. The next few days will be taxing. I’ll try to get some food for you later.”

“What’s on the menu tonight, toad’s head with a side of boiled bat wing?” I couldn’t help the sarcasm in my tone; I was mentally and physically exhausted.

Asher turned sharply in the doorway; his face softened with amusement. “Great Mother. What stories have you heard about The Black Cloth?” The laugh that followed did not match his appearance. It was sweet, melodic. He was deliciously dark, mysterious, *wrong*.

“Oh, sorry for assuming bloodthirsty crones and *shadow witches,* who kidnap and torture people for fun enjoy eating pie and potatoes like *normal* people!”

“Your imagination is wild. Colour me intrigued.” Asher smiled menacingly as he closed the door.

Gods, I’m in trouble. In more ways than one.

CHAPTER TWENTY-THREE

Asher

One day earlier…

Briar had told me that Phoebe Emberwood would make her way to the manor soon, following the kidnap of her mother. I didn't often feel sympathy for those of a higher class such as the Emberwood family, revelling in their wealth whilst the common people starved on the frozen streets, but their family wasn't like that from what I had heard and what I had seen at their Yuletide ball. They were generous and humble. Briar had gone too far this time. Even I could admit that.

"What time are you expecting your *wonderful* spy?" I asked, pulling apart supper's leftover bread on the table, dipping it into salted oil. *Damn, this bread was good.*

I was looking forward to seeing that weasel again; I successfully got under his skin the last time I saw him by stealing a dance with his girlfriend. *Ugh, girlfriend.* I also couldn't wait to see his face when I told him I was the one who invaded his mind when he was trying to be intimate with Phoebe. Hearing him tell me to get out of his head was fucking fantastic. In my own defence, I didn't realise I possessed that type of magick until it happened. I had been thinking about the night of the ball – about Phoebe; the way our bodies melded so perfectly together as we danced. She had plagued my thoughts after that encounter; something I couldn't understand had begun to bloom, wreaking havoc on my senses and *black heart.*

"He tells me that she plans to lay siege to us at nightfall tomorrow," Briar guffawed, cutting through my daydream as she sliced the skin off an apple with a tiny blade.

"And you trust him?" I asked, raising my brows in surprise.

"What's not to trust? Everything he's told me so far has been true. Without his information, Rafael would still be lording in that castle of his, acting the hero of Eskium." She poured wine into her glass and offered me the bottle.

Pouring a generous measure into a cup, I answered, "Don't you think it odd that the woman's friend and lover would turn against her? Aren't you concerned that he could betray you?"

"A thief is loyal when his coffers are full."

I sank further into my chair, letting out a sigh in irritation. "You've spoiled him with plenty of gold already. How loyal do you think he'll remain once he finds out you're not true to your word about what you promised him?"

"If he betrays me then I'll take his head. He knows that." She drained her glass, then poured another.

I studied Briar as she sipped, looking for small glimmers of doubt, but she was resolute.

When the weasel arrived, Briar began pacing the floor like a crazed animal. But she wasn't nervous; her body hummed frenetically as if she was… excited.

"Our faithful spy," I taunted him with a smirk, looking at him from the feet up. Ignoring me, he turned his attention to Briar, his gaze lingering on her mouth and lower to the swell of her breasts fighting to escape her corset. The action filled me with annoyance. *What did Phoebe see in this wretch of a man?*

"You're early." Briar's tone was frosty as she addressed him, instantly cooling the desire in his eyes.

"Yes, well. The last leg of the journey was rather rushed, thanks to the cursed beasts in Mossfall Thicket. She is just outside the gates. Her followers are not far behind."

Fools. All of them. Who would have the stones to come up against Briar? Knowing what she did to those who wronged her? This *Phoebe* was either as dumb as a rock or braver than any soldier in Frieya.

Briar made a sound between a cackle and a shriek, setting my teeth on edge.

The three of us hurried over towards the gate, Tyrus a few determined steps ahead. Nightfall had already enveloped the town of Duskbrook in an ebony veil, torches dotting the sconces of buildings like fireflies.

As we caught up with Tyrus, the Emberwood woman tilted her head in confusion.

Briar picked her up with a single look and hurled her into the air before sending her careening back down onto the icy earth. "Welcome to Duskbrook

Manor," she sneered as she grabbed Phoebe by her hair, then pummelled a fist into her face, knocking her out cold.

"Was that really necessary?" asked the weasel, his voice high.

"Oh, you're not going soft on me now are you, Tyrus?" Briar began to walk back towards the manor, and demanded, "Asher, bring her inside."

I rolled my eyes at her and gently lifted Phoebe off the ground and cradled her in my arms. I'm sure I could have just thrown her over my shoulder like a sack of potatoes, but she was injured, and it didn't feel right to be so rough with her. It was hard not to inhale her sweet, floral scent while holding her so close to my chest. She smelled of lavender and vanilla, if I remembered correctly. I took in a deep breath, filling my lungs with the night air instead.

Get a grip.

I had worked alongside Briar for many years. I'd witnessed countless tortures, murders, and maiming. I can't say I had never got my hands dirty, often taking part myself. Sometimes I regretted it. Oftentimes not. I enjoyed scaring bad men shitless, using my shadow weaving to summon all kinds of horrors. But I still felt ill at ease when Briar went after women. They always looked so delicate, so fragile, many having already suffered the rough hands of men.

Most of the brutes I ended had deserved their suffering: rapists, greedy brothel owners, wife beaters. But women like Phoebe? I wasn't sure I could say the same. She hadn't done anything wrong; she was just a victim of circumstance.

After carrying her through the manor entrance, then down the hallway to the siphoning room, I placed her down on a table. I loitered for a few moments, taking a step back and moving forward again, fighting an internal battle with myself about staying or leaving. Noting Briar's bored expression with me, I excused myself from the room, leaving Phoebe in crueller hands.

Hours had passed without a sign of Briar or Tyrus. Making my way to the siphoning room in search of them, I paused outside the door and waited a few seconds before tentatively turning the handle.

As I entered the room, my eyes met Phoebe's. She was attempting to use her powers, struggling fiercely to break free of the restraints. I approached her, attempting to get her to lie back down and was stupefied. I couldn't see her too well when we were outside the manor gates earlier; it was dark, and she was barely visible amongst the mud and muck. The first time I ever laid eyes on her at her family's ball, I knew she was special, but as she lay in front of me under the warm lights of the siphoning chamber – her face fully revealed to me – I couldn't help but stare at her; I was hypnotised.

Her strawberry blonde hair was in a messy braid, falling just below her shoulder. Her skin was so fair I wondered how she could ever tolerate the sunshine; freckles danced across her delicate nose and along the tops of her cheeks, and a faint purple bruise had started to emerge from where Briar had hit her. I frowned as I recalled how much power went into that punch. My eyes wandered to her lips, rosy, full and... I couldn't help but allow my eyes to roam further down past her shoulders to the swell of her breasts. Her shirt was slightly torn, revealing more of her shapely figure.

She was like one of those ancient statues of the goddesses – strong but soft at the same time.

I shook my head. *Stop gawping at her,* I internally chastised myself for being so obvious and for allowing myself to get so distracted. But Great Mother, she was the most beautiful woman I had ever seen. *Fuck.*

CHAPTER TWENTY-FOUR

Phoebe

It must have been days since I last saw another soul other than one of the maids who would drop off a jug of water, stale bread, and a hunk of cheese around midnight each night—leftover scraps, no doubt.

I felt nauseous. From fear. Pain. Hunger. I couldn't remember when I last ate a proper meal; I certainly hadn't been eating as well as I did when Maria was still around. When Eskium Castle was still Eskium Castle.

My side was still sore, but whatever Asher used on me had significantly reduced the pain, and the wrapping of my ribs had clearly helped. I wondered why he hadn't returned as he said he would, but then again, I wouldn't have been surprised if he had left me to rot. I hated to admit it, but I had gotten used to his company, and I found it cathartic – when he wasn't being an arsehole, of course.

Before my mind could wander further, the lock of the door to the room clicked. Asher pushed through the door with a plate full of food. A wave of emotion enveloped me, leaving me with an ache in my chest I didn't understand. *Was I relieved to see him?*

"What took you so long?" My voice was shrill in disbelief. "It's been days!"

"Nice to see you too, little phoenix. Briar has been keeping me busy." His eyes lit up with delight – I could tell he was pleased with himself about the nickname.

"Gods, 'little phoenix'?" I rolled my eyes in disgust, and snapped, "Don't call me that."

"I was called away for a few days and was assured you would be well cared for. Based on the greyness beneath your eyes, I suppose that did not happen. Quite the little grouch when you're hungry, huh?"

"You suppose correctly." I folded my arms, abruptly turning my head away from him. I desperately wanted to refuse whatever delicious smelling food he was holding, but I was so hungry I felt sick. The smell reminded me of…

"I hear this is one of your favourites." Asher interrupted my thoughts and handed me a pewter plate, and my heart sank at the food in front of me: beef wellington, roast potatoes, and green beans. One of Maria's best dishes.

"How the… is this part of Briar's cruel game tormenting me?" *Where* was *Maria? Was she okay?*

"Do you not like it?" A look of genuine disappointment adorned his face.

"This is something Maria, the cook at Eskium Castle, used to make for me. It is one of my favourites."

Asher hesitated, chewing his bottom lip as if he didn't want to speak.

My eyebrows shot up as I tilted my head. "What is it?"

"Well," he paused, scraping his fingers through his hair. "Maria is here. She's alive and well."

The plate wobbled in my hand, my grip suddenly weak.

"What?" My voice trembled, and my stomach lurched. I couldn't believe what he was saying.

"She's staying with us. She will be useful for what comes next."

"I don't understand. She works for you now? What do you mean, 'what comes next'?" My chest felt tight, my breaths shallow; I couldn't process what he was telling me.

"There's more to Maria than you *clearly* know," he said with a frown. "And Briar's plans go beyond just stealing your power."

"Stop being vague and tell me what you mean for the love of the gods." I set the plate down on the side table, not wishing to drop what Maria had cooked for me – *if* she had even cooked it at all.

"You'll find out soon enough. Now eat. Oh, don't forget this. Maria said you'd make use of the whole jug," he replied, handing me a gravy boat on a plate. As I took it from him, I noticed folded parchment beneath the jug. *What was that?*

"I feel like I'm losing my mind. None of this makes sense," I said as my eyes flitted between the paper and Asher.

"I'll tell you more another time. For now, enjoy your meal, and a message from someone you hold dear," he said as he turned to leave.

He hesitated in the doorway, and looked back at me, his features softening as he said, "I will get some fresh clothes for you once you've finished your meal."

"Oh, drop the nice guy act, I'm not buying it." My voice changed from a tremble to a snarl. "Why are you doing this? Tending to my wounds, plying me with food, fetching me clean clothes. And to top it off, a note from gods knows who, just because? I'm a prisoner, Asher. Tell me why you're helping me."

He opened his mouth as if he was going to say something; a look of indecision warred in his eyes like a brewing storm.

"Answer me, you necro fuck!" I screamed at him, throwing the first thing I could put my hands on – a godsdamn moth-eaten pillow. It hit him square in the face and he thundered towards me, stopping just before colliding with me. He was standing so close to me our torsos met. "What did you just say?"

"I said: You necro. FUCK," annunciating the last word ardently; attempting to invade *his* space in retaliation. Well, as much space as I could invade, given his height.

"You really are delightful, aren't you? I should just let you rot in here." His tall frame loomed over me, the compassion waning with every second that passed.

"Oh, there he is. Didn't take much for you to show your true colours, did it?" I said tauntingly with a saccharine smile.

"And it didn't take much for you to behave like the whiny little princess that you are."

We both stood there, chests heaving, ready to unleash words that could wound. I could feel my magick stirring, goading me to attack, despite it being impossible for me to do so.

"Fuck you!" My fists were balled at my sides as I fought the urge to punch him in his stupid face.

"Is that an offer?" His lips pulled into a shit-eating grin, so I shoved him with as much force as I could muster.

"Get out!" I screamed, pushing against his muscled frame. In doing so, I lost my footing, nearly falling to the floor in a clamorous heap.

Asher caught me with one strong hand and lifted me back up, setting me on my feet. His grip on my wrist sent shivers down my spine, and a wave of realisation hit me. *He was the stranger at the masquerade ball.*

"No 'thank you'? I'm offended." He clutched his chest, feigning offence.

I bit the inside of my cheek so hard I could taste copper.

"Eat the damn food. If not for your own sake, do it for Maria. She'll want to know that you've been given a good meal." Asher pointed towards the plate on the side table, then headed towards the door.

Grabbing the plate, I stabbed the fork into the meat and pastry and shoved a chunk into my mouth. "Happy?" My response was muffled thanks to the beef wellington between my teeth. *Gods, it was delicious.*

"I'm positively ecstatic." Asher slammed the door shut and turned the lock with a harsh clunk.

Fucking necro wanker.

Despite wanting to throw the plate of food at the wall, I finished every scrumptious morsel of the meal. For Maria, for me. Not for that bastard.

I took the piece of paper from beneath the gravy boat and unfolded it slowly. I didn't know who I could trust. *What if this was some sick joke?*

But when I looked down at the paper, I recognised the handwriting immediately. It was Maria's.

Dearest Phoebe,

My sweet girl. I am writing to let you know that I am safe and well. Our captors are not treating me poorly, though I'm not sure why. I am doing all I can to ensure you're at least fed properly, but I am so worried about you, Phoebe. I hate knowing that they are hurting you.

I still don't know why they're doing this to us.

I am trying to find out where your mother is and if she is okay.

Stay strong, sweet girl.

I love you.

P.S. This Asher fellow seems to be the only decent person here. I think you can trust him.

M

The sound of the door unlocking startled me, robbing me of the time I needed to process Maria's letter. I quickly wiped the tears from my eyes and stuffed the note beneath my blanket.

The door flung open, the metal handle clanging against the wall of the room. Two men entered. They were dressed in black robes; their hoods obscured their features.

"Told you she was a pretty little thing," sneered one, rubbing his hands together.

"Let me go first." The paunchy man sidled over to me, grabbing me off the bed before I had time to react. He gripped me by the arms, his pudgy fingers digging into my skin so roughly, I winced.

He pushed me against the cold wall and pressed his gut against me, making me recoil from the dull ache at my side. The feel of his bloated stomach and the smell of sour liquor on his breath made me heave.

"I'm going to cut you up, little girl," he threatened, trailing the edge of a blade down my bruised cheek and along my jawline, leaving a rivulet of blood in its wake.

"Get your greasy paws off me, you fat fucking bastard!" I yelled, pummelling into his doughy chest with my fists.

"I like it when they fight, don't you?" The one further away said to the fat man. "Makes the maiming much more fun."

Oh gods, no. No. No. No.

He started fiddling with the laces of my breeches, breathing heavily against me. I closed my eyes, praying to the Great Mother for strength.

I continued to pound his chest with my eyes shut tight, my fists ploughing into him with every ounce of energy I had, cursing myself for having focused too much of my attention on honing my elemental craft but never how to fight with blade or fist.

"Move your fat gut off me, you ugly piece of shit!" I slapped his hands and tried to elbow him, aiming for his breastbone. He only laughed in response, pushing harder against me. I started to panic as my chest tightened, my breaths becoming short and sharp as he began to overpower me.

The sound of a wet tear, followed by a thud, cut through the thick air of the cell. I peered over the fat man's shoulder to see that the man farthest away had fallen to the ground, hands grasping at his open neck as blood spurted out of his throat from a deep slash.

"Step away from her. Now," a deep voice boomed.

It was Asher. Fury in human form, blade still in hand, dripping with blood.

"Fuck off, lapdog," the fat man on me sneered, taking his blade away from my neck and pointing it towards Asher.

Within seconds Asher was on him, pummelling his head with the hilt of his dagger.

"We kill people like you. Not employ them." Asher's face was almost unrecognisable, rage consuming his deep blue eyes as he smashed the man's head into the wall. Blood splattered against the stone. "What's the matter? Cat got your tongue?"

The fat man cackled in response, blood trickling out of his nose.

I could barely stand, grabbing the wall behind me to steady my trembling limbs, equal parts terrified and oddly awestruck.

"Asher, stop!" I shrieked, the sound of my voice momentarily interrupting his frenzied attack.

"He cannot get away with this." Asher's face turned thunderous as shadows appeared, entwined between each of his fingers. *Shadows. Sweet gods above.*

Nebulous ribbons swirled around his fingertips and drifted onto the man's face, tugging painfully at the corners of his mouth, prying it wide open.

Then Asher took his blade and shoved it inside.

The man squealed in terror like a wounded pig as his tongue was shorn off with a merciless swipe. The screams that followed made me nauseous as he writhed on the floor. Dark, tarry blood poured from his mouth and down his flabby chest, soaking his tunic.

Asher pinned the fat man's torso with his knee, shoving the man's severed organ down his throat.

Holding his mouth closed with one palm, he watched him twist and turn beneath his weight.

Minutes passed.

The fat man's face turned purple.

Then he was motionless.

I didn't know whether to throw up or jump for joy. I had experienced unrelenting terror because of Briar, but when the fat oaf pressed himself and his blade against me, I was overcome with a sense of fear and dread I had never experienced before.

"Are you hurt? What did he do to you?" Asher asked breathlessly, scanning my face, chest, and arms for signs of injury. He delicately thumbed the red mark on my cheek left behind by the fat man. "Those fucking cunts."

"You… you just butchered two of Briar's men. Why…? Aren't you going to get punished?"

"If Briar deems it necessary, so be it. Savages like them aren't welcome amongst The Black Cloth."

How peculiar that he would find their actions unsavoury yet partake in all of Briar's horrors.

I peered down at the bloated corpse of the fat man, his face mottled, his mouth slack like the maw of a felled beast. The other man's blood continued to seep across the stone floor, filling the room with a coppery stench that turned my stomach.

"I suppose I'm to expect more of these wonderful visits from other brutes like this," I said dejectedly, stepping over the puddles of blood to perch on the end of my bed.

"No one will dare. I'll be keeping a closer eye on you from now on. I'll have someone clean this up as soon as possible," Asher motioned around him, "and here, some fresh clothes." He picked up a small pile of blouses and breeches he had left by the door and handed them to me.

"I do not understand you."

"What?" Asher's brows furrowed.

"No, I mean… You don't belong here. With Briar. You're not like her."

"I wouldn't say that," he replied, gesturing towards the two bloodied bodies – the evidence of his casual brutality.

"You saved me. Thank you. I don't know what would have happened if you..." I got up and placed my hand on his elbow. Asher glanced down at the gentleness of the touch, his lips curving upwards slightly.

He studied me as my eyes met his, leisurely taking in my features, looking at my mouth, then back to my eyes.

There was a flicker of electricity between us, like a static shock, but one that made my heart leap in my chest. There was *something* about him. He was obviously stunning, the most handsome man I had ever seen, in fact. But I couldn't figure it out. He was magnetic, undeniably alluring. *Just like he was that night at the ball.*

"When are you going to admit that you were at my family's Yuletide ball… And confess why you were there?" My voice sliced through the tension.

"I… I'll get someone to clean this up," he stuttered, retreating backwards and out of the door. "And I'll ask the maids to bring you a tub so you can wash."

I stood there surrounded by bloodless bodies and torn flesh and wondered if I would ever discover the truth about this man.

CHAPTER TWENTY-FIVE

Asher

She's a prisoner. Your enemy. You should want her dead. Her grandfather murdered your parents.

"Get your shit together," I said out loud, looking at myself in the mirror as I splashed my face with cold water, willing the thoughts of her lips out of my mind. How utterly ridiculous of me to behave this way, feeling so protective of her that I murdered two of our men in an instant. I didn't even know the damn woman, she was annoying as Hell, and regardless, she'd be dead in a few weeks.

Sighing as I left my room, I headed down the hall to find a few people to assist with clearing out the cell.

"You three. Come with me." I motioned for the men to follow, and they scurried towards me.

"Clear out the bodies and tidy up the mess. You are not to go near this woman. Understand? If you touch one hair on her head, you will suffer an even worse fate than those two bastards," I threatened, pointing towards the corpses. I turned my attention to Phoebe, who seemed to be in shock, her fair skin much paler than usual and her lips an off-white colour. The bloodied line on her cheek made me clench my jaw. *Gods, Asher. She is no one to you.*

I hurried down the stairs to the maids' quarters and was met with a flurry of gasps.

"You shouldn't be down here, sir," muttered one of them coyly.

Briar had hired young women to wait on us hand and foot, and I fucking detested it. She wanted to make a point, that she was powerful and had status – two of the many things denied to her growing up. But it made me uncomfortable. I didn't see myself as better than anyone else. Nor did I like the idea that these women were cooped up on the lower level of the manor like rats on a ship. But I needed their help.

"I'm sorry to bother you all. I'd like to have a bath prepared for… one of our guests." I asked.

"Apologies. We did not know you had guests, sir." One of them looked panicked, darting over to a clean pile of towels.

"Not exactly a guest... But they require hot water and some soap. A towel too. Would that be possible? I can take a tub up but will need help finding the other things."

"Right away, sir."

"Please. No need to call me sir. My name is Asher."

"Very well… Asher. Which room is your… guest in?"

"The holding… cell next to the siphoning room. Can I take this now?" I pointed to a wooden tub. It was very small, only just about big enough for an adult.

The maids nodded in unison.

"Many thanks," I replied, struggling as I heaved the tub upwards.

I headed upstairs, taking the steps slowly with the weight of the tub. I was slightly stronger than the average man, but it was quite a struggle; the last few steps were hurried as my forearms stung from the strain. I saw two of my men dragging a body each down the corridor; the third one had gathered up bloodied rags. I placed the tub outside the cell and unlocked the door, walking inside without a thought.

"Get out!" Phoebe screamed as she whirled around, covering herself with her hands.

I twirled in the opposite direction so fast I felt dizzy.

"Gods, I'm sorry. I didn't know you'd be… you'd be…"

"Naked?!" she screeched.

"Yes. Naked," I replied sternly, trying to calm myself despite all the blood diverting to another part of my body.

She sighed heavily. "I was trying on some of these clothes to see if they fit, you bloody idiot!"

"Would you like some help? Actually, no, I much prefer you naked." I hoped she could tell from the tone of my voice that I had a grin on my face.

"You are such a pig. Get on with whatever it is you're supposed to be doing, please."

I dragged the tub in, keeping my back to her.

"The maids will be up soon with hot water and towels. Do let me know if you need assistance," I teased, lingering in the doorway.

"Asher. Leave." Her dismissal made it clear she wasn't in the mood for games. *Pity.*

Closing, then locking the door behind me, I rested the back of my head against the door and shut my eyes. That glimpse of her naked body made me lightheaded. It was enough to damn near kill me.

"You've been spending a lot of time with my prisoner, Asher." Briar's tone had an icy edge to it as she tapped her nails on the wooden dining table in front of her. "Killing two of my men in the process. Tsk tsk," she tutted.

"I wouldn't have to if you had control of your wild dogs," I said bluntly as my leg bounced beneath the table. Despite the chill outside, the heat of the room was stifling from the roaring fireplace. I pulled at the collar of my tunic as a bead of sweat ran down my chest.

"Trying to control a sex-starved man is like trying to put a leash on a rabid wolf," Briar paused, studying the annoyed expression on my face, "and hungry wolves get desperate."

I shook my head, levelling her with a stare. "There are brothels for a reason, Briar."

The smile she returned had a malicious curve, and she cocked a brow. "You've grown fond of the pretty little bird, haven't you? Can't say I blame you, she is rather delicious. But I thought you knew better than to play with your food, Ash."

"I'm not fond of her." I swallowed the knot in my throat, anxious about what Briar's observations meant for Phoebe.

"Then why rush to her defence when those two oafs tried to maim her? Now we're down two men with no replacements."

"We annihilate men like this, Briar. That's why."

She let out a menacing laugh. "Oh Ash, I'd say you're more than fond of her. You've never been a very good liar, have you?"

"Fuck off, Briar. Just drop it." I gritted my teeth, turning my attention to the fireplace.

"You can have whatever fun with her you like, shag her until she's spent for all I care, but nothing more. Focus on the task at hand."

"I won't be shagging her."

Her mouth twisted into a smirk. "If you say so." She slowly stood up, pushing the chair out with the backs of her legs. "I want Phoebe up here within the hour, but I'm going to go pay her mother another visit first."

"You've already drained her of everything, what's the point? Just let her go, or kill her, whatever." I said hesitantly, trying not to sound too bothered.

"I have the Emberwood women under one roof. Why would I want to do that? Something about these red-headed women really makes me *wild*."

Rolling my eyes, I sighed loudly. "Except Lady Gabriella does not want your attention."

"Morals too now, Ash? Has *Phoebeee* hypnotised you so fiercely already?" she fluttered her eyelashes mockingly.

"I already told you I don't care about that bitch." The words burned on my tongue.

"Prove it. Bring her to me. Now."

For fuck's sake.

Dread seeped into my bones. I should have kept my mouth shut.

CHAPTER TWENTY-SIX

Phoebe

Within the hour, the room went from the scene of a massacre to something bordering on peaceful. The smell of lemon now filled my cell, a welcoming scent after days of mud and blood. Maids arrived with hot water and fresh towels shortly after Asher had burst into the room. He looked visibly flustered, which caused a surprising thrill to dance in my chest.

Maids came back and forth several times with jugs of hot water, interrupting my daydream abruptly. They left a bar of soap, a sponge, and a towel for me to use, filling me with excitement at the prospect of a warm bath, something I hadn't realised I missed so fiercely.

I slowly peeled the bandage off my ribcage, wincing every now and then as pangs of pain hit me. Dipping myself into the water, I groaned blissfully as the heavenly warmth soaked my skin. The mud, blood, and green salve had to be scrubbed away after days of it being caked on me, so I worked the sponge vigorously, reaching every single inch of my battered body. My ribs still ached, but the discomfort was nothing like it was before Asher used the salve and bandaged me. I wondered if any magick went into that to have expedited the healing process so much. If he had any other powers besides his shadows.

I heard footsteps outside and quickly grabbed the towel to cover myself. There was a knock.

“Are you decent?” Asher’s voice was muffled through the door.

“For fuck’s sake. No, I am not. How many times are you going to try and see me naked today?”

He stayed silent for a few seconds, no doubt contemplating a flirtatious retort.

“It’s time for more siphoning. Do not make me come in there and drag you out.”

“You know it’s not really appealing to leave this bath knowing that,” I shouted through the door as I eased myself out of the tub and huffed out a sigh.

“I’m sure it’s not. But it is what it is.”

“It is what it is,” I whispered to myself sarcastically.

I threw my dirty clothes into the corner of the room and leafed through the pile of fresh clothing that Asher had given me earlier. The options were black, black, or black. *How very Asher.*

I gingerly stepped into some suede breeches and then put my arms through the sleeves of a silky dark blouse, fastening the buttons. It surprised me that the blouse fit, hugging me perfectly in all the right places yet loose enough around the bust for my ample cleavage. There was no denying the quality of the garments; the silk felt like a kiss against my skin.

“Come in,” I called, quickly fastening the laces of the breeches and adjusting the blouse.

Asher looked short of breath as he opened the door and stared at me, pupils blown wide.

"What's the matter with you?" I asked, squinting at him in confusion.

He took his time as his eyes traced me from head to toe, taking in every detail. "Black suits you."

"I bet it does," I said confidently, watching as he smiled at me. But then his face changed, his wolfish grin morphing into an expression void of warmth and mischief. *Was he ashamed?*

He looked down at the ground, barely able to maintain eye contact with me. "I need to take you to her."

"I'm not going anywhere near that psychotic bitch." I retreated, attempting to increase the distance between us.

"Please don't make this harder than it already is, Phoebe," Asher said pleadingly, taking a step towards me.

"You're pathetic!" I shouted, my fear turning into anger. "All this power, yet you're a coward. You follow Briar around like a lost puppy. You're no better than Tyrus."

We each paced in circles, a cat and mouse game, delaying the inevitable.

Asher closed the distance in two long strides and took hold of me.

"Stop fucking around," he snarled.

"Why do you do this? Why do you follow her? You don't need her!" I squirmed under his grip, furious he was manhandling me this way. It reminded me of Tyrus's brutish touch at the Yuletide ball.

"It's time to go."

Then I slapped him.

"That was uncalled for." He said as he rubbed his stinging cheek.

"Do not ever touch me again." I went to slap him a second time when he grabbed me by the wrist.

"Stop. Slapping. Me. Phoebe."

"Let go of me." My jaw was tense, my teeth clenched as I held his gaze.

His eyes returned the intensity as he continued to hold onto me. He stared at my mouth again like he did before, making my heart beat so fast and loud I was sure he could hear it.

Thudthudthud.

Thudthudthud.

Thudthudthud.

My heart was a war drum, my blood ignited.

Being so close to him, I couldn't help but look at the silver piercing on his nose. *Gods, why did he have to have a nose piercing?*

"Stop struggling," he demanded, grabbing both of my wrists this time.

I headbutted him, knocking him backwards. *Great Mother, ouch.* I think I hurt myself more than him.

"Fucking Hell, Phoebe!" his voice was muffled as he clutched his nose. "I didn't deserve that," he said as he wiped away a trickle of scarlet from his nostril.

"What do you deserve then?" I rubbed my forehead, trying to soothe the dull ache.

Before I knew it, Asher's face was in front of mine as he pushed me against the wall, lifting both of my arms above my head. He pinned me by the wrists with his hands and anchored me in place with his hips. I was surprised to feel exhilarated as his touch set me aflame, lighting a fire low in my belly.

"You creep." I twisted under him, trying to escape whilst feigning disgust. *I wish my body would stop betraying me.*

"You want to hate me so badly, don't you?" Asher's eyes seared into mine, branding my bottle green with his blue and gold.

"I do fucking hate you!" I screamed in response, pulling against his vice-like hold of my wrists.

I frantically looked around me; towards the floor, the walls, the ceiling—my prison.

"I'm here because of you," I continued, my voice shaking from the adrenaline coursing through me. He let me go, taking a step back as if I had physically wounded him again. He took a deep breath before pinching the bridge of his nose. *Were my eyes deceiving me or was he holding back tears?*

"Because of who you are." I invaded his space this time, jabbing his chest with my forefinger. "Because of who you associate with." Despite the solid muscle of his chest, he winced.

He looked down at where I had prodded him; his gaze slowly trailed to my face. But he remained silent.

"You think you are blameless because it wasn't you that tore my father apart?" My chest heaved as I gasped for air between my words. I wanted him to feel just an ounce of the pain I felt. "You may not have dealt the killing blow, but you are complicit. Your ignorance has stained your hands with his blood."

"Phoebe –" Asher attempted to take my hand, but I shoved it away.

"No!" I paused, not quite finished with my tirade. "Why save me from those brutes just for you to deliver me to someone even more evil? It doesn't make any fucking sense!"

"Do you know what they would have done if I didn't stop them?!" he roared back.

The tightness in my chest intensified, forcing me to take deep, calming breaths. I didn't want to think about what they intended to do.

"You told me that I was privileged to have never needed to choose between being alone and being a monster. Well guess what? I would rather live a desperately lonely life and die with no one to mourn me than turn into a spineless bastard like you."

He stared at me, speechless; his expression blank.

"Don't I have somewhere to be?" I asked mockingly.

CHAPTER TWENTY-SEVEN

Asher

Phoebe could have stabbed me, and it would have been less painful. I felt the sting of her verbal assault for days afterwards. Gods, that woman knew how to wound with words.

I suppose I couldn't blame her. She had lost everything, and the only thing on her horizon was death.

Me, on the other hand? Death had always been with me; I had never been afraid of it nor too scared to wield it. Over the years. I've tortured many men, pushing them to the brink of suffering. The story is almost always the same; they beg for their god, for mercy, and for a dignified end to peacefully enter Summerland.

But Phoebe, well. She didn't seem afraid of it either. I never saw her praying or begging for mercy. Gods, I didn't think Phoebe even knew how to beg. She was too fucking stubborn.

It was that fighting spirit that had kept me going back to her room, even though I had no need. I didn't have to be her keeper; it could be anyone. And Briar had already noticed the time I've spent with her.

The first siphoning wasn't so difficult to stomach; I had only just *officially* met Phoebe.

The last time, however. Well, that made me feel physically sick. Her cries of agony and her pained expression were unbearable. On more than one occasion, I contemplated interrupting Briar, but I knew she would only punish Phoebe more.

Tyrus burst through the door, bringing me back to the present. His face was flushed from frustration, and he was huffing and puffing like a child with his toys taken away.

"What's the matter?" Briar asked with minimal enthusiasm, barely even looking up to acknowledge him.

"This is just… This is just not how I thought it would go," Tyrus said as he fidgeted in the doorway.

"What did you expect, Tyrus? That I would just willingly ignore the fact that I have a sibling? That she has powers that I can take for myself?"

"You told me that I would get to see my sister again. That you would bring her back."

"All in good time, Tyrus. All in good time," Briar said, reaching for him. "Now stop being such a dramatic fool and come here," she said, patting the seat of the chair next to her seductively. "Let me remind you of one of the reasons you've stayed loyal." Her long, red-painted fingers danced along her cleavage as she moved to sit in Tyrus's lap.

"You cannot be serious," I muttered under my breath as I looked at her, then Tyrus.

"Something you have to say, Asher?" Her head turned sharply towards me as she stroked the back of Tyrus's head.

"You have been bedding him this entire time? Dear gods," I asked, rolling my eyes.

"So what if I have?"

"And *you've* been dipping your wick in Phoebe *and* Briar?" I shifted my focus to Tyrus. "You really are a repugnant little rat." *Gods above, how could a man so insufferable have two women at his beck and call?*

"Who are you and what have you done with Asher? Since when did you give a shit about sexual loyalties?" Briar put her hands through Tyrus's hair, mussing it aggressively.

"This man is a weasel. And you've let him use you."

Tyrus sent a furious glance my way. The one I returned screamed, "just fucking try me."

"Use *me*? Oh darling, I have held all the power. He still follows my every order. Unlike some people around here."

Tyrus cleared his throat and awkwardly held on to Briar's hips as he shifted in his seat. "My sister. I want to see her."

"You will see her soon, I promise," Briar stroked his cheek, "now, shall we retire to my room?"

I didn't know why it bothered me so much, but it did. Knowing Tyrus had been bedding Briar the entire time made the betrayal so much worse. Another deceit. But if I told Phoebe, what difference would it make? The damage had been done.

Whilst Briar and Tyrus were otherwise engaged, I decided to visit Phoebe again.

Except all I ended up doing was standing outside her door, fighting an internal battle about seeing her. Despite how we left things before, I couldn't stay away, and it was driving me fucking mad.

Leaning against the door, I chastised myself for my foolishness. I had never felt this odd sensation before. I had several partners in the past, but they were mostly just lovers. There was rarely worthwhile conversation, let alone companionship, and I certainly never felt a borderline painful urge to be near them.

Pushing myself off the wall with my foot, I began to walk away, convincing myself that I needed to stop going to see her whenever I got the chance.

I halted at the foot of the stairs. *When was I ever responsible?*

Rushing back to her room, I lifted my hand to knock on the door, but hesitated. *She doesn't want to see you.*

But what if she does?

I unlocked the door, slowly opening it to avoid startling her. "Fancy a walk?" I asked as I peered round the door to find her smoothing her palms over the walls.

She jumped back in fright.

"This room *is* warded." I said, "And you will not be able to breach it. So I suggest you save yourself the bother."

She cleared her throat, her cheeks flushing a soft pink. That flustered expression often adorned her face and it always thrilled me.

"A walk? Are you kidding?" She glared at me incredulously as if I were talking in another language.

"Do you want to or not?" I huffed out a sigh. "Briar is busy. I figured you may want to stretch your legs and now is the time to do it."

"Seriously?" Phoebe shot up from the bed, a whisper of a smile appearing on her face.

"Seriously. Now hurry up or my offer expires." I popped my head out the door to check the hallway for signs of movement.

"Okay! Bloody Hell. You've given me about thirty seconds' notice." Phoebe frantically pulled out blouses and breeches from the small pile by her bed, throwing things over her shoulder in a panic.

"Oh, I'm sorry. Would you like to fix your hair and paint your face first? Shall I ask Briar for some rouge?" My lips pulled up in a grin.

Scowling at me, she raised her middle finger with a defiant look that could kill a man. All it did was make my heart race.

"What if she finds out?" She paused; several pieces of clothing pooled at her feet.

"Don't worry about that. She's busy and will be for a while." *I should tell her. No, you shouldn't; it'll upset her. But if you tell her, she might appreciate your honesty. She might also burst into tears then you'll never get to take her for a walk.*

She hurriedly put her boots on, then grabbed her fur-lined cloak off her bed.

"Now. Ground rules. One. Don't fuck about." I pointed my finger at her.

She went to speak, but I raised the same finger to signal I wanted silence.

"Two. If you run, I will chase you. And I will catch you." I couldn't stop myself from smiling at that.

Smirking, she threw her braid over her shoulder as if she was pretending not to be bothered by what I just said.

"And trust me, little phoenix. I like the chase."

This time, she locked eyes with me, looking panicked.

"Three. If anything happens out there, you head straight back to the manor. Understand? You are not to go into those woods." I gave her a stern look – we still had to be careful.

"Why?" she asked, hands on her hips. My eyes drifted to them for a second and I internally scalded myself; I could not afford to be distracted. "Tyrus told us about the beast you encountered in Mossfall Thicket. There are more of them out there and only me who can stop them should they wander into these grounds."

Phoebe opened her mouth to speak but halted as I placed manacles over her wrists.

She peered up at me, giving me that quizzical look that turned my insides to jelly.

"To nullify your power. You think I trust that you won't use your fire, Phoebe?"

"Fine. Now can we actually go for that walk or are you going to just talk forever?"

We hurried down the hallway and out of the main entrance. I peered behind me every few seconds, double checking no one was around or watching.

The cold night air hit us both like a frosty slap, causing us both to gasp.

"Fucking Hell. I forgot how cold it was," I said, teeth chattering. "Are you going to be warm enough?"

"I will be just fine."

Even if she were stark naked, Phoebe would say she's 'just fine' to spite me.

We headed towards the gardens behind the manor. Most of the plants had died or withered under the harsh frost, leaving only skeletal branches in their wake. Trees croaked in the wintry breeze, causing Phoebe to jerk her head every few seconds.

She trudged alongside me, her arms outstretched due to the manacles around her wrists. I contemplated freeing her of them but knew better – she would never do as I asked.

CHAPTER TWENTY-EIGHT

Phoebe

The moon was full, illuminating the manor in an ethereal glow like spilled silver. Howling wind filled the silence with an unnervingly high-pitched whine as it whipped up pockets of snow. *That was just the wind, right?*

I shivered as goosebumps coated my skin, and a cold feeling of dread churned in my stomach, making me feel ill at ease. Peering around the hood of my cloak, I took in the weathered building in front of me. I didn't get a chance to see much of the outside of the manor when I first arrived, having been knocked unconscious by my crazed half-sister. *Ugh. I always wanted a sister. Note to self: be careful what you wish for.*

The manor looked like it could collapse from a gust of wind at any moment, the wooden slats clapping as the breeze filtered through the gaps. There were three stories, the ground and first level were huge, and I couldn't help but wonder how many rooms there were. *How many Black Cloth members were there? Who had powers? Where was Briar's room?* Eyes trailing upwards, I noted the top level of the manor; it was pretty small, probably a quarter of the size of the other floors. An attic, perhaps.

"Come along, we're meant to be walking." Asher said, blowing warm air into his cupped hands.

"You chose a fine opportunity for it. I might bloody freeze to death at this rate." My teeth rattled, making Asher fuss with my cloak.

Asher sighed, sending a cloud into the glacial air. "I thought you said you were warm enough. Must you always be so stubborn?"

"I am used to Wintertime, but this is something else. Why is it always so cold and dark here? Is there ever a sunny reprieve?" I said, fighting the urge to say something dismissive and sarcastic.

Asher's eyes narrowed, his expression hardening. "Legend says that the night of the trials, the gods were so angry they stole the sun away, leaving Duskbrook dressed in a mourning shroud."

"The gods favoured the witches that wronged Eskium?" The moment the statement left my mouth, I suddenly wished I had rephrased the sentence. His mother and father were victims of the trials - whether they were truly guilty or not was beside the point. When he took a few moments to respond, my heart sank ever so slightly. *You forget he knows the same loss. Twofold.*

"Who can truly say whose side the gods are on? They are fickle. And callous," he replied, sadness clouding his features.

At that moment, I was truly sorry to see him look so sorrowful. Despite losing his parents a long time ago – *how old was he, anyway?* – I knew that grief never left those unfortunate enough to know its pain.

It lingered, waiting in the shadows, ready to attack and incapacitate. Sometimes it quiet, filling the mind with endless questions and doubts to counteract the painful silence. Other times, it was a scream so loud it could shred your throat and shatter glass. Our journeys may have been different, but our destination was the same – we were children whose hearts would forever be missing a piece.

"Asher," I said, voice low, "I'm so sorry about what happened to your parents."

He angled his body towards me and placed a palm on my shoulder. "You have nothing to be sorry for."

I gave him a half-smile, unsure whether to say any more. But then I said, "My grandfather was a cunt."

The laugh that escaped him came from his belly, a deep timbre laced with something splendid yet sinful. There was something so magnificent about it that it warmed me and soothed my soul, making me want to wrap my arms around his giant torso and hug him tightly. Too bad I still had the stupid manacles restraining me. *That's right. Blame it on the manacles.*

"This way." Asher gently nudged me in a different direction with the palm of his hand at my lower back, warming me. I thought *I* was naturally warm, but this man was *something* else.

"We're going out the gates?"

"Just a little. There's only so much ground to cover around the manor."

My mind wandered, drifting into an endless flurry of irrational thoughts, suddenly fretful that Asher meant me harm, and this was some sort of twisted game.

"I'm not sure about this," I said nervously, peering down at my inoperable wrists. I'd be able to do little to defend myself.

“Not sure about w–”

Asher jumped in front of me, shielding me from a lumbering beast that had just broken through the clearing. Branches snapped, shedding the threadbare trees of their final remnants of life.

“Stay. Very. Still,” he whispered, still standing in front of me, moving his weight from one foot to the other.

“Asher, what is that?”

He only glared at me over his shoulder and held his finger to his lips, demanding silence.

The sound of heavy footsteps boomed across the snowy floor. An eerie groan followed. We stood like statues, frozen in time, as the creature retreated further down the path away from us.

“Fucking. Hell. That was close.” I whispered to Asher in relief.

But it was short-lived. The moment I stopped speaking, whatever it was careened towards us.

“Phoebe! Run!” Asher roared, gripping my arm and running back towards the manor.

I looked behind me, panic flaring in my gut as the beast gained on us. It was just like one of the abominations from Mossfall Thicket, covered head-to-toe in rotting flesh, with bulbous patches across its body.

As we approached the gate, something crashed into our path, blocking the way.

“Holy shit!” I screamed as Asher pulled me back by my cloak.

“Fuck this.” Asher halted, then swirled his fingers, raising his arms on either side of his body. Serpentine shadows coiled around him in a whirlwind of black.

“Asher, you have to free me!”

"Not gonna happen," he replied, casually sending his power into one of the creatures, making shadows twine around its limbs. It toppled over, groaning as it fell. The stench of rot billowed out of its mouth, making me gag. I watched on in horror as it twitched on the floor, fighting against the gauzy ribbons.

"Come on! I can help you," I said, ducking from a fetid arm as the other beast tried to swipe me. It lurched, losing its footing, so I came down upon its head with my fists, pummelling it as hard as I could. My wrists may have been manacled, but given the right position, I could still do some damage. I averted my gaze for a second, watching the other fallen monster overcome Asher's shadowy restraints.

Before I knew it, I was thrown on my back, staring up at the coal-black sky with the wind knocked out of my lungs. Its maggoty maw opened above me, and globules of putrid saliva dripped onto my face. I squinted my eyes and scrunched my mouth shut, doing everything in my power to avoid ingesting any of its spit. It swiped at me, its talons catching my neck. A stabbing pain burned across the delicate skin. Warmth bloomed where it struck, seeping into the hood of my cloak. *Gods above, don't let me die like this.* I lifted my hands, desperately trying to feel the wound, but they were still bound together. I hovered them above my face and chest instead, hoping to protect my most vulnerable body parts.

"Phoebe, I'm coming!" Asher's voice was strained as if he, too, was fighting against the weight of one of these monstrosities.

"Asher!" I shrieked in response. A faint wisp of smoke flitted over to me, circling my wrists. Suddenly, there was a metallic snap. My manacles fell. I peered down in disbelief as they dropped to my side onto the sludgy ground beneath me.

The surge of fire beneath my skin was instant, the burn intense as my fingertips began to glow an orangey white, like metal in a forge. The promise of fire beneath my skin whispered to me, and I answered in kind, gripping the monster's face with both of my hands, searing its flesh with molten fingers. Screeching in agony, it fell backwards and away from me, swatting at its face. The flames scorched its putrid flesh, burning through it without abandon. Once its skin had melted away, the fire went through to the bone, consuming every inch of skin. Only a skull remained.

Panting heavily, I stumbled to my feet. I desperately pawed at my neck, terrified that I was potentially mortally wounded. I hissed as I felt the slashes, but fortunately, they were only surface wounds, not deep enough to leave any lasting damage.

"Phoebe! A little help –" Asher called out, being pulled along by one foot.

"How the Hell are you getting your arse beaten right now?" I joked, throwing a fireball into the hulking creature that was trying to drag him off into the forest.

"You distracted me with your wailing!" he shouted back, commanding his shadows to loop around the beast's neck. He yanked on the nebulous shadows as if he were holding a rope and brought it down, felling it like a tree.

"I'm going to turn you into ashes, you ugly fucker," I sneered at the vile creature as it tried and failed to kick out its legs, thanks to Asher's shadows keeping it pinned. Then I set it on fire, my palms outstretched, grinning as its skin turned a sickly off-white to coal black.

My eyes trailed to Asher, and I smiled victoriously, but the look he returned was wracked with concern.

"You're wounded." His thumb lightly stroked the corner of my mouth as he surveyed the slashes as if an act of tenderness like that was normal between us. Those gold and blue eyes slowly slid their gaze up to meet mine, and I could have sworn his pupils dilated.

"It's just a scratch," I whispered, my voice hoarse, searching his eyes for answers to so many questions. My hand reached up to my neck, reaching for my pendant out of habit. But I was met with nothing but my bare collarbone and sore flesh.

"What is it?" Asher queried.

"My pendant." I rushed over to the body of the beast that injured me, frantically searching the icy floor around it. My hands scrabbled in the snow – the act hit me like a brick in the face, making me picture the day I scoured snow-covered bodies in search of my mother as my castle burned. I froze, as if I had been entombed in ice.

Asher kneeled beside me and gently stroked my back, bringing me out of my anxiety-ridden stupor. He helped me search through the sooty and blood-soaked ice then pushed the body over, making it slump on its side. Underneath it lay a broken purple crystal, the leather cord attached to it singed.

"I'm sorry, Phoebe." He smoothed my back in soothing circles again as my mind warred with itself, wanting to set everything aflame out of pure rage whilst also needing to crumple into a ball and give up. For the first time, I leaned into his touch, collapsing into him in a clamorous heap. Thick arms wrapped around me, holding me tightly to his firm chest.

Being in his arms provided a balm to my broken soul, chipping away at the walls I built.

I took a deep breath, then finally allowed myself to cry in his presence.

CHAPTER TWENTY-NINE

Phoebe

I was so tired. Tired of fighting to avenge my father, of fighting against Briar's relentless siphoning, of never knowing which day would be my last. Tired of not knowing how I felt about Asher.

The opening of my cell door caused me to jump in fright.

"Phoebe! Are you alright?"

Asher lightly placed his palms on each of my shoulders and I tried my best not to drink in the vision in front of me. His shirt was unbuttoned, revealing dark hair across a firm chest. The sleeves were rolled up, showing off the tattoos down each arm – dark scrolls, like his shadows.

"Say something," he whispered so quietly I could barely hear him.

I patted the bed, inviting him to take a seat. He slowly walked over and sat down next to me; the bed dipped under his weight. The man was gargantuan, well over six feet tall, and all corded muscle.

"Tell me more about your powers." My voice was hoarse, making me sound croaky.

"This is what you want to talk about right now?" he looked surprised as he leaned over to reach the pitcher of water that was on a low table by my bed. "What do you want to know?" he asked, pouring me a glass.

"When did you discover you could do what you… do?" I slowly sipped the water, feeling instant relief as it washed the dryness of my throat.

"At the orphanage. There was this kid who would not leave Briar alone. He'd soak her bedsheets with vinegar or put rocks in her shoes. He spread vicious lies to the other children, saying Briar's mother was a demon who feasted on the blood of innocents."

I frowned. It was difficult to picture Briar at the mercy of someone else's cruelty.

"One day, after I'd been out collecting berries for the cook, I came back to find Briar in tears, drenched from head to toe in a red substance. This kid stood there with a group of others laughing his head off. I snapped. Before I knew it the kid was choking but none of us could see why. It wasn't until he collapsed on the floor that wisps of shadow unfurled from his neck and flew back to me."

My jaw dropped. "Did he live?"

"Yes, but he was never the same again," he paused, scraping his fingers through his hair, "I don't regret doing it. Briar had been endlessly tormented by him. Someone had to put a stop to it."

He stood up and walked towards the door, keeping his back to me.

"You got somewhere to be?"

"No. But I can't bear to look at you for one minute longer." He clenched his fists and I watched in awe as the muscles of his forearms flexed under his skin.

I gasped in reaction to what he said. "What the Hell do you mean?"

"The way you look at me… I can't bear it."

"What?"

"Sometimes you look at me like I'm a monster, like you're repulsed. But often, I notice a glint in your eye – the kind of glint that makes me think you desire me. If I thought for one moment that might be true, I don't know what I'd do." He rushed out of the door, slamming it behind him.

I sprinted after him, swinging the door open again, hoping I could convince him to come back and explain himself. It wasn't until I was standing *outside* of my cell that I realised he had forgotten to lock the door.

Holy. Fuck. I would never get another chance to flee.

Tiptoeing down the hallway, I listened intently to the low rumbling of voices. I didn't know where Asher's room was, but he was nowhere to be seen. I couldn't hear Briar or even Tyrus.

It was risky, but I had to try.

Thinking of my mother still being held captive, I knew I needed to rescue her first, but with no clue where she was being held, it would not be easy.

As I peered around the wall, a Black Cloth guard patrolled the main floor.

Fuck. I retreated, pinning my back against the wall. I needed to find a way to incapacitate him without creating a ruckus or avoid contact altogether and find a way around.

I dipped my body low, skimming the walls with my fingertips. Slowly walking to the end of the hallway, I took one last look behind me as the siphoning room, and my cell, vanished from my periphery. I lightly hopped onto the first step of the staircase, but it let out the faintest of creaks. The guard's head swivelled in my direction. Fortunately, it was dark, and he couldn't quite see me. As the guard began to walk towards the sound, I rummaged through my pockets, hoping to find something worthwhile to create a distraction. Aha! Some rocks. Witches always carried rocks.

I hurled one to the opposite side of the entryway, causing it to rattle as it hit the wooden floor. The guard rushed to the noise, his face bewildered as he tried to fathom where a random stone had come from.

Heart thundering fast, I walked backwards a step, my eyes fixed on the guard. The familiar burn of my magick flickered under my skin; there were no wards nor manacles to prevent me from using my magick. I took a deep breath, readying myself to attack the guard, but I hesitated – I would never escape if I created such a scene.

My bare feet sank into the plush carpet, which was oddly gratifying given I'd become used to a cold, stone floor. I took one last step backwards and was met with a wall.

Except the wall felt… warm? *What?*

I clasped my mouth, attempting to stifle the scream that was trying to escape.

"Miss Emberwood." A deep voice rumbled behind me. Asher. *Thank the gods.*

"Oh my gods! Why are you standing at the top of the staircase like you're haunting the place?" I whispered, flustered by his proximity.

“Oi! What are you doin’ up there?” the Black Cloth guard yelled; his footsteps boomed as he hurtled towards me.

Before I knew it, I was gripped by large hands and pulled into a passionate embrace. The same large hands gripped my waist, holding me closer, deepening the kiss.

“Oh, uh. Sorry, Asher. I didn’t know, uh…”

Asher pulled away from me, his eyes transfixed on my lips, breathing heavily. “I’m having some alone time with Miss Emberwood. You’re dismissed.” Asher held onto the sides of my face as he addressed the guard. I felt boneless in his hands; I was supple clay, and he was the sculptor.

“It’s just that, uh, she shouldn’t be out ‘ere.”

“Must I repeat myself? I’m taking this woman to my quarters. Now go,” Asher ordered, pulling me towards him again.

“Asher –” The guard nervously addressed him.

“Leave us!” Asher yelled vehemently, causing the guard to lose his footing slightly and miss a couple of steps as he descended the staircase.

Asher took hold of my hand in a firm grip and led me down another hallway.

Mahogany side tables and bookshelves laden with all sorts of trinkets lined the sage green walls. Paintings of people adorned every inch, portraits of the young and old. *Were any of them related to Briar?* Each painting was framed with wood and gilded in gold leaf, some starting to warp with age, revealing faint cracks along the corners. They were eerily beautiful, which seemed fitting for the young woman who was now in charge.

We were nearing the end of the hallway when I halted. A large painting consumed the space. It was a woman around my age, or maybe a few years older, like Briar. In fact, she looked just like Briar. Her hair was black as night and her eyes an enchanting icy blue. Her skin was alabaster. I stood there, mouth agape, hypnotised by the radiance of the woman. "Zayla," I whispered, as I read the inscription at the bottom of the painting.

"You're lucky it was me that caught you and not anyone else," Asher interrupted my daze and pulled me away from the portrait of the unnervingly enchanting woman.

"You're just saying that because Briar would kick your arse knowing you left my door unlocked," I whispered back with a hint of aggression.

His grip on my hand became firmer and he pulled me towards his chest.

"Less of that lip, little phoenix." His face was so close our noses nearly touched.

"You were taking advantage of these lips just a moment ago."

I should not have said that.

Asher heaved open a door and nudged me inside, slamming it shut behind him with the heel of his boot.

My chest heaved, a mixture of fear and excitement setting my blood on fire.

"You will stay in here tonight," he barked.

"I absolutely will not," I replied, heading towards the door.

"If I walk you back down there right now, the guard will suspect something. He'll think it a ruse."

"Is it a ruse? Have you not wanted to kiss me since the moment you looked at me?" *What the Hell was I doing?*

"I think you know the answer to that." The intensity in his eyes made my stomach flip. "And I think it's time you stopped pretending you don't want me to kiss you, that you don't want to kiss me too. You'd like to do more than that, wouldn't you?" He walked at me, causing me to retreat and bump into the bed.

My cheeks burned. I opened my mouth, but I had no idea what to say in response. A few painfully long seconds later, I asked, "Where will I sleep?"

Asher pointed to the enormous four-poster bed behind me. The mahogany wood and dark green and gold throws were surprising; I had expected something much more macabre. Next to his bed was a table covered in dusty tomes and papers. I noticed a leather cord necklace with an obsidian stone nestled on top. How apt – dark and protective. Just like him.

"You have got to be joking? I'm not sharing a bed with you." I laughed nervously.

"If you don't get in there willingly, I will throw you in it and tie you down." The full lips that had kissed me moments ago curved into a wicked grin, revealing perfectly straight and white teeth.

"You wouldn't dare," I replied, scowling at him.

"Really, Phoebe? When are you going to learn that there is very little I wouldn't do?"

I fiddled with the hem of my shirt, biting the skin of my lip as I surveyed his room.

"But you should also know by now that I am not going to harm you," he spoke softly, tucking a rogue lock of hair behind my ear.

My panicked eyes darted up to him, afraid of my true feelings. "I really think I should just go back to my cell."

"Do you really want to go back to that cold room and sleep in that sorry excuse for a bed? Just get in and shut up," he gestured towards the bed. "It's big enough for four people." He winked, causing a wave of embarrassment to wash over me.

Ugh. I will not be enquiring more about that statement.

"Fine. But I swear to the gods, if you so much as graze me, I will kick you in the balls then set this damned bed on fire," I stood on tiptoes, pointing at him.

"I love it when you talk dirty."

It took every ounce of my willpower not to smack him. I had never experienced such a strong urge to simultaneously punch and kiss a man at the same time before.

"Make yourself comfortable." He gestured towards the bed again. "And if you so much as summon a wisp of fire, I will know."

Reluctantly, I moved towards the bed, pensively holding the bottom of my shirt, having just realised that's *all* I had on. I pulled back the throws and slid under the covers.

It was nearly impossible not to let out a contented groan as my skin grazed the soft sheets beneath me. *Great Mother.* I had forgotten what it felt like.

Asher stalked to the other side of the bed, watching me intently. Although he kept telling me he wouldn't harm me, the look in his eyes was nothing short of predatory.

"Comfortable?"

"I really want to say no, but yes, it's wonderful." I slid further down the bed, my head nestled into the goose feather pillows, causing my hair to trail behind.

"Good night, Phoebe."

"Good night, Asher."

CHAPTER THIRTY

Phoebe

My eyes strained open, and I peered through them, taking in my unfamiliar surroundings.

A deep mahogany canopy above a four-poster bed. Endless green velvet throws and goose feather pillows.

I went to sit up, but I fell straight back down, forced backwards by a weighty feeling across my midriff.

That weighty feeling was a tanned, toned, and familiar tattooed arm.

Gods above. I'd shared a bed with Asher. And nothing happened? *Nothing happened.*

"Asher," I nudged him, "Asher, wake up."

"Hmm, what?" If fully awake, firing-on-all-cylinders-Asher was sickeningly handsome, then the just-woken-up, ruffled-hair-and-sleepy-eyed-Asher was divine.

"I can't be here. I need to get back."

"Oh, ssh. Don't worry about that. I'll just tell them I was up all night fucking your brains out, no problem."

My jaw dropped. "You will not! Now get up." I shoved him harder.

"Gods, you're not one of those annoying as fuck early birds, are you?"

"No, I'm not. Now, will you do something for me?"

"Phoebe, no need to be coy." He looked at me with a wicked grin, his sleepy face almost distracting me.

"For the love of the gods," I sighed, "I need to see my mother. I need to know she's okay."

"You know I can't do that, Phoebe." His head plopped back on the pillow.

"Please, I can't bear not knowing." I shifted closer to him, causing our legs to graze underneath the quilt. My heart lurched at the feeling of his skin against mine. But I didn't move. And neither did he.

"There is no way you will be able to without alerting Briar. And in doing so, you may put your mother at risk of further harm."

"*Further*, harm?" My eyes widened as I absorbed his words.

"We need to get you back to your cell. Briar will want to siphon you soon." He began to move out of the bed, but I grabbed him by the wrist.

"Asher, answer me. What has happened to my mother?" I pleaded with him, tugging on his arm.

"I don't know for certain," he replied, refusing to look me in the eye.

Clearing my throat, I said, "Then tell me whatever it is you do know."

He paused, looking me in the eye and taking a breath. "Your mother revealed her powers when Briar attacked her at your home. Briar had only heard from Tyrus that you had power, and that your mother had no magick at all."

My heart sank as I let go of him.

"Your mother's power has been depleted, but she's still alive," he said with a hint of optimism in his tone.

I was elated to know my mother was alive, but at what cost?

"What does Briar want with all this power?"

"Fire magick is something she has wanted to possess for as long as I've known her. She convinced herself over the years that if she could master it, or build upon it somehow, she would take Eskium, claim it in her mother's name and memory. Once she learned of your father's whereabouts, and your family's powers, she was like a woman possessed."

I bit the inside of my cheek hard as I recalled the reason why Briar had all this information in the first place. *Fucking* Tyrus.

"My mother has barely used her craft for years, so it is no surprise her power has depleted so soon. But me? How does she know she will be able to take all my power when I can attune with fire and water?"

"She is anything if not persistent."

"Asher!" A heavy knock sounded at the door, startling us.

Speak of the devil, and she shall appear.

CHAPTER THIRTY-ONE

Asher

I was in trouble. Big fucking trouble.

Something had started to change between Phoebe and me. It was like opening a door to a room that had been locked, revealing treasures beyond all imagining.

I had to get away from her, at least for a few days. Clear my head. I already made my excuses to Briar, telling her I would meet up with August to find out more about the witches he had discovered in the west.

I set off early, taking one of the ebony steeds from the stables and a satchel full of food supplies.

Despite needing to distance myself from Phoebe, I still wanted to ensure she would be okay in my absence, so I asked Maria to see to it that she was fed properly and given our strongest tea to help keep any potential infection away from the slash at her neck. Just the thought of her being injured had me clenching my jaw, making my teeth and skull ache. I had also politely requested fresh, hot water from the maids be sent to her room every day, knowing how much she cherished a warm bath.

It would be at least one day's ride to Zhadria in the west, and I planned to stay there for another few days.

Surely that would be enough to get the woman out of my veins?

Who was I fucking kidding?

I arrived at a small village around noon the following day, having rested myself and the horse for a few hours during the journey. It was a humble place, the narrow streets lined with wonky, mismatched three-story houses. A river ran alongside, and boats were moored, empty nets and ropes were strewn across the decking.

Hearing about August's adventures from Briar, I knew he frequented the local pub regularly, so that was my first stop.

The Gullible Guppy.

What a fucking name.

The outside was weathered, the shutters worn and in need of a new lick of paint. The wooden sign hanging above the entrance portrayed a blue fish with a spear through its gut. The sign creaked in the wind, short and sharp metallic whines setting my teeth on edge.

I heaved open the door and was immediately enveloped in the stifling warmth from within, along with the stench of stale beer and peanuts.

The willowy, white-blonde male I sought was not hard to find amongst the short and stocky men with unruly greying beards.

"You should have seen the size of her tits!" he shouted, sloshing the beer in his tankard as the men around him laughed. It didn't surprise me in the slightest to discover him mid-story, discussing a woman. I doubted that he was talking about Briar. “But that didn’t compare to her exquisite cu-”, he stopped, turning around in a whirl of black leathers and wool as he saw me approach.

“Well, if it isn’t my favourite shadow fucker. Asher! My man! How the Hell are you? He slapped me hard on the back. “What brings you here?”

I lurched forward, stabilising myself by bracing my hands on the bar. “August. Always a pleasure.”

“Oi! Bottle of your finest red,” he gestured towards the barkeep, who only grunted something in response, pulling two glasses from beneath the bar. He uncorked the bottle and slid it towards us.

“How is my darling Briar?” August clumsily poured the wine into both glasses, spilling some on the countertop.

“She’s well,” I said with a wince as I sipped. The wine tasted like swill, far too sharp and bitter for my tastes. *Cheap.*

“I received word that she captured that fire bitch from Eskium. I cannot wait to get back to see her for myself. Heard she’s a gorgeous, ginger-haired thing,” he said with a predatory snarl, making me want to punch his teeth into the back of his throat.

Deciding to change the subject rather than smash his head into the bar, I asked, “How are things in Zhadria? You manage to find any witches here?”

“A few. Well, I think so. They seem to have water magick, but they’re nothing special. I doubt Briar will want anything to do with them. They wouldn’t survive the siphoning anyway, they’re way too weak.”

Pushing my glass of wine away, I considered what he said, as images of Phoebe flooded my mind, knowing Briar would have continued to try and take her powers whilst I was gone. I imagined her recoiling in pain, thrashing and kicking with all her might. The sweat on her brow as she fought against Briar, her eyes wild with fear she tried so hard to conceal. None of this felt right. I wasn't sure I even wanted Briar to succeed anymore.

"Where are these water witches?" I asked.

"They work in the brothel down the way," he said, gesturing behind him.

I sighed. It was bad enough that these women had to sell themselves to dirty, drunken old men. Now we'd be luring them into Briar's web of pain.

"Can you take me to them? I want to see what they can do."

"Oh, like that is it? I highly recommend the blonde one," he laughed as he threw back his wine.

Scowling and pursing my lips, I turned to face him and ground out, "Not like that. I want to see their powers."

"You're always so uptight! You could probably do with a good shag! Haven't you had a taste of that cindercunt yet?" he elbowed me, smiling from ear to ear.

I jumped up from the barstool, knocking it back as I squared up to him, pushing my chest against his.

"Watch your fucking mouth," I hissed at him.

"Woah, woah! Calm it, Asher," he replied, retreating a few steps and knocking into one of the men at the bar.

I could feel my shadows clawing at me, desperate to break free and smother him, but I couldn't make myself vulnerable by revealing my power here. Resigned, I began to walk away from him, heading towards the exit.

"I'll take that as a yes then." He laughed, a sickening sound that made me see red. *Or black.*

Lunging for him, I grabbed him by his coat and dragged him across the floor of the pub and out the door. I hurled him to the floor and put all my weight into a punch, hitting him so hard in the face he spat blood out. And two teeth followed.

"What the actual fuck!" he shrieked, teeth coated with red.

"If I hear you speak about her that way again, I will fucking kill you," my chest heaved, my breaths laboured as I loomed above him. "Now do your fucking job and get those water witches."

We sat on an aquamarine velvet sofa in one of the women's rooms in the brothel, away from prying eyes. No one would pay any attention to two men joining two women. It was quite an opulent room, with wooden panelling on the walls and hardwood underfoot, covered by deep navy rugs. Candles were lit around the room, creating pockets of golden light in an otherwise darkly decorated room. In the middle of the space was a large bed layered with azure velvet throws and an assortment of cushions in various sizes and shades of teal. The two women perched on the edge of the bed, sat so close together they looked like they were joined at the hip. They were obviously treated well; the quality of their quarters, along with their attire, seemed to be a testament to that.

But as I looked at the supposed water witches, my heart felt heavy.

"We don't want any trouble. Please," muttered one of them.

"You're a whore *and* you're a witch. No one will miss you if you *do* cause us trouble and we have to … dispatch you," August said, smirking as he dabbed the blood around his mouth with a handkerchief.

I bristled, then took a deep breath. "You're a piece of shit, you know that?" I pointed at him, "if I hadn't already kicked your arse, I would be knocking more of your fucking teeth out right now. Do me a favour and keep your mouth shut from now on." Fury ripped through me like a scorched path.

Turning my body to face both women, I asked, "What are your names?"

The blonde one fiddled with the sleeves of her sky blue dress, nervously looking at her friend and me.

"Margot," she said quietly before nudging her friend to speak up.

"Leila," the other woman whispered. Her hair was dark brown and long, braided at the crown, then down into a long-plaited ponytail that ended at her lower back. She had thick eyelashes that framed hazel eyes, a vibrant gold and green, which matched the dress she was wearing perfectly and complimented her deep brown complexion. I may have found her to be truly beautiful at one time, but it was clear Phoebe had ruined every woman for me for eternity.

"Well, Margot and Leila. Let's see your powers," I asked in as gentle a voice as I could possibly summon.

They looked at each other again, evidently unsure if they could trust me.

I nodded, signalling that it was okay for them to try.

August sighed, dramatically crossing one leg over another on the table in front of him. I glowered at him, pissed off with his impatience.

Margot shuffled forward, hovering a palm over a lit candle. Miniscule droplets formed, like tiny raindrops, dripping onto the candle and snuffing out the flame.

"Good," I said reassuringly.

"Why do you want to see our powers? What are you planning?" Leila asked, glancing between her friend, then me, then August.

"We want to create an army of witches," August lied, "to take Frieya back. Return it to those who deserve it."

Guilt trickled through me as I held back a grimace at the lie. We were sending these women to their painful deaths.

"What if we don't want that?" Margot interjected.

August's mouth curved into a wolfish grin. "You either come with us willingly, or we take you by force."

Both women gasped, and Leila ran over to Margot and clung to her.

"We won't go! You can't make us!" Leila shrieked, backing her and Margot into the corner of the room.

"Just fucking show us! You're wasting our time!" August stomped over to them, his long coat billowing behind him like the sail of a ship. "You're going to show us exactly what you can do. Both of you. Right fucking now." Spittle left his lips as he snarled at them.

What August had failed to notice was the shadowy wisps twining around his ankles, circling his legs. I smiled broadly, amused by his lack of awareness.

"I fucking warned you, August," I said, twirling my fingers as my shadows tipped him upside down and lifted him off the floor.

"Run, go far from here. Do not tell anyone what you saw," I spoke to the two women with urgency as I held August in the air with my shadows. I would not play a part in any more maiming. I would not allow Briar to hurt anyone else.

"You fucking traitorous bastard!" He screeched, thrashing his arms and legs. "You'll pay for this. Briar is going to gut you like a fish, Asher."

I chuckled, mouth curved into a gloating smile as I said, "She can certainly try."

I managed to find another tavern further down the street and booked myself into a room, having knocked August out and tied him to the hitching post outside The Gullible Guppy. He would be out cold for some time, so I figured I'd catch up on some sleep.

As I nestled deeper into the blankets and I began to drift off, my mind was flooded with an image of Phoebe. This time, however, she was curled up on her bed at Duskbrook Manor, her cheeks sodden from tears. A dull ache filled my chest, wishing I could kiss away the hurt. *This is not something I have seen before. This doesn't feel like a dream. This feels like it's happening right at this moment. How can I see this?*

Shaking my head, I tried to empty the vision from my mind, but it didn't budge. Instead, the colours became more vibrant, the sounds of her fitful sleep so clear it was as if I was in the room with her.

Distance is working wonders, Ash.

The last time something like this had happened was when I unintentionally infiltrated Tyrus's mind. But I thought that was because I hated the fucker so much I somehow managed to unlock magick within me I didn't know was there. Maybe it wasn't because of Tyrus or hatred. Maybe it was because of…

"Phoebe?" I whispered as my body hummed with warmth, an odd sensation vibrating along my bones.

Of course, she didn't answer; she wasn't there. Feeling foolish, I turned onto my side and pulled the blanket over me. I took a steadying breath and closed my eyes.

"Asher?"

I shot upright, jumping out of bed. Stupefied by the sound of her voice, I scanned the room, expecting to see her standing there with her trademark frown. Instead, a floral scent swept past, swirling around me in a mist of lavender and vanilla. I could no longer see a vision of Phoebe, but I could *feel* her.

Just as soon as it happened, it was over. She was nowhere – not in the room, my thoughts, my senses. I rubbed the back of my neck pensively, wondering if I had imagined the entire thing.

One thing I knew for certain was that distancing myself from Phoebe didn't work – in fact, it had made it ten times worse.

I needed Phoebe Emberwood like I needed oxygen.

And I was going to save her.

CHAPTER THIRTY-TWO

Lady Gabriella

The ravens arrived, and darkness fell, scratching and clawing at her until all she could see was red. Then black.

The pain was unlike anything she had ever experienced, like being burned and frozen at the same time, a gnawing, crawling sensation underneath her broken skin.

Briar didn't just want her powers – they were simply a bonus. She wanted her to suffer. And make her suffer, she did.

After Gabriella's fire was fully depleted and Briar's taunting had ceased, ravens were released into the cell. Dozens of black wings smothered her, beaks like blades stabbing at her arms and legs.

She had never known ravens to behave this way. She respected the creature and called upon its wisdom in many moments of doubt. To use these birds this way was a disgrace. The gods would be displeased.

But as each day passed, Briar added more. So many they could barely fly in the room, their caws became deafening—a blur of inky black, a storm of ebony feathers.

Gabriella tried to protect her face, but the birds launched themselves at her. Her hands were ripped, rivulets of blood permanently dried onto the delicate skin, pulling it uncomfortably tight. Despite Gabriella's constant screams, Briar never relented. The sound of her sinister laughter echoed in the hall outside, its disturbingly high pitch combined with the flapping of wings—a lullaby of chaos.

She couldn't understand why Briar continued to hurt her when she had surrendered completely within a few days. Gabriella didn't care if she took her power; she knew there was barely anything left, and how much more powerful could she get? Gabriella was ashamed of that; she should have fought harder. Should have searched the depths of her power for something more and used it against her. But what was the point? There was no reason for Briar to release her or stop hurting her – Gabriella was of more use to her here, where she could taunt and maim her, make a mockery of the suffering she had caused.

And not just to Gabriella, but to Rafael. She told her everything. Every single detail about what she did to him. Gabriella begged her to stop; her tears and pleas were infinite as she made her relive the pain her husband went through. How he wailed as his body struggled against her powers.

She wondered where Phoebe was; if she was safe. Or even alive. *Was she going to try and rescue her? Would Gabriella ever be free of this cell?*

Perhaps this was no longer her cell but her tomb.

CHAPTER THIRTY-THREE

Phoebe

I didn't know how much time passed since I was first captured. The only way to discern if it was morning, noon, or night was when meals arrived.

Briar continued to drain my powers every few days, leaving me feeling fragile and exhausted. I'd spend a few hours in the siphoning chamber, then be escorted back to my cell, where I would sleep for hours and hours.

Despite Briar's best efforts, her siphoning was futile—she could only summon minute licks of flame.

Asher had visited me every day up until a few days ago after we ended up sharing a bed. I don't know where he was or if he was okay – he never said goodbye or told me he wouldn't be around. *What if he never comes back?*

The maids refused to answer my questions, just telling me that 'Mr Asher said to ensure you had fresh, warm water for your bath.' I was well fed, too; at least I had a full belly.

I thought I despised Asher with every atom of my being. The way he smirked whenever I rose to his bait. The intense look in his eyes when he surveyed me from head to toe. Every time he called me "little phoenix," I wanted to kick him in the balls. I hated the fact that he clearly wanted me, but I hated myself more for wanting him back. We were drawn to one another like the tide is drawn to the moon: a brutal, inescapable pull. But was I the moon, or was I the tide?

Whenever I asked him to tell me more about his life, he obliged. Some evenings we would spend hours talking about all sorts of wondrous things until the candles in my room were nothing but pools of wax – from the scorpion fights he used to bet on in Troyla, to hunting wild bears in Arleau and diving for treasure in the Avisa Waters, off the coast of Zhadria.

Despite all his wrongdoings, he had lived a rich life. In my twenty-five years of existence, I hadn't even left Eskium Castle, let alone Eskium. I suppose I shouldn't compare my life to that of a murderer who dabbled with the dead…

I never felt as though I was missing out, though. I had a wonderful family, great friends, and living in a castle was a dream. Plus, my powers made every day unpredictable and exciting.

But listening to his stories, despite the setting and circumstances of which they were being told, made me long for adventure. Which was a ridiculous notion considering it was unlikely I'd survive much longer.

In the quiet of my cell, the weight of all that had happened bore down on me like an avalanche. Waves of emotions so intense I felt sick. I missed my family, and I had no idea if my mother was okay. I didn't know if I would see Brielle or Xavien ever again.

Slipping to the cold, stone ground of my cell, I wrapped my arms around my knees, bringing them tightly to my chest. Gods, did I miss hugs. What an odd notion, to crave something as simple as a hug. I sobbed into my sleeves, soaking the fabric until it clung to my skin.

A clunking sound at the door signalled someone trying to enter.

I rose to my feet, panic suddenly invading my thoughts as visions of the two brutes who intended to harm me flooded my mind. I grabbed a knife from the side table, it was a butter knife, but I could still do some damage if I aimed for the eyes.

A shadow loomed in the doorway as golden light filtered in from the hall, causing a long dark shape to stretch across the floor. My heartbeat hammered in my chest, but then *he* appeared.

Asher. He was back. He was back. He was back. And gods had I missed him.

"Good, you're up. Look what I've got." Asher walked into the room, totally unaware of my pathetic battle stance with a blunt knife, wobbly legs, and tear-stained cheeks.

He had a tray of something in his hands.

"They're still warm." He picked something off the plate, then handed it to me—a freshly baked cookie. The sweet scent filled the room with buttery notes, causing my stomach to angrily rumble in response.

"Where the bloody Hell have you been?!" I cried out, furious that he disappeared on me. It was hard to stay angry when I had a delicious chocolate cookie in my hand.

"I'm sorry, I…I just had to get away for a few days. Clear my head."

“Well thanks for telling me,” I said sarcastically as I bit into the cookie, trying not to salivate from the rich, gooey centre. “I’ve been worried sick and bored out of my mind.”

“You’ve been crying,” he said, eyes squinting at the sight of my tears.

“Thank you, Commander Conspicuous.”

“Have another cookie. Cookies solve everything.”

A whisper of a smile passed my lips at the childlike innocence of the gesture. Cookies did solve a lot of problems, but I wasn’t sure if they were good enough for this.

I inhaled deeply, hoping it would stifle the urge to burst into tears. The soft look on his face wasn’t helping.

“I can’t do this anymore, Asher.”

“Do what?” His eyebrows furrowed at my admission.

“Wait around to die.” My voice broke. “Do you have any idea what it feels like? To be robbed of the only thing that gave you power and purpose? To be nothing but a pawn for someone else’s pleasure?”

Asher tipped my chin with his finger and stared into my eyes with such intensity I could almost feel it burn. The gold flecks of his eyes seemed to ignite, and my pulse quickened in response. He rubbed away a single traitorous tear with his thumb.

“I didn’t just come here to give you cookies.”

The corner of my mouth quirked up. *Where was he going with this?*

“I came here to tell you that I will no longer stand by and allow this to continue.” He replied firmly as his thumb gently stroked along my jaw. “I have a plan.”

My eyes widened in surprise. “What? Why? Why are you helping me?”

“Because… Because, Phoebe…” He turned his gaze away from me, his expression was forlorn as if what he was about to say caused him a great deal of pain.

As I went to speak, he put a finger to my lips to silence me.

“You remember when you asked me about your masquerade ball?”

I nodded. “I think it’s pretty obvious that you were there, but sure, entertain me. I promise to act surprised.”

“Well, yes, I *was* at your ball. And it *was* me who danced with you. I did it to get under Tyrus’s skin. I hate that fucker more than you know.”

I peered into his eyes, perpetually entranced by their colour – like sunlight filtering through the depths of the sea.

He continued. “When I saw you, sin wrapped in velvet, I had to speak to you. See you. Had I known how truly, undeniably, frustratingly magnificent you were, I never would have gone. It would have saved me many sleepless nights. Stopped this *black heart* of mine beating faster every time I recalled the scent of the vanilla and lavender of your hair. The freckles across your cheeks.”

I swear I stopped breathing.

“I have not stopped thinking about you since that night. You have driven me closer and closer to madness.”

“Asher – ”

“These eyes, so full of wonder and defiance.” He grinned as he delicately stroked his finger along my temple. “This nose, so delicate and feminine. These lips. Gods, these *lips*. The poets could write about them for millennia and never grow tired of it." He brushed his thumb across my lower lip.

It felt as though my spirit had left my body, and I was floating above, watching it all in slow motion.

He cleared his throat and took a step backwards.

"I will not allow Briar to hurt you anymore. But for now, I must leave you to rest. Give me a day or two. I will be back and I will tell you of my plan."

"Asher." My voice broke again.

He turned on his heel.

I rushed towards him, pushing him towards the closed door with such ferocity his back thudded against the wood, forcing him to let out a groan that did nothing to douse the flame of need within me.

What the fuck was I doing? It was so wrong, yet...

Taking his face in my hands, I pulled his lips towards mine, desperate to have him closer. My lips crashed against his in a desperate display of acceptance – accepting his affection, his mercy, his madness. Accepting *him*.

He kissed me back – far gentler than I expected – his tongue briefly dipping into my mouth to meet mine; he was exploring, teasing. I put my hands through his hair and gripped the back of his head, rejoicing in the surprising softness of his dark waves.

"So you did want to kiss me?" he whispered, trailing kisses along my jaw. "Why are you doing this, Phoebe?"

I pushed away from him. "Oh, gods. I'm sorry, I shouldn't have..."

"Sorry? I asked you why you're doing this. Doesn't mean I didn't want you to."

He pulled me back and held me tightly to his chest as his mouth claimed mine again. Adrenaline rushed through me so quickly I felt lightheaded, consumed by all the conflicting emotions I had experienced from the moment I unknowingly met him. Feeling so wanton in his arms, I couldn't contain the moan that fought to leave my lips.

"Don't do that. I'm barely able to control myself as it is."

"What, this?" I teased, moaning into him again as I pressed my hips more firmly into his. He grabbed me by the waist, his hands making their way up to the middle of my blouse before he paused, "Can I touch you here?" he asked, breathing heavily as he kissed the skin of my neck. I nodded enthusiastically, undoing a few buttons at the top.

Had I truly gone mad? I couldn't believe this was happening. The electricity I felt several times before had magnified to the edge of pain. *What the Hell was going on?*

"Asher, what the fuck?" I yelped. Dark swirls danced along his arms as if his tattoos had become sentient. Ebony curls of smoke and shadow skirted along his wrist and fingers, skimming over where his hand gripped my hip.

"Oh gods," Asher looked down and turned his palm over, "this has never happened before."

"What has never happened before? What is it?"

"My power… I think it's responding to you."

"What the Hell does that mean?"

"I have no fucking idea."

The shadowy tendrils began to pull my blouse open, hovering over my breasts like phantom fingers, awaiting the approval of their master.

"Asher…" I swatted at the transparent ribbons.

"I can't get it to stop!"

I was mesmerised and horrified by his magick, so delicate and sheer it was hard to fathom that anything was even there.

"This is torture." Asher muttered, resuming the kiss as his shadows began the softest of ministrations, exploring tentatively, gliding over me like gossamer.

We were interrupted by the sound of a short and sharp cough.

"Sorry to interrupt. Briar wanted to know where you were. I figured you'd be here. You don't waste any time, do you?"

Tyrus.

He gritted his teeth so hard I could see the muscle of his jawbone ticking.

Asher peeled himself away from me, covering my chest with his broad forearm.

Tyrus snorted. "Oh, I've seen *all* of her already, no need to protect her modesty."

"Shut your treacherous trap," I hissed at him.

"Didn't take long for you to forget me." He stared at me for a few moments before abruptly averting his gaze as if it had become too painful to look at me any longer.

"Because you were barely worth remembering."

Tyrus shoved past Asher as I was buttoning my blouse and grabbed me by the shoulders, pushing me out of my cell and into the hallway. I struggled under his grip, making it difficult for him to keep hold of me, but as soon as we approached the siphoning room door, he shoved me inside.

"Watch it." Asher snarled, pressing his chest against Tyrus's. He was taller by a few good inches.

"Look who I found, trying to woo the prisoner. Again." Tyrus looked smug, grinning from ear to ear.

"Gods, Asher. She's barely been here five minutes and you're pining over her like a lovesick teenager. I knew you were too fond of her. Why can't you just fuck them and leave them?" Briar snickered. "You're too close to her now, you're going to ruin everything."

She nudged him out of the way and motioned for Tyrus to assist. They dragged me to the table, kicking and screaming. Asher tried to block their way, but Briar hurled him to the other end of the room, holding him against the wall; her magick overpowered him, rendering him defenceless.

"Pathetic. You hardly know the girl, yet you would defy me just because you want to bury your cock in her?"

"Put me down. Now," Asher growled as he struggled against her invisible power.

"I'll put you down alright. Permanently, if you're not fucking careful."

"Was any of it real, Tyrus? Any of it?" I screamed as he held me down on the table, and Briar fastened the restraints over my wrists and ankles. He ignored me.

"You fucking used me but made *ME* feel like the one who was doing the using."

"It was *just sex*, Phoebe."

I spat in his face. "How fucking dare you."

He wiped the saliva away with revulsion.

"You betrayed me and my entire family for a false promise from a stranger."

"It's not false. She can help me!"

"You are beyond help, Tyrus." His name tasted like poison on my tongue.

A deep discomfort lodged itself in my chest like a thick splinter as my mind relived every moment, every word. From the first time I saw him, leaning on the bar of The Silver Sparrow, arms folded, one ankle crossed over the other. When he asked me half a dozen times to court him, I finally agreed. He took me to the brook outside the town square and brought a picnic. A godsdamn picnic. Sandwiches, scones, strawberries, and a bottle of mead. It was there that we kissed for the first time, and he was so tender and gentle for a man so determined.

But all of it was a lie. I had been fooled.

That stabbing pain returned as my eyes met his. *How could he do this to me?*

My sadness quickly turned to fury. "I curse the day we met. You will pay for this, if it's the last thing I fucking do." My chest heaved as I fought back the tears. I would not let him see me cry. "I cared for you Tyrus. Why would you betray me like this?"

He grimaced. "Well, you've already moved on. Can't be that upset," he said, glaring at Asher.

I lurched forward, unable to reach him thanks to the restraints.

"You're a dead man walking," I threatened.

He scoffed. "Coming from the one who is restrained by one of the most powerful witches this realm has seen? Empty threats, Phoebe, as per usual. This is one of the reasons I could have never truly fallen for you. You're so blind to what's in front of you. So wrapped up in *Phoebe*, you can't tell that your entire life has been a lie."

His words wounded me, leaving me short of breath. But I swallowed down the hurt.

"Do you think I have survived all I have suffered to be broken by you? You have underestimated me, Tyrus. Not only as a witch, but as a woman."

"Now, now, children. I have work to do." Briar interjected, firmly placing a palm on Tyrus's chest.

"Briar has plans, bigger plans than you could ever imagine," Tyrus added.

I scorned, smiling as I said, "Briar is *nothing* and *no one*, with magick so weak she has to steal it from others far more powerful than she'll ever be."

"I suggest you shut your mouth before I shut it for you," Briar snarled as she grabbed me by the chin yanking my face in her direction.

"Briar, come on. You don't have to do this," Asher bellowed from the other side of the room.

"Oh, forgot you were there. Out with you." With a swish of her head, Asher was thrown through the door. He landed painfully, colliding with the corridor wall.

"Get him out of my sight," she commanded Tyrus as she looked at me with a devious glint in her eyes.

CHAPTER THIRTY-FOUR

Asher

Tyrus made his way over to me, balling up his fists and pummelling into my face three times. I tried to retaliate, but I was severely winded, and my lower back burned with pangs of agony from the blast. "You really are a coward." I winced through the blows.

"Keep talking, necro. I'm nowhere near done with you." Tyrus sent another balled fist into the side of my head, putting all his weight into it.

"You think you can just take whatever you want, whenever you want it?" Tyrus was incandescent with rage as he continued to pummel me. "You think you can take what isn't yours?"

"If you're referring to Phoebe, I've not *taken* anything and as I've told you already, she belongs to no one."

"She was MINE first!" Tyrus hauled me up by the collar of my shirt, kneeing me in the stomach. The cuts and bruises on my face had already started to heal, just one of the perks of my magick. I responded in kind by tackling him, throwing him to the ground in one mighty push. I climbed on top of him and started pounding my fists into his face.

"She's yours? You betrayed her! You were the reason her father was murdered, her mother stolen away, and her home destroyed!"

Tyrus jabbed me in the ribs, gaining an advantage to hurl me onto my back.

"Have you forgotten who you are, necro? You are part of this game. You're just as guilty as I am." Tyrus's hands gripped my throat, the pressure so intense I started to see stars.

"She's blinded by your charms right now. But she'll soon realise you're as much a part of all this as I am."

I extended my arms, palms upwards, hovering them on either side of Tyrus's body. Black mist eddied round my hands, then my forearms, as a deathly whisper echoed through the hallway.

"What the fuck is that?" Tyrus frantically turned around.

"A promise kept," I responded, headbutting him.

Tyrus recoiled as blood pissed from his nose. He opened his eyes to find a shadowy figure standing in front of him, weeping and wailing; its mouth open unnaturally wide.

"Fuck!" Tyrus shrieked so satisfyingly loud I couldn't help but laugh.

"Is that how you normally speak to your sister?" I taunted.

"Celeste…?! Gods, no." Tyrus rose, clambering up the wall to get away.

"You did say you wanted us to bring your sister back." I looked on as the black figure followed him, sinewy arms reaching out and clawing. I got to my feet just as a blood-curdling scream sounded from the siphoning room.

Phoebe.

I dashed to the room, nearly tripping over myself in the process. Phoebe expelled another painful howl, her back arched in agony as Briar violently pulled fire from her, twisting and turning her hands in disjointed movements.

"Briar, stop!" I boomed, sprinting across the room. I ran full pelt into her, tackling her to the ground, breaking the siphon. Phoebe let out a gasp of air.

"You stupid fucking boy!" Briar scratched at my face, her long nails digging into my flesh.

I had begun to summon my dark energy when something shook the manor with a powerful force. Shouting could be heard amongst the thudding against the building.

"They're inside! They're inside!" yelled a voice, followed by the sounds of metal clashing, and glass breaking.

Tumultuous footsteps hammered down the hallway towards the siphoning room. I clambered towards Phoebe, hoping I could shield her from whatever was about to enter.

In the doorway appeared three people: one young messy blonde-haired man, a girl with brown skin and a cherub face, plus an aged gentleman wearing an eclectic variety of velvets and corduroy.

"Get away from her," demanded the old man. The younger two were each armed with an axe and daggers.

I stepped to one side, raising my hands to display I meant no harm.

Briar tried to lift the old man with her cold stare but was met with resistance.

Phoebe. Her face was contorted, eyes transfixed on Briar.

In a matter of seconds, Briar was hurled backwards and pinned to the wall.

"Impossible," she muttered, her face aghast that Phoebe could summon her powers whilst restrained *and* in her siphoning room – a room with wards designed to nullify the powers of everyone else but The Black Cloth. The same room that had prevented Phoebe from using her magick. Until now.

I cautiously approached Phoebe in a bid to untie her, petrified that she was hurt but confused that she could use earth magick. I thought she could only commune with fire and water.

"Not so fast, dark one," yelled the girl.

"I want to help her," I insisted, not taking my eyes off Phoebe.

"Back the fuck away. Now." The blonde lad sidled up to me, axe aimed at my throat, with one arm heavily bandaged. He was brave for someone with such an incapacitating injury.

Phoebe stirred. Her face was soaked with sweat, the usual rosiness of her lips pale.

I exhaled in relief. "Phoebe! Thank the Great Mother."

The three strangers looked at each other quizzically but remained poised to attack.

"Asher. What's going on?" Phoebe whispered, trying to reach me with a strained hand under the buckles.

I studied the three newcomers. "Can I please get her out of these restraints?" I tentatively hovered over Phoebe's wrists and ankles.

The old man nodded, and the posture of the younger pair relaxed, the axe lowered from my throat.

Phoebe pensively rose from the table to try and see who I was talking to, wincing as every inch of her body cried out in pain.

"Oh my gods." Phoebe broke down in tears. "Oh my gods, I can't believe it's you." The young pair threw their arms around her, squeezing her so tightly she yelped. "So good to see you, Xavien and Brielle. And you, Jefferson," Phoebe added, her face a much warmer colour than before. "How is your arm?"

"Never mind that. Where is Tyrus?" Xavien frowned, looking around the room.

"He set all this up. He has been sending information to Briar for gods knows how long. He's the reason she knew where to find my father. How she knows about my powers," Phoebe seethed, her face twisted in anger.

"I don't… I don't understand." Brielle's wary eyes shot to Xavien, then Jefferson. "This can't be true."

"It is, I'm afraid to say," I interjected.

"And who in the name of the gods are you?" Jefferson crossed his arms defensively.

"I'm Asher. Asher Rune."

"Well, Asher Rune. There's a reason you're here. And on the wrong side. Explain yourself."

"I trust him. I don't bloody know why, but he's saved me at least two times already," Phoebe added.

Just as we were all catching our breath, Tyrus stumbled through the doorway.

"Tyrus, what the fuck have you done?" Xavien yelled, striding towards him and bunching his shirt in his fist.

"Fuck off, Xavien!" he snarled.

I lurched towards Tyrus, throwing him backwards with my shadows, Phoebe appeared beside me, a steely expression hardening the soft features of her face. Her eyes were like two amber stones, and flames flickered from her fingertips.

"You piece of shit," she shouted, launching a fireball in Tyrus's direction. He dodged out of the way, running out of the room and down the hallway.

"Stop him," she commanded me.

I lifted my hand causing a wave of black to envelope the hallway, blocking the exit. Tyrus slammed against it, assuming he would simply pass through.

He pressed his back up against the shadowy wall, frantically looking for a way out.

I clicked my fingers, and his spectral sister reappeared. The screams that escaped his lips were intensely gratifying; genuine terror consumed his face. His ghoulish sibling snarled and snapped at him; her putrid breath was stifling, turning the air of the corridor rancid. He whimpered and scrunched his eyes closed.

"Celeste, it's Ty… Please. Please don't hurt me," Tyrus whimpered, keeping his forearms in front of his face.

Phoebe pushed me to one side. "Asher. He's mine."

"Phoebe, don't do this!" Brielle shrieked as she, Xavien, and Jefferson looked on in horror. "You're not a killer."

"I *wasn't* a killer." Phoebe corrected her. Her face was devoid of all warmth; even her freckles seemed faint.

"You don't show me any mercy, but you willingly run into the arms of *him?*" He gestured towards me. "How do you know that he had nothing to do with your father's murder?"

"Phoebe, you have my word that I did not lay a finger on your father." I leaned towards her, attempting to touch her arm.

Phoebe's eyes darted between Tyrus and me, before distancing herself from me with a few short steps.

"I swear to you, I did not harm him," I repeated, the tone of my voice urgent, pleading for her to believe me.

Tyrus smirked, revelling in the seeds of doubt he'd planted in her mind, before saying, "You've barely known him for five minutes! Seems you're no longer a little cocktease."

She ripped her gaze from mine, then lunged for Tyrus, throwing an impressive punch that knocked him back into my shadowy wall with a heavy thud. She gripped him by the throat and muttered some words under her breath.

"Please don't do this!" Tyrus begged.

"Please, what? Don't kill you? Too late for that." Her grip tightened as the flames in her fingertips skirted along the column of his throat.

"Phoebe!" Brielle shrieked, clinging to Xavien. They looked on in horror as the air in the hallway began to turn foul with the smell of charred flesh.

The skin on Tyrus's neck turned black, patches of flesh turned to ashy flakes as she burned him from the inside out. He gargled painfully, blood and smoke seeping from his mouth in red-hot ashen globules like lava seeping over rocks. His eyes rolled into the back of his head, leaving lifeless white globes in their wake. He fell to the floor as his skin continued to flicker and burn.

CHAPTER THIRTY-FIVE

Phoebe

I should have felt physically sick from taking a life with such brutality. Especially a life that I cherished.

But I felt nothing except icy numbness mixed with a gratifying sense of retribution.

“She’s next,” I said in a voice I barely recognised.

“Phoebe, you must stop this.” Jefferson tried to block my way to the room where Briar was still pinned to the wall.

“Get out of my way,” I sneered at him, shoving him to the side causing him to stumble into the wall.

“Phoebe, don't do this. This isn’t you.” Xavien attempted to pull me back from Briar, but I shrugged him off, not fazed by his protests. Gaze still fixed on Briar, I grinned at the way she had been pinned to the wall like a taxidermy moth, I said, “This is exactly who I need to be. I’m going to make you suffer even more than my father did.” I was so incandescent with rage I would have loved to have cut her head off right there and then and be done with it. But something inside of me had already snapped, and I wanted to drag the pain and suffering out for as long as the bitch could endure.

What kind of horrors should I inflict upon her? I wanted to see her writhe in agony, just like she did to my father. And to me. I wanted her to feel like she needed to escape her skin, just to find some relief from the pain. I'd watch with delight as the flesh melted off her.

How could I forget? I had arrived at the manor with the elixir I had bought from Luna's Light.

I glowered at Asher. "Where is the elixir?"

"I don't know what you're talking about," he replied, rubbing the back of his neck.

Clenching my fists, I snarled at him as I screamed, "Liar! Tell me where it is before I add you to this trophy wall."

"Let's go home, Phoebe," Brielle muttered as she attempted to approach me.

"I'm not leaving this place until this monster is dead and my mother is safe. And Maria."

"Phoebe. Please." Asher pleaded with me, his face stricken with turmoil.

"*Please? Please?*" I mocked, "Bring me the fucking elixir, Asher."

"No."

His defiance filled me with burning rage, so hot I thought I would breathe fire and turn the entire manor to ashes around me. I raised my hands on either side of me and moved my fingers in a claw-like motion. I had no idea what I was doing, but I could feel something brewing and bubbling beneath my skin. It wasn't hot like my fire; it was cold and rough and pulsing, like the wind.

The tables began to shake as my power took hold; the candlesticks toppled over, leaving small pools of waxy puddles on the wooden floor.

"I am the daughter of the elements," I said in a voice alien to me – much deeper, darker.

I could feel energy surging through my veins as objects began to move around me. Was this… the earth element again? My power was evolving after weeks and weeks of trauma and pain, and I hadn't even realised it.

"Phoebe, can you hear us?" Xavien's voice was a distant echo. Yes, I could hear him. But I wasn't going to answer, and I certainly was not going to relent.

The room churned and whined as my power grew stronger, shattering the vials that sat on the shelves, sending shards of glass into Briar's pinned body.

She recoiled from the pain as scarlet rivulets trickled down her cheeks and neck. *How was my power working in this room? It was supposed to be warded.*

"It can't be…" Jefferson mumbled, eyes squinting as he looked in the direction of Briar.

I heard a distant howl as a large glass vial flew into the room and into my hands. Bright yellow in colour. *Widow's Kiss.*

My friends looked on in horror as the cork sprung free without a single touch of my fingers.

"I can't wait to watch the flesh dissolve off your cursed bones," I grinned wickedly at Briar, signalling the vial to head towards her.

A few droplets escaped, leaving pools of corrosive liquid on the floor. It bubbled and smoked as it burned through the wooden planks beneath my feet, leaving tiny craters in its wake.

I let the elixir teeter above her head, toying with her like a cat with a mouse.

"You know what this is?" I asked her with a smirk.

"Don't. Don't do this," she pleaded, frantically looking at the others in the room, her eyes filled with sheer terror.

"Don't do what? This?" As I went to lift the elixir, something hit my hand, and I dropped the vial, sending it crashing to the floor.

"Phoebe, no!" Jefferson yelled, looking down at the broken vial as its lethal contents narrowly avoided our legs. It burned through floorboards, filling the room with a noxious smell.

My wicked grin began to wane.

"Why did you do that?! What is the meaning of this?" I threw my weight into him and pinned him against the wall.

"I couldn't let you do it, Phoebe. I… I couldn't."

"Why?!" I growled.

"Because I think that girl is my granddaughter."

CHAPTER THIRTY-SIX

Asher

The woman before me was no longer the Phoebe Emberwood I thought I knew.

I should have been the one to kill Tyrus; she shouldn't have his blood on her hands. Perhaps if I had been the one to take his life, she would have been able to keep her fury under control. I knew how much she wanted Briar to suffer, but the Phoebe I knew wasn't disturbed. She would never seek to gain some sick satisfaction in the prolonged suffering of others.

The Phoebe I knew was kind. Sentimental. Loving. *Stubborn.*

Staring at the woman before me in awe and terror, I could no longer see Phoebe Emberwood. This woman was a wild spirit unleashed, one of fire, rage, and hatred. She was searing pain. Wrath. Resentment.

But she was still my little phoenix.

And I would let her soar.

CHAPTER THIRTY-SEVEN

Phoebe

"She's your *what?*"

The room fell silent. My vision blurred, and my chest tightened as if the walls were closing in on me.

"I didn't know… I didn't know she was alive," Jefferson mumbled, scraping his fingers through his wild hair.

I frowned at him, totally perplexed by his words. "What are you talking about?"

"You know her as Briar. I know – *knew* - her as Inara. The black hair and pale blue eyes, just like… Zayla's."

My eyes lingered on his, noting the striking resemblance. "Jefferson, you're not making any sense."

"Zayla Dreed… She was my daughter. Once she became coven leader, she changed her last name to Ravenquill, relinquishing her connection to her mother and I."

If Jefferson was her father, and he had been married to Maria…

"Dreed..." My mind ticked over, pieces of the puzzle coming together. The mother's family name was the one that was passed down to the next generation, meaning…

"Maria. Maria is…Zayla's mother?"

He nodded solemnly.

The revelation was like a punch to my gut. In fact, a punch would have been less painful.

If mothers passed their power to their daughters, did that mean that Maria used her magick for evil too?

"How could you keep this from us?!" I lunged for him, but Asher grabbed me, pulling me back towards him and holding me to his chest.

"Phoebe. Let him talk," he muttered against my forehead. His touch soothed me, snuffing out the wildfire roaring through my mind and body.

"After Zayla was killed, we joined your father in trying to find Inara. But when we arrived at the orphanage, the building itself was gone, torn down, like it had been consumed by the eye of the storm. There was not a single trace of her left. We thought she had perished in a freak accident."

I stepped out of Asher's hold and paced the floor, pushing down the nausea that was building in my stomach. All this time, my father had *more* than just a good friendship with Jefferson and Maria; he had been their son-in-law.

He continued, "Maria used her air magick for simple domestic tasks, to aid her cooking. She never once used it to harm a soul." Jefferson clasped his hands together. "I promise you. We had no idea that Inara…Briar was even alive, let alone that she was this person. We didn't know she inherited any powers at all. Please. You must believe me."

My knees buckled under me, but Asher held me up with his hands. Somehow, I managed to keep Briar pinned to the wall with an invisible force I didn't seem to have any control over.

She had been silent the entire time, her eyeballs white in surprise.

"Maria and I separated shortly after Zayla… Shortly after Zayla was killed. Maria blamed me for her death. She said I could have stopped it." His gaze slowly turned to Briar, the icy blue of his eyes lined with tears. "We swore to your father we would never tell anyone."

I couldn't believe what I was hearing. *"We fell out of love,"* Maria had told me.

"Another cowardly man. Eskium really is full of useless patriarchs." Briar finally spoke, her voice oozing with disdain.

"Inara. We loved you. I promise you. We loved you so much," Jefferson spoke through pained sobs.

She scoffed in response. "You're right, old man. *Inara* did die. She died the day her mother did. The day her father abandoned her and left her behind. When her grandparents forgot about her. You're not my grandfather. I have no family." She spat the last word out.

For a whisper of a second, I felt genuine sympathy for Briar. She had faced true horror at such a young age, with no family to help her through it. No one other than Asher. But it really didn't matter what she had been through; she murdered my father – that made her unworthy of redemption.

Swallowing the knot in my throat, I turned my attention towards Jefferson. "This is far from over."

His head dropped dejectedly, barely able to speak through tears as he said, "Phoebe, please. Forgive me. Forgive us."

I ignored his pleas, turning to face Asher. "Where is my mother being held?"

"She's in one of the outbuildings, underground."

"Once I find her, I am out of here," I sniped. The amorous exchange between us was fleeting, a moment of weakness. I could never care for him. He was the enemy and always had been.

"Phoebe, please," he begged, trying to take hold of my hand. "There is something happening here. More than we can contemplate." Asher grabbed my arm, drawing me back towards him so close my nose almost met his chin.

"Even if there was a tiny glimmer of that connection before, trust me now when I tell you it is severed. This is insane!" I said as I moved my head away from him, trying hard to keep my voice steady.

Asher gently turned my face with his forefinger and thumb on my chin, forcing me to meet his gaze. "Then let us face insanity together."

I stared up at him for a few moments, breathing deeply as I tried to fight past his charming words. Shoving him away instead, I rejected the sentiment. "Oh, save it. I have no need of this," I said, watching the way his expression changed from hopeful to hurt, "or you. Take me to my mother. Now."

Asher walked out without saying a word and motioned for me to follow. Xavien and Brielle started moving towards me, but I put my hand up to halt them, shaking my head in dismissal – a silent plea to stay put.

I scanned the carnage in the room: members of The Black Cloth were scattered, cornered. Dozens of bodies lay lifeless on the ground. Several others were fleeing.

In the hallway, Ivi and Olivier Blackthorn skewered a man with a garden fork, nailing him to the wall. Arryn Merek had another in a headlock, twisting the hooded figure's head beneath his thick arms. The splintered crunch that followed made my stomach turn; it was so visceral it was almost as if I could feel every one of my own bones break.

Ezra was duelling two men at the same time, delivering flying kicks into their bellies. He lifted some of them into the air, throwing them backwards into the wood-panelled walls. He no longer hid his power, using it to aid him as he fought. I felt a pang of regret. Ezra had concealed his magick for many moons – until he met me.

Suddenly, a black-cloaked figure lunged for me but was blocked by Asher's huge body, shielding me from a blade. Asher wrapped his hand around the assailant's throat, lifting him in the air as if he were light as a feather, then threw him to the ground and stomped on his head over and over again. His skull squelched under Asher's boot like a rotten pumpkin. Blood-soaked and broken teeth rattled across the floor, along with bone and brain matter. I could not contain my revulsion and violently vomited onto the floor. "Bloody Hell, Asher," I said, wincing as I wiped my mouth with the sleeve of my blouse. He shrugged, unfazed by the gore he created, guiding me outside.

It was pitch-black and eerie, and I swear the same beady yellow eyes stalked the bushes as they did in Mossfall Thicket. Asher gestured towards the wooden door as we approached a stone outbuilding. "She's through there and down the stairs," he said coldly as he sauntered past me. The swift breeze he left in his wake, along with the smell of sandalwood and spice, coated my skin in a layer of goosebumps. I shook my head, trying to clear my senses. It didn't matter what I felt before – it was a mistake and no doubt a result of him showing me an ounce of sympathy and comfort whilst I was held captive.

We headed down the stony underbelly of the outhouse; the walls were lined with torches that forged lively shadows across the brickwork.

"She's in that room." Asher pointed to the last room along the corridor. "Let her through," he ordered the guardsman who was outside the door.

He unlocked it with several metallic clunks, then swung the door open.

There, upon a heap of blankets, lay my mother.

"Mother!" I gasped, running towards her and falling to my knees.

"Ph…Phoebe?" She reached out and grabbed my arms.

It was only then that I noticed.

Her eyes were grey, no hazel colour. Her face was scratched with dozens of cuts.

"Mother. Your eyes! What happened?" I couldn't hold back the tears as I gripped her cheek.

"She has taken all my power, Phoebe. And with it, my sight." She traced the lines of my jaw with her fingertips, then moved her fingers delicately across my nose and then my eyelids.

"My beautiful girl. Are you okay?" she whimpered, clutching my arms.

I embraced her tightly, sobbing heavily as I stroked her matted hair.

Clearing the tears from my face and steeling my resolve, I spoke with confidence, "We're getting you out of here. Now."

"Help me get my mother to safety," I demanded, short of breath from propping her up as we walked from the outbuilding.

"Of course luv, she can stay wiv' me at the inn. We'll get goin' immediately." Arryn replied, wiping the blood from his hands on his breeches before scooping my mother up into his arms in one effortless movement. He was a giant brute of a man, 'built like a brick shithouse' as Xavien would say.

"Brielle, Xavien. You must leave. Get out of here, I will catch up with you," I urgently requested.

"We're not leaving you," Brielle shouted, grabbing me by the shoulders.

"I can't see anyone else get hurt. Go!" I shoved her backwards, causing her to tumble against Xavien, who winced as his injured arm was knocked.

I mouthed my apology to him.

"Mother, you must go with Arryn, Brielle, and Xavien. They will protect you." I took her face in my hands and kissed her cheek lightly.

"My darling girl, please, come with us." Her sobs were like a knife to my heart. I desperately wanted to go home – to be with my mother and friends. But the risks were now too high, and I was a danger to them. I needed to get as far away as possible.

"Go now! You must go now!" I yelled, signalling Arryn to leave. "I will meet you back at Eskium." I lied.

My mother tightly held onto my hand until it was no longer possible, her arm outstretched as she desperately tried to grab my fingertips. I had only just gotten her back, and I was already saying goodbye.

Asher followed me as I rushed towards the siphoning room to finish what I had started with Briar, only to find Jefferson with his arm around Maria as they stood in the doorway. For a brief moment, I was taken aback by their closeness.

"Where is she?" I roared as I pushed past them, circling the room.

"Phoebe, please. I can fix her! Just give me a chance." Jefferson pleaded with me, clasping his hands together.

"Where the *fuck* is she, Jefferson?"

"Phoebe, enough blood has been spilled. You must stop." Maria tried to take my hand, but I swiped it away. I was livid with her, torn apart from the lies and the deceit. She was the closest thing I had to a grandmother, and she had kept this from me.

"Do not touch me!" I yelped, my voice breaking as tears began to fall down my cheeks.

But then it hit me. My father was the one to blame. Not Jefferson and Maria. They had kept his secret; they had been loyal to a fault.

"We meant you no harm, Phoebe. You must believe us. Please, we love you."

Maria's pained sobs were the last thing I heard as I was swept up in a turbulent cloud of smoke.

CHAPTER THIRTY-EIGHT

Phoebe

I awoke in surroundings I didn't recognise. My hands and feet were bound to a chair in a room smothered by cobwebs, and I began to panic as memories of being taken from the manor crystallised.

"The manor is in quite a state thanks to you."

A strange voice sounded from the shadows and out walked a tall, willowy man with white-blonde hair and eyes so dark they almost looked entirely black. Beneath his thick, dark cloak, he wore a deep blue leather jerkin and breeches. A glint of silver at his waist caught my eye – a dagger.

"I must admit, I am impressed. But I'm not too happy about what you were trying to do to my beloved Briar. She is very special to me, you know."

"And who the fuck are you?" My voice wobbled.

He jabbed my chest with a dagger, just enough to make it sting but not enough to puncture the skin. I recoiled at the sharp pain as he continued to twist the knife.

"You think what Briar did to you was bad? Oh, you have no clue." His head jerked as he circled me like a bird of prey ready to swoop and kill.

"You guys love to talk, huh?" I let out a long yawn, mocking his self-importance and showmanship.

He raised an eyebrow. "We love to fight and fuck more. Which one would you like to do first?"

"Oh, I'd love to fuck. Not you, though. Not my type," I replied with a saccharine smile.

"Not your type? Let me guess, you prefer them much more dark-haired and tattooed?"

I glared at him, exasperated that I had to deal with yet another sarcastic lunatic.

"He won't come for you, you know," he said tauntingly, circling me like a predator.

"You think I give a shit about Asher?"

"I don't think. I know."

"I don't give a damn about that necro piece of shit," I lied. I didn't know how I felt about that handsome, shadowy man, but I knew I *did* give a damn.

"Oooh! You made me go all goosepimply," he waved his fingers over his forearm.

Sighing, I said, "Just get on with… whatever *this* is before I die from boredom. You're like the male version of Briar. Kind of disturbing when you think about it. What was your name again?"

"August. And trust me, you won't forget me in a hurry. Much like my darling Briar, I like to take my time." He traced the knife along my arm slowly, digging into my elbow. I felt warmth on my skin and looked down to see a bead of blood trickling down my arm.

He continued. "There is so much you don't know about yourself, Phoebe. So much power underneath this delicious body of yours. Do you want me to help you find it?"

Why did this arsehole think I didn't know about my powers? Did he see what I did to that room? "Whatever mind games you're trying to play won't work. I'm well aware of my powers."

Cocking a brow, he said, "Oh, I don't mean your elemental powers."

His eyes lit up as he sliced the skin on my forearm with a swipe of his dagger. "We are going to have so much fun, Phoebe."

Tick tock.
Tick tock.
Tick tock.

A grandfather clock stood in the corner of an otherwise bare room. Cherrywood and copper, worn at the edges and layered with cobwebs, like it had been standing guard for many moons. The ticking was torturous, but the chiming. Gods, the chiming. The brassy sound seemed to reverberate through me, persistent, nauseating vibrations that rattled my bones.

August was right; I thought Briar's attempts were painful; his were excruciating. My arms were covered in cuts, mostly shallow, yet they peppered my pale skin in angry red lines. The burning, stinging sensation never ceased, and my skin felt tighter as the wounds healed. He enjoyed toying with my consciousness, pushing me to the point of no return and then bringing me back again. He made me feel as though he could take me against my will at any moment, his eyes lingering on my chest or a hand placed on my shoulder or thigh for too long.

In brief minutes of clarity, I wondered where everyone was and if my mother and friends made it home safe. 'Home' didn't exist anymore, but it was better than this purgatory.

As time went on, my will to survive grew weaker and weaker. I dreamt of the peace of death. The absence of pain. The end of fear. Before I passed out from the agony or from exhaustion, my final thoughts always drifted to Asher. That pissed me off. *Why, of all the people or things that I could think of, did I think of him?*

It was only then that I realised that it was finally the end for me. I wept and wept until my cheeks burned from the tears and my eyes were sore. My lungs ached as I gasped for air, and my heartbeat galloped as the image of all that I had lost consumed me, leaving me breathless to the point of pain. I was alone. And no one was going to save me.

But I wondered: what if I no longer wanted to be saved? Why aimlessly wander the realm with nothing but shadows and ghosts and whispers? I was a lighthouse with no keeper—a featherless bird with no flock.

"Phoebe?" a spectral voice whispered. I hesitantly turned towards the sound as the room filled with flecks of silvery grey light, followed by the comforting scent of sandalwood and spice.

It couldn't be. I must have been hallucinating. Perhaps I was already dying.

"Can you hear me?" It whispered again. It felt so close, almost as if I could feel breath on my face.

I nodded. Not sure if this conversation was happening in my head or not.

"Good. That's good."

I looked around the room, August was nowhere to be seen, and I was certain no one else was there. *But I was asleep, wasn't I?*

"Keep focusing on my voice. Imagine I'm with you."

"I'm dying, aren't I?" I asked, my eyebrows knitted together, "Is that…you, Asher?"

"Yes, little phoenix, it's me."

"Asher? No, this can't be. This is all in my head. This is all in my head. How? How are you doing this? Fuck, fuck, fuck!"

"Yes, I am in your head, but my voice is real. This is real. I need you to stay focused on my voice, okay? I'm coming to get you."

"What? How? How is this even happening?"

"I can send messages to you. A little something I discovered back when I left you for a few days to go to Zhadria."

"Don't be ridiculous." I couldn't believe it. *Was it even possible?*

"How do you think I'm talking to you now?"

"Because this isn't actually happening, and I've gone fucking crazy!"

"You don't remember when this happened before?" he asked, his voice not quite clear. Like the sound after an echo.

I tried to think about what he meant, not remembering what he was referring to.

"Oh, my darling Phoebe. I'm not far. I can feel it. Can you?"

There was no denying the pull I suddenly felt. But I couldn't wrap my head around what was going on. It was all too bizarre to possibly be real.

"Stay with me, Phoebe. I'm almost there."

My eyes brimmed with tears. *Was this real? Was I really going to escape? Was it Asher?*

The smell of sandalwood and spice overwhelmed me, causing a flurry of goosebumps to glide across my skin.

He was here.

I peered down through half-open eyes, my arms swaying in front of me. The ground was vanishing beneath me, moving so fast that my head began to spin.

"Phoebe, you still with me?" Asher's voice broke through my daze – he was carrying me over his shoulder. "August is not here; we need to leave before he gets back."

"Fine. Please put me down before I vomit all over you."

He slowly placed me on the floor, but I stumbled, my legs giving way after being tied to a chair for gods knew how long. He caught me just before I hit the ground. I felt a rush of relief to be in his arms, comforted by the way he enveloped me into his warmth.

"Will you have the strength to travel?" he asked through ragged breaths.

I nodded. I wasn't sure I could do it, but I had to try.

"Rest now, Phoebe. We will reach sanctuary soon."

"Oh, I don't think you will." August's voice sounded from behind us, his tone dripping with arrogance.

Asher jumped in front of me, shielding me with his massive body. His act of chivalry caused my stomach to tingle with butterflies. *My protector.*

“Know this,” Asher paused before taking another step and invading the other man's space.

“For every mark on her body, you will suffer ten times as much. You will understand true agony. You will beg me for mercy, and I will take great pleasure in denying you of it,” he snarled, clenching his fists at his sides.

August feigned a yawn. “You think I’ve forgotten about that stunt you pulled in Zhadria?”

“I sincerely hope not,” Asher mocked.

“Besides, you can torture me all you want; you will never win. The Black Cloth will hunt her for the rest of her days. You will not be able to protect her forever.” A maniacal laugh escaped his lips as he threw his head back.

Asher snapped. He unleashed his shadows upon August, launching them with a ferocity I hadn’t seen since we encountered those monsters at the manor. Violent ribbons of black smoke coiled tightly around August’s limbs like a serpent, weaving up his body and down his throat.

Wrenching them back, Asher pulled on his power as if it were a rope tethered to August’s insides. The white-haired man clutched his stomach as it churned from the force of the shadows, goggle-eyed as he cried out in agony.

“Asher, just end him. We need to move,” my voice was croaky, acid burning the back of my throat.

Asher faced me, his expression devoid of any warmth. “I want to hear him apologise to you.”

“Don’t be foolish. We don’t have time for this!” I yelled in exasperation.

"Come on, August. Say it. Say you're sorry," Asher sneered.

August's cries were muffled as he clutched his stomach.

"I can't hear you." Asher grabbed his face and pressed his fingers into the hollow of August's cheeks, forcing his head towards me. "August, apologise to Phoebe. Now."

"I'm thworry." August could barely speak the words, thanks to the vice-like grip Asher had on his face.

"Hmm? A little louder." Asher dipped and tilted August's ear towards him.

"Asher, stop it! He can't even talk with you gripping his face like that," I said abruptly, my patience waning; I was worn out and in pain.

"Oh, but August loves to talk, don't you, August? Apologise like you mean it."

August's tongue stuck out awkwardly. "I'm tho thworry."

"That's a bit better. But you know what? I don't think it's enough. Kiss her feet."

"Oh, for fuck's sake, Asher. This is enough. I want to leave." I grabbed Asher by the elbow and attempted to heave him backwards. *This bloody man.*

"Get on the fucking floor and worship her." He shoved August to the ground and held him down with his boot. "Crawl to her."

"Oh my gods, we are not doing this. I mean it, Asher. I'm leaving." I sighed heavily and headed outside, finding a horse that Asher must have taken from the manor.

In a flash, Asher's shadows blocked the space in front of the horse and danced around me. My pulse thrummed against the sudden invasion of my space as the nebulous swirls skirted along my chest – my thoughts immediately drifted to what his shadows tried to do before when we were in my cell.

A dragging sound interrupted my drifting thoughts. August was crawling along the floor on his belly, his legs trailing behind.

"This is one of the worst things you have ever done," I huffed in Asher's direction, folding my arms.

"You remember I choked someone to death with their own tongue, right?" He laughed, that dark, velvety laugh that had no business being so charming.

He did have a point – that was *far* worse.

The sound of August dragging his bloodied carcass across the floor was nowhere near as satisfying as it should have been, and I forced myself to look away as he stared up at me with bloodshot eyes, kissing the tip of my boot.

"Okay, can we go now?" I shifted my weight onto one hip; I was ready to leave and be done with Asher's games.

"Do you feel worshipped, my little phoenix?" Asher raised an eyebrow. His gaze roamed over my body so arduously, it was like he was undressing me with his eyes.

"A broken man whimpering at my feet and staining my boots with his blood is not my idea of worship." I wiped the tops of my boots on the ground underneath, trying to remove the remnants of August's suffering and shame.

"Maybe you'll let me worship you one day," he paused, "but for now, seeking vengeance in your name will have to do."

In an instant, vicious black swirls engulfed August, smothering him in a cloud of dark silver. His mouth opened to speak, but Asher's powers slid over his face, entombing him in a shroud of shadows.

CHAPTER THIRTY-NINE

Phoebe

When I opened my eyes, it was daylight. *Where was I?* I started to panic, throwing a blanket off and hurling myself out of bed. *Blanket? A bed?* A stranger's bed. It wasn't until I saw *him* nestled on a sofa amongst some cushions and throws, that I remembered what had happened. *Whose house was this?*

I went to tiptoe past him when he rose, flinging his legs out and accidentally tripping me up, causing me to fall on top of him.

"Oh gods. Sorry," he said through a husky, just-woken-up voice. His hair was untied and ruffled, the dark brown waves gathered around his neck. He wore only his underclothes.

Great Mother, what a sight to wake up to. I didn't rush to move off him; the warmth of his hair-covered chest was so inviting I could have stayed there. There was just *something* about him that made me feel safe.

"Comfortable?" he teased, placing a hand on my hip. My heart fluttered at his touch, but I swatted those feelings away. I pushed myself off him, tugging the shirt I was wearing down to try and cover the tops of my legs. *His shirt.*

I studied the humble dwelling. "Whose house is this? How did you find me?"

"It's one of our safe houses," he paused, "And I can't really explain how I found you. I could just feel you. I followed that connection until it was almost too powerful to bear. Then I drifted into your mind. Saw where you were and recognised it as one of the many safe houses we own."

I looked at him bewildered, unable to process the information. "Drifted into my mi…?"

"We cannot stay long. Let us eat, wash, then be on our way," he announced as he stood up.

His body was lean, his toned chest layered with coarse dark hair, a faint line of which peppered over the muscles of his stomach, down towards his belly button… And further again. I could not dull the delight in my eyes as I drank in the olive-skinned perfection of his body, my skin so fair compared to his. Visions of the two of us entwined filled my mind, a tangling of golden muscle with snow-white tender flesh.

"So… Hungry?" His voice penetrated the thick silence – and my wandering thoughts. I squeezed my eyes shut, unaware of how long I had been gawping at the mostly naked man in front of me and unsure if he was asking if I was hungry for food or him.

"Excuse me?" I responded nervously.

"Food? Do you want something to eat?" he smirked as his eyes lit up, rejoicing in my evident distraction.

My eyes roamed the small and cosy space to divert my attention. The hearth took up most of the room; the large pale cream and grey stones were charred with soot, an ashen reminder of many a meal shared here before. Warmth from the fire seeped into the room, taking away some of the chill that seemed to have taken permanent residence in my bones.

"A necro with culinary skills? Who knew?" Smiling at him, I perched on a stool next to him.

"Don't call me that," his reply was curt as he placed two eggs into a pot of water above the flames of the hearth. The boiling water bubbled away, filling the small space with the sounds of pops and spurts.

"Well, that's what you are," I raised my eyebrows at him, trying to coax a reaction. I had put up with his antagonisation for a long time; it only seemed fair to return the favour.

"Would you like me to tell you what we call people like you?"

I squinted, confused by his comment. "People like me?" I asked, grabbing two small plates.

"Yes."

"There is no name for us." I grinned, reaching for a loaf of bread on a side table. I gingerly picked it up and turned it over, inspecting it.

"The princess has no idea. Adorable," he said teasingly, lifting the eggs out of the boiling water with a ladle, then placing one on each plate.

I glowered at him as I took a bite out of the tough bread, turning my head abruptly as I ripped the crust. "Where did you get this?" I asked, mouth full, waving the bread at him.

Asher shook his head and laughed. "I swiped it from the kitchens at the manor before I left. To find you."

An ache flared in my chest thinking of Maria.

Handing the bread to him, I cut into the egg then placed a small piece in my mouth. I couldn't help but groan at the flavour–rich and wholesome, perfectly cooked.

Great, he can cook too.

"That good, huh?" he asked, his eyes glinting with delight as he watched me devour the food.

"If you could stop being good at everything, that would be great."

"You have no idea how *good* I am at *some* things," he winked, taking the dirty plates and putting them in the sink.

Oh my gods.

My heart thumped in my chest and I could feel a warm flush creep across my skin.

"Bathing room is through there," he pointed, seemingly unaware of how flustered he had just made me.

Reluctantly, I headed to the bathing room to freshen up. I rinsed off the dried blood caked underneath my fingernails, trying my best to get rid of the evidence from what happened the day before. When I splashed my face, I was horrified as the murky water swirled in the sink. I was filthy. I went to lift my shirt, *his shirt*, off and over my head when Asher yelled from the other room.

"Fuck!"

"What is it?" I rushed out, frantically searching Asher's face.

He had tied his hair back with a leather cord and dressed in lightning speed, sheathing two blades against his thigh. "We need to leave. Now." His voice was urgent, causing me to panic.

"What? Why?!" I shrieked, grabbing my things, hurriedly climbing into my breeches, and hopping into my boots.

He shot a panicked glance out of the window. "Quickly, Phoebe," he spoke as he pushed me out of a door towards the back of the house.

Asher lifted me up and onto his horse, then slid behind me, anchoring my hips. He nudged the horse with the heel of his boot, sending it careening out towards a dusty path.

"You're going nowhere!" a booming voice sounded behind us.

We rode ahead furiously, weaving in between trees and dodging low-hanging branches.

"They're gaining on us!" I yelled, turning around to see the four blackened figures on horseback, their dark cloaks billowing in the wind.

"Use your powers!" Asher bellowed.

I raised my palms, screwing my eyes shut. The skin on my hands tingled, and flickers of flame spat out at my fingertips, then smoked into nothingness.

"It's no use, Asher. I'm not strong enough!"

Asher lifted his right arm; his hand held high in a claw as threads of black crawled upwards. The threads turned to ribbons, to waves. Suddenly, the ground underneath us rumbled; whispers of shadowy clouds seeped out of the cracks. To our left, the earth crumbled, and cadaverous hands clawed their way out. I looked on in horror as other pockets of earth erupted with more pallid digits breaking through the mud and clay. Swaths of the undead–Asher had summoned corpses, dozens and dozens of corpses. The ghastly hulks staggered towards us, jaws dislocated, decayed clothing tangled amongst their bones.

"Asher… Asher!" I clamoured.

"Calm. They will not harm us."

"This is what your power can do? Great Mother."

"How turned on are you right now?" he whispered into my ear, his stubble grazing against my lobe. The feel of it sent a shiver through my body as I imagined feeling the roughness of it against other parts of me.

"You are insane."

"Insanely good at saving your arse. Again."

"I wouldn't need to keep being saved if you weren't one of the reasons I'm in danger!"

The undead groaned as they dawdled past us, ignoring us completely, and headed towards The Black Cloth.

The echoes of painful wails filled the forest air. I looked behind to see the boned abominations leaping towards the horses, clawing at their necks to reach the men that were saddled atop them. The dead overwhelmed them, crawling over their bodies like flies on excrement.

Blood sprayed through the air as they were taken down one by one, their flesh shredded into meaty strips as rotten teeth devoured them.

CHAPTER FORTY

Asher

With any luck, my power would have stopped The Black Cloth from finding us any time soon.

Feeling somewhat content that we were out of immediate danger, the frantic gallop of the horse slowed to a canter, giving us a reprieve from the glacial wind lashing at our faces and from the jarring sensation of a turbulent horse ride.

In our frenzied hurry to escape, I hadn't realised how close our bodies were, Phoebe's back molding into my chest perfectly like the most gorgeous little spoon.

The shit my brain comes up with because of this damn woman.

But it wasn't just the closeness of her, the feel of her full hips under my hands as I held onto her. It wasn't how my stomach somersaulted each time she spoke, the hypnotising lavender and vanilla scent of her hair. It was the time-slowing, heart-pumping feeling I felt when she was in danger. An invisible thread pulled taut to the point of breaking, sending me damn near out of my mind. I had put everything on the line for her, betrayed my closest companions. I would kill for her. And other than the fact she was beautiful, brave, and cunning, I had no idea why I felt so at her mercy. Why I believed it had to be me, only me, to save her. To keep her safe.

What did it all mean? Did she feel this too?

"We're going to have to stop for the night. We'll continue in the morning. There is an inn about half a day's ride from here," I said in a low voice, slowing the horse.

"You cannot be serious," Phoebe replied, her tone void of any enthusiasm.

"The horse needs rest, as do we. And darkness is upon us." I gestured towards the sky awash with colour – deep purples and pinks, like a fresh bruise.

"You're telling me that we're going to sleep in the forest?" Phoebe shivered as she pulled her cloak to her chin.

"Are you scared, Phoebe?" I teased but watched her face for any hint of unease.

"No. Of course not."

"Liar." Smirking, I squeezed her hip.

"The thought of sleeping in a pitch-black forest, with the horrors that lay dormant below and vengeful Black Cloth on our tail isn't exactly appealing."

"I'll protect you," I whispered into her ear as she leaned further into me.

The horse slowed to a stop, and I swung my leg over and slid to the ground, extending a hand to help Phoebe down from the horse.

"I can do it myself," she recoiled from me, her expression barbed with frustration.

"Go on then." I crossed my arms and smirked, knowing that she was going to struggle but too obstinate to accept my help.

She awkwardly dragged one leg off the horse, desperately clinging to the reins as she slid ungraciously, her legs dangling.

I appeared behind her and placed my hands on her hips. "You're so fucking stubborn," I said, gently placing her on the floor.

"And you'll take any opportunity to touch me." She pushed my hands away and twirled around, her back facing the side of the horse.

"I don't remember you stopping me before." I stepped closer, my chest flush against hers. I was so much taller than her that her breasts grazed underneath my pecs.

"What are you doing?" Her eyes darted up to mine as she tried to take a step back, bumping into the horse.

"You're cold."

"I'm fine," she snapped through chattering teeth.

"You look and sound it. Come. Let's find somewhere to sleep," I yawned. "I'll make a fire." I was exhausted, but if Phoebe couldn't summon her own fire, I needed to do something to keep us warm.

We walked a few paces into the woods, which was not as easy as I had hoped, given that there was barely any light to be able to see, and my boots slipped on the icy leaves.

The wind had started to pick up, blowing through the snow-laden trees with a ghostly whistle, causing flurries to obscure our already poor vision. I held tightly onto the reins of the horse for fear the beast would bolt as the winds grew in strength; the last thing we needed was to end up stranded and having to walk to the inn.

As we approached a clearing, I tied the horse to the thick branch of a tree, hoping that I had picked an area that was sheltered enough. Phoebe slumped to the floor and wrapped herself in her cloak.

"The whole "I'm annoyed at you" act is kinda old now, Phoebe. And you kissed me, remember? So, what was that all about?" I tentatively queried as I began to prepare the ground for a fire.

"Nothing," she locked her arms around her legs and looked at the ground, continuing to avoid my eye contact.

"It sure didn't feel like nothing." I paused for a few moments, contemplating whether I should continue teasing her or demand she look at me. "Do you often kiss strangers when you're emotional?" *Teasing it is.*

"Shut up!" she yelled, throwing a ball of snow at me.

It hit me square in the shoulder, filling me with even more gall to fuel her temper.

"I expect to receive another kiss soon, given your current *emotional* state."

"I swear to the gods, Asher… Shut the fuck up. Don't you have a fire to make?"

I smiled to myself – flustering Phoebe had become one of my favourite hobbies.

The silence of the forest that followed was crippling as I pondered, my thoughts racing and my heart pounding all because of this stubborn woman who would surely be the death of me.

If death was graced with a face like hers, I'd welcome it with open arms.

I started on the fire, bashing stones together over a modest collection of branches and twigs. Sparks illuminated the mossy ground underneath us, and five or so attempts later, the sparks landed in the woody pile. I released a lengthy blow from my lips, causing the sparks to jump and ignite.

"Quite the outdoorsman."

My heart galloped in fear for a second, not realising how quiet it had been before Phoebe spoke.

"I look forward to your fire returning so I don't have to gather sticks and stones like a child." I observed her as I continued to kneel, hovering my hands above the growing flame.

Phoebe's brows drew together, and she chewed her lip as she stared at the fire, her bottle-green eyes illuminated by the angry orange hues. I wished with all my might that I could chase those fears away.

"That should burn for a few hours at least. Let's try to get some shut eye," I groaned as I stood, my back aching from the exertion of the last few days.

Nestling down with my back flush against a dead tree, I pulled my cloak over myself. Phoebe followed suit a few steps away. I watched her as she fidgeted, moving from one side to the other, throwing her cloak over and off herself several times, letting out exasperated huffs and puffs. When she finally settled, I could hear her teeth chattering as the cold night swept over us, coating us in a light dusting of snow.

I debated sliding behind her, knowing that I would be able to keep her warm throughout the night.

"I'm going to make a suggestion which you will likely decline," I whispered.

She sighed. "Oh, Great Mother. What?"

"We should lay next to one another for warmth."

"You'd like that very much, wouldn't you?" she spat out through chattering teeth, peeking out from beneath her cloak for a moment.

"I'd like for us to not freeze to death."

She moved her cloak from her face again and glared at me. "Nothing to do with wanting to be close to me. Again."

"As lovely as your body is, my motivation is to simply survive the night."

Phoebe didn't say anything. I took a deep breath, shutting my eyes, wondering what was going through her mind.

"Well?" I pushed for an answer.

"Fine," she huffed as she rolled over, her back to me. "But keep your hands to yourself."

I crept over, slipping behind her. I slowly moved my hand underneath her cloak and rested it on her stomach.

"What did I *just* say?!" she shrieked as she turned her head to look at me.

"This is the best way to keep warm!"

"You're a deviant."

"A deviant who wants to keep you alive and well." *Who'd also like to fuck you senseless.*

"Goodnight, Asher."

"Sweet dreams, Phoebe."

I nestled my head into the crook of my elbow; my right arm remained draped over Phoebe, my palm delicately placed on her. She fidgeted. A lot. At times it caused me to stir underneath my breeches. Phoebe eventually fell asleep, which meant I would no longer be tortured by the feel of her backside pushing against me.

I couldn't believe this was happening. Phoebe Emberwood *was* just a silly girl with powers who lived in a castle. Now, she consumed every single thought that entered my mind. I wanted to protect her. I wanted to look after her. I wanted to do *other* things too. But I couldn't think about that too much with her pressed so closely against me.

Phoebe suddenly pushed into me, letting out a faint, breathy moan as she said my name.

Gods above and below.

"Phoebe…?" I asked, eyes wide with shock.

"Huh? What?" She shot upright, startled by my voice.

"You just said something," I said huskily as I attempted to adjust myself without her noticing.

"Of course, I didn't. I was asleep, you bloody idiot." She let out a lengthy, frustrated sigh.

I grinned from ear to ear. "Well then, you talk in your sleep."

"I do not."

"Oh, you do," I said, grinning from ear to ear.

"What did I say then, smartarse?"

"You said my name."

"Piss off, no I did not."

"You most certainly did."

"Oh my gods, shut up!" her voice was shrill as she slapped me on the arm. "If I said your name, it would have been in anger, not whatever it is you're thinking." A blush dusted her cheeks.

"Phoebe, if that's the kind of noise you make when you're angry, I must try to piss you off more often."

"Turn away from me right now!"

"Why? Worried you might push your backside into me again and feel what you do to me?"

She gasped and roughly shoved me. “Turn. Away.”

“Very well.” I shifted onto my other side, my front facing away from her. Phoebe laid down, her back against mine. “See you in your dreams,” I whispered into the night.

CHAPTER FORTY-ONE

Phoebe

We awoke at dawn and began riding shortly after. Asher said he knew of an inn not too far away. I sincerely hoped he was right; I longed for a warm bed and an even warmer bath.

Being so close to him on the forest floor last night did not do me any good. I had fought against the strange feelings I had been experiencing and was ashamed I had already succumbed to the temptation back at the manor. *What did that say about me, that intimacy even crossed my mind with all that had taken place? That I felt so consumed by him?*

"It should be up here on the right," Asher whispered, leaning forward into me ever so slightly as the horse slowed to a stop. The stubble along his jaw lightly grazed my cheek, interrupting my internal monologue.

"Thank the gods." I clasped my hands together akin to prayer.

True to his word, an inn appeared in the distance: The Tipsy Toad. Smoke billowed out of the chimney, seeping into the surrounding forest in grey puffs. The inn was a modest size with a small garden running alongside it, surrounded by a rickety fence. Beds of lavender dominated the space, the scent of which filled me with a sense of calm I hadn't experienced in what felt like forever. I peered up at the magnolia stone walls that were partly smothered by ivy. It reminded me of Brielle's family home. My heart felt heavy with sorrow.

Asher hopped off the horse and extended a hand to me, helping me down in one graceful swoop. I decided to allow him this time after making such a fool of myself before.

He leaned over the fence and plucked a sprig of lavender, twirled it between his fingers, then handed it to me.

"To go under your pillow to help you sleep," he said with a half-smile.

"Thank you." I reached up and touched the tip between my collar bones, missing the heaviness of my amethyst pendant and the way it made me feel connected to Brielle.

He smiled softly at me and headed towards the entrance. When he turned his back, I couldn't help but feel grateful for the thoughtful gesture.

The cosy hum of the main room filled me with an overwhelming feeling of comfort as I stepped over the threshold. The smell of beef stew and ale filled the air – I could kill for a drink.

"What can I get for you?" the innkeeper asked, drying the inside of a glass with a cream cloth.

"Can we have two rooms please?" Asher asked as he leaned against the bar.

"We only have one room available. All booked up because of Yule tomorrow."

Yule was tomorrow? I could have cried. There would be no family feast, no exchanging of gifts. I glanced at Asher and was surprised to see a smile plastered on his face. *Why the bloody Hell did he look so smug?*

Wait – did the innkeeper say there was only one room?

"There's only one room?" I asked Asher, giving him a bewildered look.

He shrugged, grinning as he said, "Come on. It's not like I planned this."

"Do you want it or not?" the innkeeper interrupted, his tone impatient.

"Fine. Guess we'll take it." Asher seemed reluctant as he put a handful of gold coins on the counter and retrieved the key from the innkeeper, sauntering off towards the stairs.

I followed behind him, dragging my heels. Apparently, the gods wanted to keep us as close together as possible.

Asher unlocked the door and lazily walked across to the four-poster bed and slumped down. It looked regal, the velvety burgundy throws and plump pillows inviting, much like Asher's bed at the manor.

"Oh my gods, I forgot what this felt like." Asher groaned in contentment. A deep, rumbling sound that did me absolutely no favours.

The wooden floors were covered in colourful patterned rugs of varying reds, and a large mahogany dresser nestled against one wall, several candles scattered across the top of it. To the right of it, a beautiful large mirror with delicate gilded edges.

"Are you going to do the whole "refusing to share a bed thing" again or are we passed that now?" Asher asked, taking off his cloak.

I went to speak, but hesitated. The bed wasn't as big as the one at the manor, but it wasn't going to be cramped. Surely, we could share it without having to be close. I still didn't feel like I could fully trust him, but my exhaustion and hesitant desire had caused my rage to go from a wildfire to a simmer.

"You can share it with me. BUT. But. You will not cross the line of cushions."

"Line of cushions?"

"I'm going to put cushions and pillows between us." I gestured towards the middle of the bed, gathering cushions and pillows to create a divide.

"Great Mother. If I wanted to take you against your will, I would have done it by now."

My eyes widened in horror.

"You wouldn't have been able to stop me," he added, bridging the space between us. I gazed up at him, doe-eyed, as all the air left my lungs. *He was* so *tall.*

"But I'm not that kind of man," he whispered, taking one step backwards.

I could barely think thanks to the wild hammering of my heartbeat, looking at the stunning man in front of me.

Who worked with Briar.

Who turned against his people to protect me.

Who was a murderer.

Who kissed and touched me so passionately that I nearly fainted.

"The bathing room must be through there." Asher pointed behind me, interrupting my train of thought.

I walked towards the door and gingerly opened it. A large bathtub sat in the centre of the room, a rolled top with brass feet. It was the best thing I had seen in ages.

"I'm going to freshen up before we eat," I called out, trying to carry my voice to the bedroom.

"Go ahead."

Perusing the various soaps wrapped in hessian, I lifted one to my nose. Peppermint. The fresh scent tingled my nostrils; the smell reminded me of the mint hot chocolate Maria made on Yule's eve.

"You okay in there?" Asher called to me from the other room. "Is there anything else you need?"

My heart leapt in my chest as I contemplated telling him exactly what had been going through my mind since I met him. I bit my lip and coyly approached the doorway.

Asher got up from the edge of the bed and strode over to me in a few steps; his eyes fixed on mine.

"I don't know." I looked down, unable to bring myself to look at him.

"Then let me help you decide." His gaze was intense, flitting between my eyes and my lips before he took my face in his hands and pulled me towards him, claiming me in the most bruising of kisses.

For a few seconds, it felt like my skin was on fire, ablaze with lust and unspoken words as his tongue met mine, exploring, seeking. I pulled myself away from him, my palms placed firmly on his chest, my breaths heavy.

"No. We can't do this." I turned away from him, but he pulled me backwards, pinning my back to his chest.

"You mean to tell me you still don't know what you want? That you haven't thought about what could happen next? Even my shadows can't resist you." His breath was hot as he spoke against the shell of my ear, his mouth lingering over the soft skin of my neck.

"You keep denying your urges, Phoebe. How much more proof do you need? When August took you, I *felt* you. Through thoughts alone, I felt you. And I found you. And I fucking saved you," he paused, "I will always save you, little phoenix."

"Stop fucking calling me 'little phoenix', it's pathetic," I hissed, pushing backwards and hurling myself into the bedroom.

"Bullshit."

"You're a liar. A murderer. You cannot be trusted. It doesn't matter about how I feel, or how you feel. It's just lust! And nothing else!"

My indecisiveness was wearing *me* thin; gods knew how frustrating this must have been for him.

"Just lust, Phoebe? Have you felt lust like this before? Did Tyrus make you feel the way I make you feel? Don't deny it, Phoebe. I know that you have been fighting this, how you convince yourself you don't want this, but deep down you know. You know that this is something more."

His words overwhelmed me with such debilitating ferocity; it was an effort to stay upright.

"Tell me. Tell me right now that you don't want this. Me."

"I don't. I don't fucking want any of this!"

He shook his head, pinching the bridge of his nose.

"As you wish." The hurt in his voice created an unexpected pain to take root in my chest. I watched as he started to gather up his things.

"I will help you get as far away from here as you can. I'll keep you safe. But nothing more."

"Where are you going?" My voice broke as he reached for the door handle to leave.

"Figured I'd sleep elsewhere, maybe the stables."

"That's not necessary, you can – ."

Before I had a chance to say he could still share the room with me, he walked out.

"Whiskey, double," I said curtly as I awkwardly positioned myself on a bar stool. *Who invented these things?* It was too small for my arse and too tall for my legs, so my backside jutted off the edge and my legs dangled like an infant. I might as well have sat on a godsdamn horse.

The unmistakable sound of drunken men caused me to turn. Two louts sat in a dusty booth in the corner of the inn, surrounded by empty tankards.

"Another? You look like you need it," the innkeeper dragged my glass back towards him and poured a generous serving.

"You have no idea."

Draining the last remnants into my glass, the innkeeper mumbled something about getting more whiskey, then shuffled into a small room behind the bar.

That glass of whiskey did the trick. A warm, fuzzy feeling coated my throat, down into my belly, then danced over my bones.

"Alright, sweetheart?" My moment of whiskey-fuelled tranquillity was interrupted by one of the drunken louts. He was a young lad, seemingly a few years younger than me.

It took every ounce of my self-control not to roll my eyes at him. I was tired of the games men played. There was not a single man in my life I could trust. Even when my father was alive, he still harboured a secret that got him killed and put my mother and I in peril. And Tyrus? Well. I still couldn't wrap my head around that level of deceit.

"You ain't from around 'ere, are ya?" he asked, eyeing me up from boot to breast.

"Nope." I sipped the whiskey, refusing to look at him.

"Well, you're the prettiest looking 'fing that I've seen in a long time." He placed a clammy palm on my thigh. "Tell me your name then."

"What's yours?" my voice dripped with ice as I took his hand and dropped it from my thigh.

"Tommas. And this is Sid." He gestured behind him to the sullen-looking man still sitting in the corner, a good few years his senior and far less attractive. He grunted in my direction as he took one long swig of his drink.

It's not that Tommas wasn't good-looking – he was tall and stocky, his hair a beautiful golden colour, shaggy and wispy, curling at the tips. But he was a booze-addled creep who seemed to think he was allowed to touch me.

His hand returned to my thigh, the grip much harder this time. "Stop playing hard to get with me, woman." He edged closer, filling up the tiny bit of space that remained between us.

"It's not going to happen. Fuck off," I sneered, hopping off the stool.

"I only asked for your fucking name, you little cockteasssse," he slurred, grabbing me by the elbow and pulling me back.

"Do you want to know my name, Tommas?" a deep voice sounded from the corner of the room.

"Who the ffffuck are you?" he slurred again, just as he was met with a brutal punch to his face.

Asher.

"I know you're used to paying for it, so you don't know how to treat a woman, but *really*?" Asher pummelled into him once more as I remained glued to the floor, watching in astonishment at his brute force and the rage in his eyes. I wanted to intervene, but I couldn't bring myself to do so.

"Is she your bird or somethin'?" Tommas wailed, trying to protect his face with his forearms.

"Why do I have to keep reminding degenerates like you that this woman belongs to no one?" Asher drove his boot into Tommas's ribs two or three times before hauling him up by his tunic.

"Get the fuck out of here before I slit your throat. If I see you again, I'll cut off your cock and beat you to death with it." Asher shoved him out of the room and wiped the sweat from his brow. His drunken companion scurried out behind him, knocking over chairs as he stumbled out the door.

"Are you alright?" Asher asked as he panted, his chest heaving from exertion or anger; I wasn't sure which. "Did he hurt you?"

"Thank you… I'm okay. It's my fault, I should have made it clearer that I wasn't interested."

"Don't let me hear you say something like that ever again." Asher's voice was hushed as he placed his thumb and index finger under my chin, intently looking into my eyes. "There is no need to be a brute. And alcohol or no, you deserve to be treated with respect."

I nearly choked on the lack of oxygen in my lungs and the rapid beating of my heart as my brain tried to process his words.

"Let me run you a bath and get the stench of that pest off you." Asher placed his palm on the small of my back and led me back to our room. "And to say sorry about earlier."

I was so confused. I had become so consumed by Asher that I no longer knew what to think anymore. What was right or wrong. If I hated him or wanted him. So focused on every little detail that even a simple conversation ended up in an argument or embrace.

He was so fucking irritating and enchanting; I didn't know whether to stab him or kiss him half the time. From the dark brown waves of his long hair to the glinting silver of his nose piercing. Those deep blue eyes splashed with stardust, so complex and surreal they soothed and flustered me in equal measure. But it wasn't just his looks. Of course, he was an absolute sight to behold, but he had done more for me in less than a month than Tyrus had in two years. A truly ridiculous thought, but true, nonetheless.

And he was right. He saved me, time and time again, he saved me. I'd be dead if it weren't for him. My mother would likely still be imprisoned.

Maybe it was time to let him save me from myself.

CHAPTER FORTY-TWO

Asher

I yanked the metal taps of the bath and with one short and sharp squeak, the water came rushing out, slowly filling the room with steam. I scattered flowers and oils that were in tiny jars on the shelf above. Lavender and vanilla. That was her, alright.

"Here," I said softly, calling her into the bathing room.

She appeared in the doorway, a tired smile across her perfect face. She looked so exhausted, I just wanted to wrap her up, put her to bed, and stroke her hair until she fell asleep.

Great Mother - who the fuck was I anymore? This woman had ruined me.

"Thank you. This is wonderful."

"Your majesty." I bowed to her, then turned the taps off.

Her expression became unreadable, almost quizzical like she was trying to figure out a puzzle.

"Talk to me," I urged her forward.

"I just… I don't know who I am anymore. Where I belong, or who I belong to." She bit her lower lip, and a deep line formed between her brows as she leaned into my touch.

Gently, I pressed the sides of her shoulders with my fingertips, conscious not to be too forceful.

"Phoebe, I have told you and countless others before. You belong to no one."

"Asher?" She said my name so quietly, it was almost a whisper.

"Yes?"

My eyes followed her fingers as she began unbuttoning the shirt and I took a step back, astonished. She looked at me doe-eyed as she said, "What if I want to belong to you?"

A wave of emotions coursed through me. Surprise. Joy. Doubt. *Desire.*

"Is that what you truly want?" I could hear my heartbeat in my ears.

She nodded.

"Really?" My feet were glued to the floor, trying to conceal my urgent need to touch her.

Nodding again, she said, "Because it doesn't matter what I try to think or feel. I can no longer deny that I've not been able to stop thinking about you. About the first time we ki…" she trailed off, looking down at her feet, out of bashfulness or uncertainty – I wasn't sure. But I thought I was going to collapse. The steam didn't help matters as it filled the room, making it airless and humid as it billowed around us.

She finished unbuttoning her shirt and grabbed me. Pulling me down into a fevered kiss, she gripped my arms as I bit her bottom lip, tilting her hips into mine in response. There was an urgency in her touch – much like when she kissed me back at the manor –

with a desperation so potent it seeped into my very skin, chiselling her name into my bones like an epitaph.

“Do you want me to touch you?” I asked huskily, voice laced with heat as I peppered kisses down her neck, then along her collarbone. Pressing one finger against her open shirt, I moved downwards onto my knees and stared up at her, as if she were a deity and I the worshipper. She offered me a coy smile as I smoothed my palms down her stomach, dancing just past the apex of her thighs and along her calves.

“Say it,” I ordered, drunk with lust. “Tell me you want me.” I took a deep breath; the silence deafening as I waited for her to speak. *She* held the fire magick, but *I* was the one who might combust from the tension in the room.

“I want you.” Her voice was quiet, quivering at what those three words would set in motion.

“Then take this off,” I demanded, pulling at the bottom of her shirt.

The hungry look she gave me as my face hovered so close to her thighs damn near took my breath away.

“What else do you want?” she asked, dropping the shirt to the floor, gaining confidence minute by minute.

I stared at her breasts, then my eyes lowered to her breeches, tugging on them lightly.

“Breeches. Off.”

She leisurely untied the laces, taking her time with a bewitching smile on her rosy lips. Sliding the breeches down until they fell to her ankles, she gracefully stepped out of them and kicked them to one side.

I realised then that her undergarments were the only item of clothing left.

"These too." I hooked a finger underneath each side of the fabric, gliding it downwards, consuming me with so much anticipation it was hard to see or think straight.

Gods above and below, this woman is perfection.

"Your turn," she replied with a smirk, biting the tip of her finger as she eyed the evidence of my desire for her beneath my breeches.

I kept my focus on her as I rose to my feet and pulled my shirt over my head, tossing it to one side. I untied my breeches, letting them fall to the floor.

Her eyes lit up, drinking me in. She went to reach for me, but I halted her with a gentle palm over her hand. My gaze trailed over to the bath behind her. It was big enough for both of us; there was no way I was going to let her bathe alone.

"Ladies first," I coaxed her gently.

"I already told you I am no lady."

"No. You're a queen," I said, taking hold of her hand and kissing it as I gently slid into the bath with her.

"Come, lay here." I patted my chest as I pressed my shoulders against the back of the tub. She moved to lay on top of me, her back to my torso. I smoothed soap over her arms, her stomach. She flinched at my touch.

Shit.

"What's wrong?" I asked, suddenly fretful that I'd taken it too far.

She clutched her sides in an attempt to hide the soft flesh there.

"I want to touch and taste every single inch of you. I will worship every single *curve,* so you know just how fucking delectable you are."

My heart raced as my hands roamed upwards, lathering her breasts, feeling the hardened peaks of her nipples. She grinded into me in response, causing the warm water of the bath to billow out against our thighs.

"Impatient, aren't you?" I anchored her against my chest with one hand, the other roamed towards her right breast. I squeezed and teased as I kissed down her neck.

"Don't toy with me now that you have me where you want me."

Pouring water over her hair, I massaged soap into it in tender circular motions and she threw her head back in response, luxuriating in the comfort of my fingers. Rinsing the suds and smoothing the strands, I caressed her neck with the softest graze of my knuckles. "I've wanted you since the moment I laid my eyes on you." I nibbled on her lobe, then whispered into her ear, "you're the most beautiful woman I have ever seen."

My hand drifted along her hip, and my fingers danced lower. "That night at your ball. Do you know how much restraint it took for me not to steal you away from him? I would have killed him there on the spot."

"You made your interest in me pretty clear," she chuckled, stroking my arm as she looked up at me.

Peering down, I couldn't help but notice my golden skin against the moon-white of hers. The dark swirls of my tattoos were so wickedly different from the russet freckles that dappled her porcelain skin.

"I'm going to explore you slowly," I teased, gently touching her, the sensation causing her to gasp and buck her hips up towards my hand. The sudden movement rippled the water around us, spilling over the bath. "And maybe my magick will join in too," I added, as wisps of smoke began to corkscrew from my fingertips.

"Asher, *please,*" she moaned my name again as she attempted to move off me, but in one swift motion, I lifted her and stood up, balancing myself with my other hand on the edge of the bath. Our wet bodies slid against each other as I placed her down on the floor.

I cupped both sides of her face and pulled her lips to mine, moaning into the kiss with an appetite for her so fierce it made my head spin. Everything was too much, yet not enough. *I was finally kissing her again; touching her, devouring her.*

We walked out of the bathroom, our mouths still locked, hands seeking purchase on wet skin.

She padded backwards slowly, never taking her eyes off me. My gaze never left hers either. She tentatively sat on the edge of the bed and shifted herself further upwards, scooching past the line of cushions she made earlier and throwing them off the bed.

Then she slowly opened her legs.

Gods above, what a sight to behold.

I moved on to the bed, smoothing a palm down her calf then along her ankle. Dipping my head, I nibbled the inside of her thigh, then sucked the pillowy flesh, leaving a faint red mark behind. My jaw brushed against her soft skin before I languidly slid my tongue over her centre in painfully slow licks, teasing her with every glide.

"Oh my gods," she moaned as my magick danced across my fingers and onto her body. It lingered over her most sensitive spot, stroking as my tongue worked. My shadows glided upwards to her breasts and circled her nipples, causing her to gasp. She gripped my hair as my mouth ravished her, my tongue working in strong, circular motions. My magick had never done *this* before Phoebe came along.

"I need *all* of you," her tone was demanding, eyes brimming with burning desire.

"Patience is a virtue, little phoenix," I responded with a devious grin, speaking against her skin as I hooked my arms under her thighs, angling her hips higher, eliciting a wondrously hypnotic sound from her.

As her breathing quickened, I upped my pace, gripping onto her thick thighs. She let out an ecstasy-filled scream as she came undone beneath me, her legs trembling so hard the bed shook. I smiled against her skin again, lifting my head with a smirk to say, "So about that line of cushions to keep me away?"

CHAPTER FORTY-THREE

Phoebe

I awoke to find Asher standing by the window in only his underclothes. I waited a moment before speaking, watching as the muscles of his back flexed and tensed. A thrill flurried through me, remembering what we did the previous night.

Instead of interrupting the silence with words, I walked up behind him and looped my arms around his waist.

He stiffened as I gently placed my cheek against his back and squeezed him ever so slightly. His heart was thundering in his chest, causing my own to gallop in response. Slowly turning himself around, he unfurled my arms from around his waist.

"I'm sorry, I just-."

But he pulled me into an embrace, his huge arms engulfing me in the warmest and tightest hug I had ever experienced.

Oh my gods.

I felt his chin rest at the top of my head and a low rumbling sound came from his throat – a sound of contentment.

Nuzzling into his bare chest, I wrapped my arms as tightly as I could around his chiselled torso. He stroked my hair, his thick fingers weaving through the strands, causing my skin to turn to gooseflesh.

I didn't want this moment to end. I felt so safe, so at peace. Two things I had forgotten existed.

"I have something for you." He spoke into my hair.

Peering up at him, I searched those gold and blue eyes for answers to so many questions. He tucked a rogue strand of my hair behind my ear, his warm fingers grazing the soft skin. I was so distracted by the gesture that it took me totally by surprise when his lips met mine. He was soft and gentle as he took his time, kissing me slowly. It was like the start of a storm, electricity in the air amidst stifling warmth, followed by tiny droplets of rain. A promise of something more. Of something powerful.

Peeling himself away, he padded over to his satchel and retrieved something. It was wrapped in a small leather pouch and wound with twine.

"What's that?" I asked as my brows pinched together.

"A gift for Yule," he handed me the pouch.

I studied him, totally awestruck.

"Go on." He nudged me and motioned towards the bed.

Unwrapping the pouch as he sat beside me, I felt overcome with emotion as I pulled out a pendant. Amethyst.

"To replace the broken one. I know it's not the same but –"

Asher didn't have a chance to explain before I wrapped my arms around his neck and kissed him, branding him with the intensity of my joy.

“We leave in ten minutes.” His voice was like a clap of thunder, clearing the air to make way for something much cooler and far less exciting.

I hesitantly peeled myself away from him and began to pad over to the bathing room.

“What in the gods?” Asher looked concerned as he peered out of the window again with his arms braced against the frame. “Men. About a dozen.”

“Black Cloth?” I rushed to his side, peeking around his shoulder.

Asher opened the window hesitantly. “No, they look like normal townsfolk.”

“Come out, you bastard!” yelled one of them, waving a torch.

“What’s the meaning of all this?” The innkeeper sidled outside.

“Go back inside, we only want that fucker upstairs.”

Tommas.

“Oh for fuck’s sake.” I threw my arms up in exasperation.

“Stay here,” he commanded, cupping my cheek.

“I will not!” He should have known I rarely did as I was told.

“Phoebe, I don’t know what they plan to do. You’ll be safer here.”

“I am coming with you. It’s my fault that the bastard is all riled up.” I said, quickly getting dressed.

“What did I tell you before?” He planted a light kiss on my lips and began dressing, sheathing two blades.

“I can help. I can use my fire.” I matched his pace, mirroring his movements as he prepared to leave.

"You still need to rest."

I raised an eyebrow; his definition of rest was very interesting indeed.

"Sexual pleasure is good for you," he replied with a wink.

"I don't want to be squirrelled away like some damsel in a tower. I'm coming with you, and that's the end of it."

He sighed deeply before taking my hand, leading us downstairs and out through the main door.

"Now, now, fellas. What's all this about?" Asher stood tall and proud, unwavering like an ancient tree.

"You got in the way of a good time, then kicked the shit outta me," Tommas said, folding his arms.

"Good time for you, sure. But I don't think the lady was going to enjoy it."

"I don't give a fuck."

"What did you just say?" Asher's gaze seared into Tommas's.

"I said –."

"Never mind. Not interested." Asher launched himself at Tommas, hurling him to the ground. But the other men descended upon him, trying to stab him as he brought blow after blow down on Tommas's head. Asher's shadows fought back, knocking weapons out of hands and pushing bodies backwards. The shadows lashed out like tentacles, disrupting every attempt to maim him.

Just as Asher was gaining the advantage, more men arrived. Their bodies smothered him, crawling over him and pulling hard on his arms and legs. The sight of him, bloodied and bruised, brought me right back to the night my father's body was dumped outside the castle. I screamed and punched and kicked to release some of them, threatening them with wisps of fire. I wanted to summon an inferno, but my power only simmered, barely enough to even light a candle.

A low rumble sounded, then the earth split beneath the group of men as a fetid stench seeped into the air. A boned hand appeared in the dirt, clawing for purchase, but it was trampled under the feet of several men.

"Stay down, whore." A man spat at me and shoved me to the ground, causing pain to lance through my kneecaps.

I looked on as Asher lay lifeless, his eyes red and purple from countless assaults on his face.

He needed me.

I could do this.

I could be the one to save him this time.

I don't know what happened next.

"I am the daughter of the elements," I bellowed, heaving myself off the floor. The men turned towards me and began making their way over, sneering at me with animalistic snarls.

My body began to heat; I felt the rage and the terror rising to the surface as I twirled my fingers and summoned flames on each fingertip. I needed much more than this if I was going to stop them. If I was going to save Asher.

"Get the fuck away from him," I commanded, my voice otherworldly, deep, and pained.

"Fucking hell, I'm out of here!" shrieked one of the men as he ran in the opposite direction.

"I said. Get the fuck away from him. Now." My voice boomed as the short flames at my fingertips rose higher and higher, gaining strength and size as every second passed. "Touch him again and I will incinerate you."

The men looked on at me in horror or astonishment; I wasn't sure which, glancing at the ground then up at me – I had no idea when I began floating in the air. My power was evolving, turning into something far more frightening and volatile.

Their incertitude decided their fate. I launched a fireball at the men, smacking two of them in the stomach, and engulfing them in violent flame.

Suddenly, my back was in searing agony, as if I was being torn apart from the inside out. I yelped as the pain deepened, burning and boiling within me. My skin felt like it was being stretched, the stabbing sensation overpowering me with every jab and jolt. I tried to crane my neck to ascertain the source of the agony.

What in the gods was that?

Feathers? *Wings.* The pain accelerated, blinding, burning, searing. It was so paralysingly painful I began to see stars. Within a few minutes, ember wings protruded behind me, taking me high in the air.

"Phoe-be…" a strained voice called out to me.

My eyes lingered over his bloody body, fuelling the fire within me further. *Asher.* I reminded myself.

Before I knew it, my whole body was encased in his darkness, and I felt my flames flicker out like candles in a breeze.

An overwhelming feeling of adoration consumed me, and when I glimpsed Asher, broken but alive, staring up at me with tears in his eyes, I fell to the ground with a thud, and the heat inside my body cooled. A thin layer of shadowy plumes laced around Asher's limbs as he crawled over to me and cradled me in his arms.

"Phoebe, can you hear me? Speak to me."

"Asher." I gripped his wrist as he stroked my cheek.

"I thought you were gone. I didn't think I'd get you back."

I began to weep as my power completely subsided, surveying the carnage before me.

Dozens of burned bodies, smoking and hissing. A trail of molten destruction from outside the inn to the lip of the forest made my heart sink in my chest.

"Phoebe, your rage will destroy you."

"My rage is all I have left!" I bellowed, balling my hands into fists so tightly the bones of my fingers twinged. Chest heaving, I stared into those blue and gold eyes like he was the cause of and solution to my pain. In many ways, I suppose he was.

He reached out, taking my hands and nestling them between his palms, enveloping them in his comforting, protective warmth.

I hesitated, breathing deeply as I placed one of his palms over my heart as if he could soothe the ache that had made itself a permanent resident there.

"If I quell this rage inside me, what would I have left?" My eyes stung as tears began to creep to the surface, traitorous pearlescent droplets betraying me. When I was around him, I never seemed to be able to stop the tears from flowing. He was the only one who could break down the walls I'd tried so hard to build with the simplest of words, the softest of touches.

He waited for me to continue, distress clouding his features.

"Once that anger is gone, only sadness will remain. And I cannot cope with the sadness, Asher, I can't. It makes me feel like I'm in the depths of the sea, but I can't swim. Like I'm fighting a losing battle against something that wants to drag me down until there is no hope of ever reaching the surface again."

"Why are you so afraid of your sadness? Hurt doesn't make you weak, Phoebe." His voice was so quiet; it was almost a whisper.

"Because it means that I will truly be alone."

"Do you think the sun is afraid to rise after it has been consumed by the night?"

Bewildered, I looked at him, exasperated by his choice of words. "But I am not like the sun!"

"You are to me!" he roared, taking hold of my face. "And not just the sun. You're the sun *and* the moon, beaming light and ethereal darkness. Beautiful and dazzling like the stars in the sky. You are hope and joy and life, Phoebe, and you should not be confined to the prison of your rage." He brushed my hair out of my face. "You are too beautiful, too special, to be eternally angry."

I wept so hard my stomach ached, and I could barely catch my breath. Stroking his cheek, my thumb tracing along the bruises and cuts already starting to heal. He winced as I caught one particularly gruesome wound.

"You have called me 'little phoenix' this entire time. Did you know?" I asked through pained sobs, sniffing incessantly.

"I had no idea that you could shift. I've never met a witch who could."

"Then why did you call me that?"

"Because, Phoebe, you rise and rise again. You keep fighting, keep soaring, keep coming back. You will not be beaten. You will not stand by and do nothing, even if it means you tear yourself apart. You are the most infuriating person I have ever met, and I bloody adore you for it."

"We will be each other's ruin. We must stop... whatever this is," I whispered as tears trailed down my soot-dusted cheeks, the words stinging me like shards of glass.

"Too late for that, little phoenix. I am yours and you are mine, until the gods claim us." Asher leaned in and planted the softest of kisses on my lips.

"Or I do."

The guttural sound of metal through flesh interrupted our embrace. I opened my eyes to find Asher clutching his chest, blood dripping through his fingers. He gasped, his eyes white with panic as he tried to speak.

"Asher! Asher! I battled to put pressure on his wound, but the blood kept pouring out, seeping through my fingers in thick crimson rivulets.

"No, no, no. Asher, do not leave me. Please do not leave me," I begged.

His eyes began to close as he slumped to the floor. His arms went limp.

A shadow loomed over us, shrouding us in darkness.

It was August, polearm in hand, its tip coated in Asher's blood.

"What have you done?" I screamed. Flames erupted from my mouth and showered him in molten waves. His skin blistered and popped. He tried to run, but I sent orbs of flame his way, one after the other exploded against his back, searing through his leather jerkin, then his skin. The orbs were so powerful, they burned through his flesh and into his body, appearing out the other side. He fell to the ground instantly, a lifeless, burned-out husk of a man.

I spun around, throwing myself to the ground beside Asher. I tried to bundle him into my arms, but he was too heavy, so I curled up alongside him and stroked his face, barely able to see through the tears that flooded my eyes. I couldn't believe it. I couldn't believe that he was gone. Taken in the blink of an eye.

How much suffering was I to endure? Could I not be safe and secure? Was it too much to expect to be happy? My chest heaved through the sobs, making it difficult to breathe.

"I told you not to leave me. Why did you leave me?" I thumped his chest with my fist. "You can't be gone. I won't allow it." I pushed him, causing his body to slump backwards.

"Wake up, Asher. Wake up." I continued to poke and prod him; I grabbed him by his shirt and shook with all my might. "Please don't make me face what comes next without you."

Pressing my face to his chest, I wept. Mourning the loss of him, the loss of what could have been. I remained there for a few minutes, numb from shock. My heart and mind were slow, yet fast. Time stood still, yet hours seemed to vanish like snowflakes in the breeze.

When I arose, I scanned the area through swollen eyes.

Corpses littered the ground in blackened piles, each one marbled with veins of fluorescent red. The fury I felt before was a raindrop in the ocean compared to the unrelenting, all-consuming pain and rage I felt at that moment.

Eyes transfixed, I began to launch my fire towards the forest. I wanted everything to burn.

Trees crackled, turning black within seconds, causing the bark to splinter and break. The flames coiled around the trunks, sending flaming tendrils to the treetops and setting the leaves ablaze.

Hurling myself up into the sky, I hovered above the wreckage, my new molten wings leaving embers in their wake. I thought I could hear my name being called as I glided over the forest, charring any last remnant of lush and green life I could see.

I wanted to dance in the ashes of the fallen, paint my face with the dust of their bones.

I would bring about ruin to anyone who dared cross me, no matter the cost.

Epilogue

I landed on the ground in a storm of sparks and embers, revelling in the power I had unleashed.

Then, darkness.

I was no longer awake. I was dreaming. And something else was here.

I turned on my heel slowly, preparing myself for an attack.

Great Mother.

A tall figure cloaked in black. It emanated nauseating energy, an odd vibrating noise, filling me with dread.

But if this wasn't real, then was I really in danger?

The figure paced up and down the path in front of me, revealing strange coloured eyes underneath its hood.

"What do you want?" My tone was firm as I tried to conceal my fear.

My darling Phoebe.

A familiar voice sounded from the figure. It was gravelly and soft at the same time. *No. This couldn't be. Wake up!* I commanded myself. *Wake the fuck up.*

It's me.

"This isn't real!" I shrieked, staggering backwards towards the woods. I tripped over the root of a tree and fell onto my hands, landing painfully. I willed my power to make itself known again, to no avail.

The figure stalked slowly towards me. I was helpless, with nowhere to run, no weapon to hand, nor any magick to wield. I winced and clenched my eyes shut as I prepared for it to attack.

Instead, I was met with a cold press against my cheek. It was cradling my face. I gingerly opened my eyes to see the figure retreating.

Phoebe, calm now. It's me, your father.

No fucking way.

Listen to me.

I looked at it again, pinching myself.

Asher summoned me, but I can no longer feel him. I do not have long before I return to my eternal resting place. You must stop this, Phoebe.

"Asher summoned you?" I yelled, my voice high pitched in surprise. "What are you talking about? Asher is… Dead." The last word was strained as I tried to keep my tears at bay.

Phoebe, I did not allow you to use your powers because I knew what you would be capable of.

If you allow your emotions to overwhelm you, you will never return to what you were before. You will be able to create carnage and ruin wherever you go. Every time you shift, you will lose a fragment of your human form.

"I don't understand! This doesn't make any sense."

I'm sorry, my darling. You must stop this. You must.

Tears stained my cheeks, creating estuaries over my soot-covered skin. "I can't do this."

You can do this. You must. You must save him. He is the shadow, and you are the sun.

Have you felt it? The pull? Gods, if I'd have known that this bond still existed, I would have done everything in my power to have moved away from this realm.

"Bond? What…? I need to wake up. I need to wake up right now." I battled against my own body, I thumped and slapped and pinched, willing myself to snap out of this stupor.

The deafening sound of cawing brought me back to reality. I looked up to see hundreds of ravens circling the air like a cyclone, consuming every inch of sky. A figure walked through the mist.

"Hello again, little sister."

Author's Note

I still cannot believe this is real. How the frick am I writing the author's note… for MY BOOK?

I loved reading as a child and enjoyed writing as a teen (hello, fanfiction!). But in my late teens and throughout my twenties, I was so consumed by anxiety and depression I lost all interest in hobbies. I had zero concentration and absolutely no desire to pick up a book. It wasn't until the loss of someone very close to me that things started to change. This combined with the impact of the pandemic on the world turned a switch on in my brain. In the autumn of 2021, I discovered a little book called A Court of Thorns and Roses and things haven't been the same since. I owe Sarah J. Maas a debt of gratitude because that book was the catalyst for so many amazing things.

To my husband, thank you for putting up with my writing and reading madness, reminding me to take rest breaks and to drink water. For giving me direction when I couldn't see a way through, telling me how proud you are of me, and reminding me that it's okay to feel overwhelmed.

To my mum, who has always encouraged me to reach for the stars and who will forever be an inspiration to me. Your strength and resilience are unmatched; I hope that I continue to make you proud.

To my stepdad, I miss you every single day. Writing this book helped me to slowly heal and rebuild, and the threads of my grief will forever be sewn into this story.

I must also thank the Bookstagram community.

To two people in particular: Cass and Brit. You two have been my cheer squad from day one and endlessly supportive when the imposter syndrome kept getting to me. I thank you from the bottom of my little goth heart for the time and effort you put into helping me get this book published and for your friendship. Brit, you also edited Emberwood and what a dream you have been! Thank you for treating my first book baby with such care. She wouldn't be where she is today without your wondrous insight and attention to detail.

To my incredible beta team and author friends: Cass, Lucy, Aimee, Caity, LB, and Gem. I cannot thank you all enough for beta reading Emberwood and helping me get the story into shipshape. Your support means the world to me - I feel so lucky to know you all! And Gem, thank you so much for all your guidance with the technical stuff and navigating the complicated world of self-publishing!

To the ARC team & hype hive – what an incredible bunch of people you are. You helped spread the word about Emberwood and lifted my spirits when I felt like giving up. Thank you!

And finally, to the human who has read this far. Thank you. Thank you for picking up my book and giving me a chance. I hope that you enjoyed my story and are looking forward to the next instalment: RAVENQUILL, coming 2023.

P.S. If you're sitting there thinking, "I'd love to be able to write a book", or "I wish I could do this," I'm telling you that you can. It doesn't matter how long it takes. It doesn't matter if you don't know where to start, or where to finish - your story deserves to be told! Self-doubt is a bitch, but you can kick her ass.

About the Author

Erin is a lifelong lover of fantasy fiction in TV, cinema, and literature.

When she isn't reading or writing about fantasy worlds and magic-wielding girls, she enjoys gaming, live music, and snuggling on the sofa with her husband and cats.

Made in the USA
Las Vegas, NV
04 October 2022